WAKUWAL

(Dream)

A story of *daione sidhe* and the Great South Land.

A story to heal troubled minds and broken hearts and to help lost souls find their way home.

Peter Botsman

Valentine Press

First published in Australia in 2017 by Valentine Press

Valentine Press
P.O. Box 527,
Bellingen NSW 2454
www.valentinepress.com.au

National Library of Australia
Cataloguing-in-Publication entry:
Creator: Botsman, Peter
Title: Wakuwal/Peter Botsman
Edition: 1st edition
ISBN: 9780994515711 (paperback)
Notes: Includes bibliographical references.
Subjects: Spirituality – Australia -- Fiction
          Historical fiction – Australian Fiction

Front Cover: Detail from "Gurtha" (The Sacred Fire of Mata Mata), 2016, P. Batumbil Burarrwanga. Back Cover: Detail from "Wurrkadi" (Larvae, maggots & grubs), 1998, John Mandjuwi Gurruwiwi. Images used with the permission of the artists and family.

Printed in Australia, U.K. and U.S. by Lightning Source.

Warning: Please use this book with care. The author acknowledges the generosity and kindness of spiritual leaders responsible for the many stories and images that are mentioned in this text. Like all deeply important and sacred spiritual texts and images, Aboriginal paintings, images, dance and stories deserve the greatest respect. Designs on skin and bark and the stories associated with them are the provenance of clan elders and spiritual leaders. It is hoped that readers who gain an interest in Aboriginal spirituality, up to 30 times older than the bible, from any part of this book, will make the effort to consult with the relevant Aboriginal authorities to learn more. There is no substitute for learning and studying directly with Australian Aboriginal elders and leaders. One of the hopes and outcomes of this book is that more Australians will come to understand in practical detail that there is an obligation for every Australian to nurture, protect and celebrate the people and leaders of an ancient culture, older than our Graeco-Roman historical heritage, that is still living and strong. Aboriginal elders and holders of traditional knowledge are truly the unacknowledged Professors and Spiritual Leaders of our future Australia.

Bukmak and all people of Aboriginal and Torres Strait Island descent, this dhäwu (story) and djorra' (book) contains the names and paintings of people who have made the journey to Burralku (land of departed spirits) and beyond... Much of this work comprises the author's dreams, imaginings and made-up stories. Many words, stories and images mentioned belong to the malas of the Yolŋu people of north east Arnhem Land.

The author is thankful for the generosity, guidance and patience of Aboriginal friends and family, particularly Ms S D Gurruwiwi and Mrs P B Burarrwanga. All mistakes and errors are the responsibility of the author. Any profits from this text are shared and devoted to the independent Yolŋu development and cultural protection of Mata Mata and Gi'kal homelands in North East Arnhem Land.

Spelling: Conventions for Yolŋu words and names in written language are an evolving science. One of the best sources is the online dictionary created by John Greatorex and Ms S D Gurruwiwi amongst others: http://yolngudictionary.cdu.edu. au. It should be noted there are many different clan languages which are proudly protected with their own sounds, spellings and conventions. In this text we have made best endeavours to use the best and most contemporary spellings agreed on by Yolŋu scholars including Ms S D Gurruwiwi, the co-author of several dictionaries. Ms Gurruwiwi, who passed away in 2016, was an inspiration and mentor to the author. The author and his friends have carried on as best they can. Invariably things can go astray, so the author wishes to acknowledge his debt to the many Yolŋu eyes that have helped this text as best they can. Difficulties are compounded by imprecise spelling of words from the spoken word for which the author is wholly responsible. Added to this is the concern of sacred words finding their way through anthropological and other written texts into everyday speech and language. All care has been taken. The author wishes to apologise in advance to any Yolŋu or Aboriginal and Torres Strait Islander people if words or names are perceived to have been incorrectly used and invites feedback for future editions and for future understanding between balanda and Yolŋu.

Special thanks to Lyn Gain and Valentine Press for attention above and beyond the normal publisher's responsibilities, provenance and duty of care.

For yapa, dhuway, dji_lwurr and ŋän̪di Barbara

The Djan'kawu saw the Dreaming Man climbing the dharpa.[1]

From the 1980s, Peter Botsman, a fifth generation descendant of an Irish convict, began to witness Yolŋu Aboriginal ceremonies in North East Arnhem Land. His friendship with Yolŋu elders unlocked a series of dreams from his own life. Wakuwal is a story of these dreams. It is a series of dreams of ancestry and hopes for the future. The stories that came from the dreams are an attempt to come to terms with the European invasion of the great southern land.

Can European and Aboriginal Australians interact in a meaningful way? What were the blockages and opportunities over five generations and over 200 years? Can there be points of commonality in spirituality and life? In a famous song by Yothu Yindi, Dr M Yunupingu sings of the feeling of reverie that comes over Yolŋu people in ceremonial activities and song: *"... the rhythm of the yidaki bilma, Carried us far away back to the dreamtime, Back to another place this is a different dimension. Only us Yolngu will ever know."* ('Yolŋu Woman',1989)

The Wakuwal dream world is not the 'different dimension' that only Yolŋu can see, it is a new kind of connection that gives some understanding of the precious quality of Aboriginal culture as 'the voices of the land, sea and sky'. The assumed superiority of European culture that still defines European and Aboriginal interactions dissolves. Aboriginal Australians must lead Australians into the next era of Australian history, not the other way around. In so many ways non-Aboriginal Australians do now want to learn and to find the connectedness that is the basic, essential fabric of Aboriginal life.

Table of Contents

Rakunydhirri Waŋgalkal (Deadly Tempest)

The sun is blotted out of the sky - look there - a lethal mist spreads across the earth.

THIS STORY DOES NOT BEGIN AT BURRALKU. It is the story of our time, not of time's beginning. It is a story of the latest invasion. Despite calamity after calamity, there might still be hope... I tell you this story from the uncreated conscience of the soul. I tell you to escape nationality, language and religion. I tell you so that you can escape from the prison and the stilted mind. I tell you so that you too can learn to feel and start again. I speak gently and humbly to those who have been visited by the sweeping cycle of death and destruction. I ask for forgiveness so that we might restore some magic and light back into this dark world.

Who am I? Ha! My name is unimportant, for I have many names. I am one of the *daoine sidhe* - little people of the hills. I come from Éire. Of me, nothing is material. I am the guardian of the hearth and home. A light was kept for me constantly burning by devoted nuns for a thousand years until a time came when men knew better and homes became houses and land became nothing more than soil. I am a spirit being. You can see and feel me. I am with you always. I am a stag of seven tines, a flood across a plain, a wind on a deep lake, a tear the sun lets fall, a thorn beneath the nail, a wizard that sets the cool head aflame with smoke, a spear that rears for blood, a salmon in a pool, a lure from paradise, a hill where poets walk, a boar ruthless and red, a breaker threatening doom, a tide that drags to death, an infant that peeps down from the unhewn dolmen arch, a womb of every holt, a blaze on every hill, the queen of every hive, the shield for every head and the grave of every hope! I was conceived as a thought from the mind of the world. I live with owls and snakes. I play in olive trees.

I counsel generals. I am your divine intelligence. I guide the hand of painters and weavers. I am the muse that whispers in your ear. I am the dream of a child who struggles to tell. I am older than the piper's stones.

We 'little people' are greatly feared by those who came to invade our ancient lands. For thousands of years we repelled fierce warriors with our magic and song. This was a time before the written word and the civilised mind. There were many lands and disconnected kingdoms and cultures. But even we magical beings of Éire had no inkling of the myriad spirits, lives and civilisations far beyond our shores. We were but youngsters compared to them but yes, we were all too familiar with invasions and death.

There is more to who we are. The ringing bells for the 7am mass call us to prayer. They ring loud and long to attract strangers, sinners and vagrants who have lost their way.

Time and space are nothing to us. Our ancient lands and kingdoms are under mountains, lakes and even under the sea. We appear and disappear in your world. When we are at play, very sensitive boys and girls and old men and women can sometimes feel our presence. We may appear as a breeze in trees and leaves. I think you know that we can fly! When we fly, time and space shifts. We can take our friends with us, but our greatest power is to *place thoughts in minds* even through the words on this page. You are flying with me now. You see us all the time but rarely do you recognise what you are seeing.

Birds and animals know better. When you hear dogs barking at night, seemingly at nothing, there is usually some faery flitting about. It is natural for us to change and shift and transmogrify. We just turn our minds and we are they and they are us. We feel and experience nature in the same way as the creatures we become. If you look very closely you will see us. Perhaps an animal will be noticeably larger... or perhaps it will have a little shimmer of light around it. These are the clues. Like birds and animals, we can sense when great changes are occurring.

You know that animals can sense a storm or an earthquake or a great wave hitting the shore before it happens? We faeries had these feelings of trepidation in that year without a summer when the sun did not shine and plants did not grow. Dry fog hung over the land. Potatoes rotted, wheat and oats shrivelled. There were strange murmurings across Éire. The people were soon starving. Old men and women looked to the heavens, crossed themselves and asked themselves what was awry. Something far beyond our world had changed. Something deep within our world had also changed. Men were altering the flow of waters in the countryside, smoke and steam were creating new powers. Burning coal vomited smoke and absorbed the hands and bodies of small children. It was one of those times where it is hard to understand what was going on. We were travelling far and wide, alert to new vibrations, trying to understand why the life-giving power of the sun had left us. A lone machine travelled across the maze, a hare ran out alarmed, shocked and fearful. It was a new age, a time of crowds when people fell by the wayside.

THE FOG THAT ENGULFED THE WORLD was something different from that friendly old man who hugged rivers and fell and rose in valleys and the crevices of mountains. This was a fog of despair, death, depression and desolation. This was a time of horrors and chills when the dead walked the earth. We prayed each day for the ancient winds to blow away the gloom. We prayed to the hero of the deep wood, dim seas and dishevelled stars.

I was drawn upwards to the sky seeking clear air. I wanted to be with the wind and to direct it downwards. In the gloom, I lost track of myself. I lost track of time. Was I flying for days or weeks? I was calm, serene, lost in my thoughts, and quite literally lost. I was searching, searching... but for what?

> *The grey winds, the cold winds are blowing*
> *Where I go.*
> *I hear the voice of many waters,*
> *Far below.*
> *All day, all night, I hear them flowing*
> *To and fro.*[2]

I had this instinct to fly higher. I wanted to get above the fog that covered the land day-in and day-out. Something drove me on. Higher and higher I flew. I was too delicate and I called on all my energy. In my mind, I became *jiir,* I felt the power of the wings take over my being. Now I could fly as high and as far as I wanted.

As day turned into night and night into day, I flew ever higher. But there was no clarity in the air. How I longed for the rays of the sun! How I longed to see the stars in the sky but there was nothing except grey. It was like flying in a great soup. I had no concept of north or south or east or west or even up or down.

No wonder the crops would not grow. No wonder feelings of gloom took over the people's spirits. My mind turned to the earth where it had rained incessantly for over 100 days. People left the countryside for the cities tramping over muddy roads. They were looking for work, looking for food, looking for a dry place to sleep.

What was causing this chaos? Had the sun left the sky? Was the earth twisting on some new orbit moving out into an unknown galaxy? Who had upset the forces of nature?

As time went on I had this feeling that something over the far horizon was clogging up the sun. It gave me an instinct to fly even higher. I needed to see. I felt the air thinning. My feathers and down allowed me to endure the cold and I flew ever upward. There were tiny sheaths of ice forming around my breast but I had to go farther.

I don't know how long it was but suddenly the atmosphere became clearer. I was miles above the earth gliding through air currents that came from space. A silver trail of dust particles followed me. I saw the heaventree of stars with humid night-blue fruit and found here the wandering island of winds.

It was in this refined air above the world that images that had entranced the world came to me. I was a ball of confusion. Some things were familiar and others were strange. I saw the young Daedalus reading the covers of books at Wetherby Road. He was devouring knowledge in the great house with Corinthian columns, that grand house with its sweeping orchards, there for an instant then demolished for flats and subdivided into little boxes for crazy ants. His vibrations moved forwards and backwards. He was the scholarship boy seemingly from nowhere and yet, through him, ancestors began to sing and a great and true dynasty was to begin. The cousins were there. Baby tookoo jumping from the train at Carwarp. Easter, the incense of the Red Cliffs church and the glorious cousins Jill and Ginny riding horses; Jo dreaming and being chased by boys; Melanie, even then, pondering the Middle East; Matt studying Red Fin and knowing early that these questions of earth were beyond the farm and that other futures would emerge. The great man Uncle Bill loading bags of grain and marking sheep in the Mallee heat. Past and future which was which? I was so high I could feel the ancient gods. I could sense another journey of ancestors and spirits beginning. I could sense Djanda on the sands. I saw the lost warrior, master of exploits and pain. I remember how I guided him home. His spirit revived me. I heard his words... "brothers in hardship, we can't tell east from west, the dawn from the dusk, not where the sun that lights our lives goes under the earth and where it rises. We must think of a plan at once, some cunning stroke."[3] I had found my way before. What a blessed relief to see the morning star over the horizon shining down to earth. I sensed other travellers millennia before me.

In this thin air, high in the atmosphere, a new consciousness came into my being. It astonished my Celtic mind for it was older and wiser than my known world. Older than any monolith, older than even the entrancing stories of the ancient warrior. It was far older than the great healer of Nazareth. It was a wisdom of earth never known to my kind. It was a spirit that came from even before the beginning of our human time. I could feel a place beyond my imagination pulling me. It was drawing me to it but at this moment I had only thoughts for the hardship of Éire and the tribulations that men and spirits faced. I just wanted to understand what was happening at home. I just wanted the sun to shine on the land.

THROUGH CRACKS AND HOLES the universe unfolds. A myriad flow from the far past and future: patterns, paintings, machines, beliefs, journeys, relics, telephone numbers, texts,

5

poems, conversations, dreamings... Clues or follies? Your eyes or mine? Or just the musings of some stranger? Seaweed rolling in and out with the tide, no identity, no family, just nothing. There will be great tribulations ahead. Death is not the end. The pathway to the top of the hill begins. The man, the dog and the gypsy eating the apples freely. Oh, the tourists invading the churches and the manikay on their vacations and work experience philanthropic tours! Ignorance is the enemy - if it takes hold all is lost. Let us paint to inform and illuminate, like so many have done in your cathedrals and churches. They are old, but we are much older. "Do not be afraid. That is one of our friends from Baralku, Banumbirr. She is telling us that all is well at home - Djankawu told his sisters. The rising rays of Walirr, spread and light up the shore at Yalanbara." [4] The morning star greets us every day. It guides us. It tells us all is well. Its light shines towards the promised magic land of gentle people. It is an old friend and confidante. It makes us comfortable when danger is near. It consoles the tears that bring up the sun. It shows the direction of life. It rises up on the string during the late-night sky and is pulled downwards in the day. It is a flag from the paradise. It shows us where we have come from and where we are going to. We have adopted you church man. Are you wise enough to understand what all this means? Your holy man was condemned and so we have been. Let us comfort and understand one another.

HIGH ABOVE THE WORLD I prayed and consulted my guides and masters. Was the world to be lost in fog? Was there to be no redemption? Would the world of men lose their magic, their loved ones and their lands? With these thoughts came determination. New strength and renewed energy surged through me.

The ancient gods favoured my efforts. *'Accept this gift nymph immortal, beauty, bride of Noman, you of the windy wilds of Connemara. Heed you well lessons of the sailor of old, the bureaucracies of churches and men, the silly, lost ponderings of 7 Eccles St and the pain of worlds that are disconnected from spirits, planets and the unseen guides of life.'* [5] On their way to

Ithaca with a house load of suitcases and boxes from Lae. There on the streets of New York City catching taxis and a bus. The little boy was ashamed of his adventurous parents. Why were they so naïve? Could we be murdered and all our possessions stolen? And yet here was a destiny forged from the books read late at night by candlelight. The great man, the dreamer, the teacher pulling his family to higher heights so they could see. And she too full of life and willingness so determined that it would be good for children to have these adventures and so it was.

Oysters! growing on the timber floating far out to sea.[6]

It was there in the wide ocean I saw them paddling, steadily following the morning star. Guthaka circling excitedly. A bag made of the skin of a Highland cow came floating to me. In it were the bawuthu of the world? There were unfamiliar, tricky, playful, gundawirwiryun winds: bärra', buḏuyurr, bulunu, djalathaŋ and the faithful ḻunŋgurrma - a wind to cheer even the heartless and hardened. Time would reveal their meanings and purposes.

Then I saw the whole picture. On the edge of the earth a great fire was burning. Its smoke and haze had shut out the sun. Most of the earth was covered in dust. I could see great clouds billowing north. Dust was blowing out over the oceans and lands. A great mountain had exploded into the sky sending ash and smoke to the very edge of the blue atmosphere of the earth. So that was it! My heart leapt! Surely even this great fire would have to go out!

As I flew above the earth I sprinkled dust from my wings. It seemed a futile gesture. I called on the great spirit of the seas. I called my familiar winds Boreas, Eurus and Aparticias to blow. For many hours, there was nothing but even more confusion. Eventually the smoke haze that covered the earth began to break up. Then, oh joy, Helios appeared and I could see that sunlight began to bathe the earth.

But now something new appeared to me.

As I looked towards the far horizon I could see thousands of little fires burning on great plains. I sensed the gentlest of peoples also waiting for the cataclysm to pass. They were cooking yams in the morning coals and keeping warm. I longed for home and the warmth of a kitchen hearth. I was so tired. How long had it taken me to get this high? How long would it take me to drift downwards? I knew I had drifted far far from Éire. But I had found a cause to our problems and with renewed spirit I plunged back into the grey, now willing myself downwards.

As I flew I wondered about heaven and earth, about the world, my people and faery magic. My thoughts cheered me and helped me on the long journey downwards. Many things came into my mind. I was excited to understand what had caused the year without a summer. But I also knew in my heart that a new spirit had come to me and that the world itself was changing. Was this terrible fog a warning?

A bearded man came to me. He was dreaming of a paradise in a dingy town of vomiting plumes of burning coal. A dustman was dressed like a king. A revolutionary illusion and the promise of conflicts driven by committees was imagined. I saw how wrong this 'news of nowhere' dream was and yet I too felt his quest to see. I too dreamed of an unlimited world of sacred *djäma* and love. But it would not be so easy to reconcile these worlds.

As I flew downwards I saw great pillars of smoke curling upwards from towns and cities and these great plumes were raining down soot and ashes. A great odyssey was beginning for me and the people of Éire. The tramping over muddy fields would continue beyond Éire. I knew that as the crops had failed in the year without a summer, more and more people were moving away from the countryside. High in the sky I could also feel the fragility of the earth. If an eruption like this could shut out the sun, then what of these great human fires of coal? What was the new destiny that Demodocus had signalled for the earth and the people? What was the future?

All of these questions ran around my consciousness but now I had to find my way home. I was circling around and around for an eternity. It slowly dawned upon me that I had flown to the end of the world and travelled far beyond my land. I just knew that I had to fly away from the direction of the great fire.

I knew somewhere in the north was Éire. I began to look too into my heart and ask for guidance on the journey back to earth, back home.

Ever downwards I went, I had to be careful not to go too fast, I flew in long spirals, watching attentively for any sign of land, of earth and of where I was. At last after what seemed an eternity I sensed that I was getting closer to land. Was I imagining it? Could I smell the scent of the forest and gardens? Could I hear the faint strains of a fiddle? I was thirsty, weary and hungry. Down and down I went.

Gradually the grey haze cleared. Through the clouds I could see the land. It was one of those days in the countryside that faeries love. The sun was shining again and there was something else. There was music!

I am a dance you will learn.[7]

ROLY POLY!! My heart skipped a beat. How I wanted to dance! I could see in my mind's eye the activities below. Summer had returned in all its glory.

Clear, fresh, cool gapu, sparkling with life and light, babbling and gurgling, darted round rocks below me. It made little whirlpools and undulations as it ran into deeper parts of the brook. Wrens and finches jumped from twig to twig chirping sweet messages. Bees were buzzing, taking nectar from the summer flowers.

It was just as the season should be. Faeries were everywhere. If you looked at the edges of the water where the sunlight sparkled, you could see little faery splashes. If you listened very carefully you could hear tiny squeaks of delight.

Oh, of course! It was May Eve! How wonderful – one of the three great faery festivals of the year, everyone was celebrating the warmth of the summer sun. Faeries playfully tossed wisps of grass around. They made great whirly-whirl swirls of leaves in the air.

The small number of people working in the fields looked up, and the older ones knew that the faeries were at play. It was just what I needed to soothe my troubles. Down I flew to drink sweet water and join the festival.

Faeries are the greatest musicians and singers. *Roly-Poly, Pretty Peg, Pigtown Fling, Hexham Races and the Whistling Postman* could be heard across the meadows as faeries danced and sang to celebrate the coming summer. In the sunlight was the glimmer of gossamer wings, little shafts of gapu flew up as young, cheeky faeries dive bombed each other in the stream.

In small bends of the brook, banquets were being prepared. Honey nectar delivered by hundreds of bees was set out in little acorn goblets. The aroma of asparagus and corn gently roasting carried upwards. The delicious smell of fresh bread and cottage pies carried in the breeze making the field workers hungry for their lunch. Even in ordinary times faeries create special picnics, treats and surprises, but today of all days, to celebrate the summer a great banquet of food and drink was prepared. We faeries believe that a magnificent feast brings luck and good fortune to all.

I was being drawn ever downwards to what was happening below me. I remember feeling the sun as it emerged from behind the clouds. Perhaps it was because I had flown so far, that as I flew downwards I became disoriented and I forgot whether I was bird or spirit.

Down I went. I could hear voices and I knew that once I was on the ground I would know where I was and what to do.

Suddenly all the faeries looked up midst the celebrations. They saw me gliding and wheeling downwards. What was this giant bird of the sea doing so far inland? Why was it heading straight towards the celebrations and why were its feathers so dirty and ruffled? Many faeries flew up towards me and soon I could feel them propping up my tired wings. Together they guided me ever downwards.

Soon I was on the ground with dozens of faery eyes looking at me. I had never seen the costumes or finery that the faeries were wearing.

The little faeries laid me down on a cocoon of grass. I could see that they too were confused.

I was still a sea eagle. I lacked the energy to move back to my faery form. I tried to say who I was but only bird sounds came from my mouth: *gnarly birdy gathering, a Runa little, Doolittle, preallotted, pouralittle, wipealittle, kicksalittle, verytableland of bleakbardfields! ... Our pigeons pair are flewn for northcliffs. The three of crows have flapped it southenly, kraaking of de baccle to the kvarters of that sky whence triboos answer; Wail, 'tis well! ...Her would be too moochy afreet. Of Burymeleg and Bindme-ollingeyes and all the deed in the woe. Fe fo fom! She jist doeshopes till byes will be byes. Here, and it goes on to appear now, she comes, a peacefugle, a parody's bird,[8] Awk, Awk, Awk... crows looking for bits of damper, picking up bits of plastic, paper and string... see the crows coming now appearing on the buŋgul ground.*

"Rest!" a hundred faery eyes told me. For the faeries knew that, despite my incomprehensible babble, something was up. They could see that I was no ordinary bird that I had come a very long way and that it was no accident I had appeared to them.

I was drifting back and forward from bird to faery mind and to different places in time and space. The grass was so soft and the music all around me was so comforting, I closed my eyes just for a minute.

CARRYING THE ENORMOUS DHARPA up the hill, too much for any man, let us take the load and share the burden. Emerging from the sacred fire beneath the sea, creating people, animals and all the ingredients of the world. This was fire hotter than a volcano, holy fire, cleansing, creative and true. Here are the mystery beings, the waŋarr, known in such detail and clarity. The learned judge and the wisest and most trained minds could not comprehend the exquisite detailed codes and meanings of the painters. Gaweriŋ, Janggarin, Birrikiidji, Manggarwuy were truly connected to the wise Guwak (koel cuckoo). [9] The greatest creative minds of the mainstream world looked on with awe and incredulity. Some had an inkling, a tingling at what was before them. They saw the technique and skill unlike any other. But not many had the patience, wisdom and knowledge to really see. It has taken many lives to get to this point of just beginning and asking the right questions. For who were these beings? Did they come from another planet? Perhaps! Millenia before the mind of modern man, these mystery men came from the sea with foam criss-crossing their chests. They brought culture, law and guardianship to the crude beings that walked the earth. Along with the sisters they taught men and women how to live. They created a paradise of heavens, earth and sea and showed us all how to love this place. It will take another five generations or more for us to become more than just beginners. How wonderful for us of this time and place to have this challenge and, finally, these teachings! Men of god and language can start the journey. They got their toes into the waters. Now it is time for the rest of us. If you want to learn, be ready to strain your brain. Be contemplative and thoughtful like a wise old man sitting on his verandah looking out to the paperbark tree at Mata Mata. Be open. Dream.[10]

"And the wise choirs of faery begin (numerous!) to be heard."[11]

I HAD WANTED SO BADLY TO DANCE but I was exhausted and my bed of grass was so soft. I fell into the deepest sleep. As I slept, midst all the festivities, I began to dream. Oh, I must tell you, a faery dream is something special! When faeries dream, things happen!

Our dreams are like yours but they light up the earth. Bystanders come with us into these dreams as we move to other places and times. Our innermost thoughts and desires light up the sky. Have you heard of the Northern Lights? In this great night-swirl of colours and shapes are faery dreams. Sometimes it is as if the whole world changes from a faery's dream!

There can be no secrets amongst faeries. Soon everyone had picked up my vibration. At times like this faeries often wake each other up because they don't know what they are in store for. But no-one in the faery throng wanted to wake me. They had seen me turn from a dishevelled sea eagle back to tired faery form. They knew that the dream would tell them more about my journey and my spectacular entrance. Soon all of the faery host gathered around wondering and watching expectantly at what would unfold.

I, of course, had no power to control my dreams. I had zoomed in on those little fires I had seen when I was high in the atmosphere. Now I was flying high in the sky above a strange new land. A marvellous vibration filled the air, it was a sound like no other. How different it was to the music of May Eve. The musical vibration carried new spirits and life we could barely imagine. It was the yidaki heraldry of a lost paradise!

"Lovers gather and give each other shade,
relief from the direct sun.
Stay close by that community.
Be shade with them, until yourself
are full of light like the moon, then like the sun."[12]

A BEAUTIFUL WOMAN, LALLA Bakitju Gunda,[13] was showing children white flowers. She was speaking a language that was barely comprehensible to me. "When you see these flowers *Djinpu* the oysters are plump, juicy and ready to harvest. Manymak!" and with that she nodded her head.

"Our seasons have returned to normal, all is well with the world again," she said to her sisters and fellow hunters. But in her mind were the strange sunrises and sunsets that had appeared one after another for the past year. The women had continuously sung and cried at sunrise each day. Eventually, they thought to themselves, things had been put right again. Everyone was relieved but Lalla was still a little on edge and apprehensive. Something was not quite right even now.

Up and down the coast family groups were gathering. On the rocky shores women and children with keen eyes were gathering maypal with razor sharp axes and knives. It was a happy scene. The people were celebrating and a great bounty was at hand. The smell of burning eucalyptus leaves wafted through the air. Oysters with wild herbs from the mangroves were roasted.

What were these aromas and these sounds? Nothing was familiar. Cedar trees towered in ancient forests and we watched with wonder as warriors ran unimpeded for miles. There were spirits of the land that the faeries had never seen before.

Shells were thrown into great piles. For many generations, since the dawn of time, ancestors had also feasted at this same place. Lirrwi – the charcoals of past campfires strewn around the beach were a great comfort and guide. Life carried on. The coals symbolized past fires, adventures, great hunters and bountiful seasons. In the evening twilight, the people and the spirits congregated to celebrate the day. Clouds, winds, sand dunes and colours of the land - all were imbued with meanings that grandparents would explain slowly and patiently to young children: 'This is the place in which the ancients also ate maypal. It is your home. It is our home. It will always be our home. You must nurture this memory."

There was dance, music and rhythms that we faeries could barely comprehend. Songs of lightning, dolphins, turtles, clouds, rain, lizards and snakes all followed in a progression that was never changed. Each family had its place within the universe and land and sea to rejoice, nurture and celebrate. The dancers would flick the sand from their heels and make shapes and forms like clouds in the air. As old men would sing of whales the great beings came close to shore splashing their great tails, breaching the surface and diving in appreciation.

How was it possible for people to have the same ability as we spirit beings to summon and communicate with nature and animals?

In the night, tucked snug into beds made from grass and woven mats, children slept as the dance and song went on into the early hours.

How different were the countless specks of light and bright stars in the sky? These too carried new meanings and stories. Bukitja Gunda and the old people talked to young children pointing upwards explaining constellations and stars. "See the dark emu? The sisters paddling their canoes."

A new day began with a bright star low on the horizon. Voices rang out across the camp. Great hunters boasted of their plans for the day and the food they would provide for their families. In this early morning time, people began to think ahead. Women spoke of the size and quality of oysters, mussels and yams. Parents carefully showed young ones the plantations and orchards of fruit. There was a oneness of the people with the land. Life itself was gentle poetry.

There were clever and mischievous spirits (mokuy) lurking. These spirits would play games and tricks. People would get lost. Children making too much noise were teased until they were rebuked by their mothers. In thick parts of the forests and gullies ghost beings and galka (sorcerers) walked the land. In deep caves beings that were part human and part animal lived with their wives and children.

Lalla and her people knew of these spirits and beings and their special majesty. The land was alive with meanings. Children were wild and free. They learned to be safe by experimenting freely and trying new things without paternal or maternal interference. They listened to their relatives and family and respected the places they visited and the unknown mysteries of the world. The stories of spirits and strange creatures helped children to grow up with reverence for tricky and dangerous places. Just like leprechauns, elves and goblins, the strange spirit beings had their place in the world. Without them the world would lose its magic.

Old men and women would gently sing of spirit places and things. In freshwater ponds and wells in the sea Lalla could look beyond normal life to the past and the future. These experiences were very much the visions of life that spirit beings would see.

How could ordinary people see the same things as faeries? The glimmers of sunlight and the shimmers of the ocean all had meanings, you only had to look in a special way to see them.

Suddenly gasps and cries went up from the faeries.

There were old men and women looking into a well of fresh water in the sand and they were looking at the faeries themselves. Lalla and her friends could see the May Fest activities. They too were shocked at the sight of the faeries.

Mokuy? They asked themselves.

Spirits from another land and place! How could this be?

Yol dhuwala? Who is here? Who is this? They asked each other.

A slither of electricity ran through all of us. A lightning bolt of energy was welding our fates together. As we confronted each other through the miraculous dream we faeries realized the people of the South Land were celebrating the same things, the produce of the land, its magic and its power.

Most of all, like us, the people of the South were recovering from a very strange year in which summer had not appeared at all and smoke and ash had rained from the sky. The faeries had blamed themselves and thrown everything into their May Fest celebrations, the new people had thrown themselves into ceremony, song and dance. Not just human life but all life was challenged by the failure of the sun to nurture the earth.

Across these worlds now things could return to normal... but would they? Could they? Why had we connected? What was the meaning of this dream? Faeries looked at each other in bewilderment. Where was this land? Why had the magic of two worlds come together? Was it an omen? A warning? All these questions ran through our hearts. On the other side of the world Lalla and her sisters asked themselves the same questions. The only clue we had was the warmth we immediately felt for each other. The faeries recognised there was something ancient, magical in the dream, something older than the parables of our forefathers and mothers. Somehow, we also knew that in the future faeries and the people of the South would be friends and allies. We knew these things but we also knew somehow that the year without a summer was the beginning of something that would test us all.

WALTJAN: WITH A JERK and a start I woke up. A light mist of rainbow-coloured rain was falling. What a surprise to find the entire faery band gathered around staring intently at me. I was as bewildered as anybody. We faeries rarely talk as

16

humans do, we don't need to. We see the images of each other's minds and feel the murmurings of each other's hearts. Faeries harmonise in this way, there is rarely much need for talk or words. The whole faery contingent live in a field of positive vibrations that create energy and life, and in a subtle way, they keep all around them happy, including the birds, animals, flowers and trees. But now there was need for talk. All the faeries stared into my eyes and suddenly all the joy of May Eve evaporated and only the sounds of the babbling water could be heard. I could not make sense of my strange dream. But the faeries could see why I had been flying so high and so far. They had the same troubles that had so worried the magic world of Éire. I stood up to address the assembled faery host. I did not know what I would say. I just let my heart do the talking.

"I am Brigit, princess of Éire, strength beyond strength, protector of home and hearth, friend of owls and eagles, holder of wisdom, weaver of souls, custodian of justice. I am searching for answers. All of the magical beings, the sheoques, merrows, leprechauns, cluricans, ganconaghs, pookies, dullahan, leanham shees, far darig, imps, and far sidhes are asking ourselves the same questions. Why in our land are so many children starving? Why are whole families in rags travelling up and down the highways and byways? The very spirit of the land seems changed.

"The far gorta, faeries who wander the countryside begging for food in times of trouble, have appeared. Banshee wails can be heard each night. The sound of the lonely tin whistle playing *Faeries Lament* is heard in each valley and garden. Mothers' eyes are red, fathers' are bent and hagged, they are worried about their children."

I could see in the eyes of the faeries around me that they deeply understood my feelings. Soon messengers from other faery gatherings arrived. All were eager to understand my startling entrance and my strange dream. All of the faeries wanted to know more and they wanted to know immediately.

Suddenly one of the faery host stepped forward. She wore a green tunic with tiny golden embroidered birds running down her shoulders to her sleeves. Her ebony hair was swept back under a beautiful silken scarf the colour of moonlight. Her eyes shone. "I know of you, dear Brigit, for a thousand years a lamp was kept perpetually alight in your name, and your famous goodbye to all 'May you stay safe and warm' is revered by all of us. I am Tanaquill, great grand-daughter of the faerie queene. I feel your life. I feel your pain. The same troubles have also come to our lands. This year without a summer has led to great hardship. But there is something more than just this change in our seasons. The whole world seems to be changing. The light in your temple is no longer kept. It is as if people no longer have homes, they have lost their connection to the land. The whole countryside is full of wanderers and lost souls."

My mind and those of all the faeries turned to the strange year in which there was no sunlight. I had heard of Tanaquill. Now I knew where I was. I had landed far from Éire, across the Irish sea, in the great islands to the North. Our faery kingdoms were linked but there was seldom contact. Tanaquill's words reverberated in my heart. "That is why we have celebrated May with such joy this year," Tanaquill continued. "It has taken all our faery magic to bring back the light, the flowers and even the bees. Your dream is an omen to us that beyond the seas we are connected and that our worlds are connected. I could feel the old men and women so far away asking themselves similar questions."

A faery spirit with eyes of oysters and hair of seaweed then ushered me forward and bade me speak more. Faeries are usually reluctant to say too much, but words came gushing out.

"The sun was blotted out from the earth - a lethal mist was spread across the earth just as the ancients had once prophesised. The clouds were filled with soot and when I flew into them I became black. After the mist, we saw women and men who were usually so happy in their gardens, silently weeping as they leant wearily on their pitchforks and rakes.

"Potatoes were withering in the ground.

"Even the best gardeners could not grow a crop.

"A disease of mouth and foot came upon the cattle... so that the beasts simply lay down and could not walk.

"Rumours and wild stories were transmitted across the land. While there was whisky in the jar - men and women sought solace in addled chaos. Others threw themselves on the sorrowful mother. Quis est homo qui non fleret.

"All this heartbreak! I could not bear the gloom and futility. I found a lonely shepherd tending to his herd and watched him weeping. His sorrow moved me. 'Weep no more, woeful shepherd, weep no more!' For something must come of this. Éire cannot be weighed down with false beliefs and suspicions. We will find our way!"

Then I remembered how I came to be flying. "I followed a cart laden with grain, corn and barley, it came to a ship. I followed it out to sea. That is how I came to be so far away from my homelands. Why was this precious food being taken away from the place it was needed? Can you tell me?" I asked urgently.

Tanaquill paused to think. As her mind turned to all these things, all of the faery troupe looked deeply into each other's eyes. They saw in each other's minds visions of people leaving the countryside, of towns and cities being overrun by people who had nowhere to live. Men were creating factories in which machines powered by steam were served by hundreds of men, women and children. Ominous chimney stacks and whirring, jarring machines were doing the work that master weavers had once done, they were creating fabrics and clothes in far greater quantities than had ever been thought possible... The simple life of the countryside was changing.

So, this was where the precious food from Éire was going. The faeries looked back at me and I understood that ships from many places were bringing food and resources for this new empire of machines. Something filled my heart with despair for I knew this was a gloom and a fog that would not disappear so easily. This was a great shift that would require all our energy over many generations to appease and moderate. It would engulf us all. It would link us all to a common destiny. We would survive or fail together.

As one, the faeries flew in their minds over the earth. They saw a dank, dusty, musty cotton factory where hundreds of children were working. None had a smile on their faces. Most were dressed in rags, and all were hungry. Giant wheels spun and pistons pushed looms back and forth. In the shadows of the factory women were sweeping up the cotton off-cuts and unthreading giant bales.

We faeries knew of the beautiful weavings that had been completed by the master stocking-makers in which the most brilliant colours of nightingale tails were spun together with intricate shades and types of cloth. I knew of the skills of Irish weavers. Now I saw machines completing yards of fabric over and over again. The faeries' eyes turned to the sight of the despondent stocking-makers with their small looms huddled on the side of roads. I looked into the future and I saw the great weaver of mandelas, created from the dyes of the earth, weaved from pandanus fronds, sewed with fire and rainbows. All was not to be lost but at this time ghost-like whirring of machines hummed and drowned out all that was human.

A small faery came forward. She showed us stocking-makers with clubs and iron trying to break the great power loom which monotonously churned out yard after yard of cloth. The master stocking makers wanted to free the women and children from the factories and send them back home to the countryside. But these machine breakers were soon captured and sent to gaols where they languished in misery. We faeries saw how the world was changing dramatically. In many towns, ghastly scenes unfolded, police came in to break up the protests against the machines, women and children left the countryside and came to work in the industrial centres and towns. The dyes and wastes polluted the water, the rivers and streams became a stinking gravy of toxic sludge.

Worst of all, families lost the capacity to grow their own food in the countryside, many were forced out of their cottages because they could not pay the rent. Thousands slept in the streets. But others grew intoxicated with the power of the machines. They amassed greater fortunes than kings and queens, they grew fat from the wealth created by the drudgery of the new slaves of industry...

As the faeries looked into my eyes they slowly connected our worlds.

They saw that faery magic itself was under threat. People were drifting away from the ancient world of magic and nature to a world of cities, buildings and machines. We could see more and more people living in tiny spaces. Even the fields themselves would be over-run with machines and threshers that would replace the summer harvest work of thousands of men and women. The food and cloth that once all had a hand in producing was to be produced by machines.

Our collective emotions and feelings send a vibration across the countryside across all of the domains and regions of faery land. Even the cranky, hairy, petulant goblins said they were willing to help.

Normally such magic creatures are so focused on themselves that the mortal world of human beings simply does not even register with them. They just carry on their business. Now everyone was tuned into what was happening in the human world.

In the past, we had seen kings and queens and great armies do battle. We had fought invaders and won and lost great contests, but no-one had seen the likes of what was occurring. The health and magic of the world can be measured by faeries and spirit beings. The life of the wild countryside was being transformed. Magic itself was in danger. There would be more of everything, but nothing would be the same. Food would not taste as good. Fabrics would lose their intricate charm. At the May Eve festival, strong feelings were felt across the assembled throng. Like seers in the faraway land, we knew what had to be done. We had to protect the children. We had to protect the future. We also knew that in some way, that we did not yet understand, we were connected with the strange land and people of my dream.

That night across England, Ireland, Scotland and Wales thousands of faery lights could be seen across the night sky. One by one the faeries landed on the shoulder of a little child in need and remained with them. In the factories children slept under their machines. In the streets children slept in rags down dark and cold alleys. On the outskirts of towns children wrapped themselves in whatever materials they could find and slept in ditches. Wherever the children were, faeries found them. Our job was to keep the magic alive within each child. I led the way in Éire, Tanaquill in England. As I made my journey home I watched as thousands flew down to the cities of Manchester and Leeds and London.

I flew back over the Irish Sea and down to the Irish countryside. The Irish faeries had also tuned into the developments and they were also on the move. There were fires ablaze and angry crowds in the towns and countryside. In all these places, we snuggled up to the hearts of those who needed comfort.

We whistled *The Faery Reel* to cheer the hungry and warm the cold hearts of the people. No-one wanted to dance but our vibrations of hope and love were like a little flame burning in the night. Hearing the music gave everyone a message of hope, from the darkest hours better things would come.

New tunes were learned and played. Gradually even in these times the spirits of the people revived. Adversity created new dreams of times when no-one would be hungry. "I will never turn a needy person away from my door." "The land is for those who respect and love it not for those who claim to own it by means of paper and police."

Across Éire, families still had to find food and sustenance. It was a daily task and to survive required the greatest endurance and ingenuity. The children dreamed of potatoes.[14]

This time as I was flying a vision began to form in my mind. I could see that we spirits and faeries were linked to the people of my dream. The year without a summer was an omen. In the great reorganisations, people would face the greatest tribulations. Midst all this we faeries had to hold on to the ancient magic.

We had to sew our magic into the children and into the new forms of the world. I would dedicate myself to this great quest. When the children were hungry I would sing to them. When a family was cold I would make them laugh. I would teach each child that no matter what happened it is how brave and fearless you are in your heart that matters. I would teach them that magic can change the world. I would teach them that there is magic in everything and it is only when people forget this that troubles abound. Magic, spirit and the natural cycles and vibrations of the earth had to live on.

CRACK! BANG! BANG! BOOM! WALLOP! WHOOSH! Rain bucketed down. Wind blew the giant eucalypts so they doubled over, lightning struck and limbs came crashing to the ground. Was it the same storm that appeared before young Hicks saw the distant mainland? The water spouts that came and went year after year. The camp was tucked snuggly behind a south facing sand dune in their shelters of bark. Some of the men and women had used the time to paint the bark slabs that sheltered them and kept them perfectly dry. Up in the mountains above the shore the people sheltered in hollowed out rocks and caves. Everyone was comfortable, warm and happy. They had, of course, anticipated the storms. The people had roamed the land during the pre-wet season, dancing and rejoicing as new shoots of vegetation sprouted. The great snake started to spit water into the air to form rain clouds. The people continued on their way dancing as they went. The great wititj rested under hills and suddenly stood up to strike creating lightning. The lightning struck trees. The storms were a welcome clean-up of the land. The lightning snake was shooting growth and vitality through the land. The rivers and streams would run strongly and clean up the debris and make it easier to hunt. The grasses and plant life would thrive and so too the animals. After the year of strange seasons, the great storms were welcome. Everyone was content and uplifted by the storm, everyone except the white-haired wise man, Dilkurrwurru Wataŋgurr.[15] There was already a kind of telepathic relationship developing between me and the people of the Southern Lands. I could close my eyes and see how Dilkurrwurru Wataŋgurr tossed and turned in his sleep. He kept on coming back to the strange vision. When he had looked into the sacred well he had seen me and strange little beings with lights.

He was overcome with a feeling of trepidation. The troubles of many thousands of miles away were coming to his shores.

The people of the South, like us faeries, did not need to use many words. Their words were interconnected with feelings, hand movements and a sense of spirit. I liked these people very much. They were tuned to the land and its meanings. The people of the land still had something that we in Éire were losing. Their lands, seasons, winds, the cycles of life and death and their spirits were so interconnected that magic accompanied them as they moved through the lands.

But Ḏilkurrwurru could sense that the fate of his people and of the lands across the seas were becoming intertwined. Just as I had flown the length and breadth of Éire, over the Irish Sea to England, searching for answers, now the old men of the great South Land were communicating through dreams and song. It seemed danger and evil were to engulf both worlds. There were stories of marauding vessels and of sticks that spat fire and lead.

Great ceremonies were being held. In music, song and rhythm, messages about the future were forming. Warnings were being issued.

No-one could understand what was happening on the other side of the world. But the vibrations and tremors of meaning were entering into the unconscious thoughts of the wise old men and women. Dreams of signs, squiggles and marks on thin strips of bark made people sit up in their beds. What was this world of strange beings approaching them? Ḏilkurrwurru knew of the pain of war between people, but over the millennia laws and ceremonies and marriage obligations had been devised to ensure that knowledge and magic survived the battles of foolish and greedy leaders. Flashes of the world of the faeries came to Ḏilkurrwurru. He saw thousands hungry, starving and dying. Troubles, war and dislocation were coming.

SAVIOUR MEETING ṆÄṆḎI ON THE TERRIBLE DAY, heal sacred mother, dhoku' has been cut down. The bees and chips of wood are flying everywhere.

24

was glistened by tears. He was trying his best to remain brave and strong but now the tears were flowing freely.

Many warriors decided that they must stay and face the white ghosts. Others began to gather what they could from the season's harvest.

"Go, old man take as many with you as you can, but we will wait and gather Bunya nuts and bring them as winter foods to sustain us in our new lands."

For many days people debated Dilkurrwurru's visions. They could see faces in the storm clouds of the summer. Willy-willies kicked up sands on the beaches. In the end, no-one doubted Dilkurrwurru.

So, a great pilgrimage began. Dilkurrwurru and the other old men and women led their families along the ancient paths that were used to connect songlines and ceremonies. They knew exactly what to do when they were approaching new lands and peoples, they must indicate that they came in peace. At each point on the boundaries of other peoples' lands they waited for the emissaries of different communities to meet and welcome them. They respected Dilkurrwurru as a white-haired and learned man. At each community word of the catastrophe that was to occur continued to spread.

Some warriors began to prepare for war. The great warrior Windrayne saw the bedraggled coastal group making their way over the mountains with no supplies at the wrong time of year and he thought they were the victims of a great feud or war between clans. He asked the old man what had happened. When he looked in Dilkurrwurru's eyes, he knew of a strange new force in the land. Immediately he adopted the men, women and children into his Wiradjuri clans and he began preparing for his own war with the new intruders.

"We must make preparations to protect our traditions and knowledge for the generations to come... Our family lines will protect our heritage... But in the worst circumstances let us place our knowledge in the trees and the earth so that at the right time in the future... our culture will once again blossom and our wisdom will emerge again," Windrayne said Dilkurrwurru nodded.

Windrayne was preparing a strategy of war, he would give Ḏilkurrwurru enough time to protect words, meanings, ceremony, so that future generations could find them once again. It was an enormous challenge. For what repositories would survive the tumult of time?

What signals would be left to attract the people of the future to understand the needs of the lands and the seasons?

Just as Ḏilkurrwurru had prophesied, strangers did come. At first, they stayed close to the rivers and harbours close to the sea. The people of the South Land tried to talk and negotiate with them. But not only were the customs of these people hard to understand, they brought with them firewater and strange diseases and sicknesses.

Windrayne saw that any animals that came with the white ghosts must be immediately slaughtered before they conveyed their evil malevolent spirit to his people. This brought many warriors into direct combat with the Europeans.

What strange ways of living and dressing and communicating these newcomers had. Their animals were not free but were kept within boundaries. Yet in the new land, enclosures did not hold them and the animals wandered miles. Wild long-horned zebus wandered the cow pastures and could not be quietened. Sickness and pestilence came on even before the white ghosts themselves could be seen.

Worse still the white ghosts would kill their own with a rope and lash a man's back until it was bloody and raw.

In these early times of contact between the people and the new comers, many died of fevers and colds. Many were severely punished for killing the cows, horses and sheep that ate the pastures of the kangaroo, emu, wallaby, echidna and wombats.

At night beyond the frontiers of conflict with the white ghosts, Ḏilkurrwurru would take his people on a journey. He would write the lessons for future generations in the sky. At night Ḏilkurrwurru would lie in his shelter and look as if he were sleeping but when all was quiet he would fly up into the night sky and look down on his people.

Ḍilkurrwurru was on a spirit journey. Up a ladder to the Milky Way he would go and there he made powerful medicine to ensure that no matter what happened in the physical world, the power and spirit of his people would always be strong.

The message sticks were sent east, west, north and south. It was nothing for an Aboriginal runner to cover one hundred miles in a day. Through all the territories and regions, Ḍilkurrwurru Wataŋgurr's warnings were conveyed. Everyone began to look up at the sky at night and to read the messages that were being written in the Milky Way.

The white ghosts were making their main camps in rivers and harbours where they could moor their great ships.

There was activity on the mainland but the great prevailing winds sent their ships southwards along the bottom of the continent. The biggest settlement was in the southern areas of the mainland and the islands.

Even with the fastest runners the message sticks could not warn the people of the impending danger. Ḍilkurrwurru concentrated on sending his warnings via meditation. He concentrated on his dreams and hoped his warnings would appear in the old men and women's minds across the plains and over mountains, along the great rivers and into the interior deserts and western shores. Ḍilkurrwurru and the other old men had their work cut out for them. Too many people were dying. In great ceremonies, the old men would sing the spirits of the dead back into the bodies of those that had died. Then they would catch the spirits and place them in the soul of their wives or children.

Sometimes when many people were killed the spirits would be placed in trees ready to emerge for new people at better times ahead.

Only a small number of those who remained behind to gather the last season of bunya nuts ever came over the dividing range. The white ghosts brought disease and death to even the greatest warriors and it did not spare women or the smallest child.

It was as if aliens had landed from another planet. Only in the very north of Australia where visitors had been trading with the people of the Great South Land for hundreds of years was there any immunity from the new perils that came to the southern shores.

Dilkurrwurru knew that his people had to wait and to live to fight another day. The rhythm of a thousand generations had been disrupted by the white ghosts. But the people who remained were strong. They had seen a time when the whole of their land was covered in ice. They had battled with giant marsupial monsters. They knew of the great beings and animals that had created the shapes and forms of the land.

Time was their friend. For no matter how long it took and how big the tribulations, the spirits and their guardians would prevail.

There were little glimmers of hope. Dilkurrwurru wondered at the tiny being that had appeared in his dreams. He felt peace and comfort thinking of her presence. Through her he could also see that many of the people who were coming to the South Land had suffered the same tribulations and troubles that his people had suffered. Through the little being Dilkurrwurru could see a time when the culture of the white ghosts and the culture of his own people would be mutually respectful. Men and women would study the ways of the people of the coast and they would resurrect their understandings and meanings. They would come to know the laws of the land and nature. Dilkurrwurru saw too that the great lands on the other side of the earth would also one day pay homage to the knowledge of his people.

No matter how bad the troubles Dilkurrwurru knew that his people would survive and prevail. He instilled this in his children and grandchildren: "Our spirit is so imbued in this land that nothing, not even death, can take it away. It will be there waiting for other little children to hold a tree, take a handful of sand and breathe the air, to look up at the Milky Way and see the world through our eyes."

All this unfolded in Dilkurrwurru's mind; but all over the continent there was crisis, torment and death.

"They live in a tranquillity which is not disturbed by the Inequality of Condition. The earth and sea of their own accord furnishes them with all things necessary for Life."[19]

OLD MAN FOG CAME TO ME, random bullets fired across the world. He was a mist and yet he was a man. Not that great lethal blanket of soot and dark, but the cloud that brings rain and hovers in the clefts of hills and makes babies. He was from the far, far past and from the far future. He was a liar and yet he told the truth. He was someone to fear and someone to admire. He was a profound, philosophical being that grandparents would tell their grandchildren about to make them wise. I knew all too well of his nature. I had grown up with imps and their shenanigans. The world of magic is full of such beings who seem to represent one thing to a young mind and then mean something else to an old one. They are there to make you think and see. But who was sending me this being and why? I had to look deeply to find an answer.

Then I saw. Shot in a shoulder the warrior recoiled in horror. Most of the lead and buckshot hit shoulders, arms or legs so as not to kill. But in these times of exploration and first contact even shots that did not kill resulted in a slow death. It was one thing to remove a spear head, it was another to remove a tiny ball of lead. Wounds festered and warriors died slowly and painfully.

I saw a great ship hit a reef. I saw the crew run a sail around the boat and plug the hole in its bow so that it could find shelter for repairs. Up the coast it ran, listing to one side, with all eyes desperately looking for a place to land. Luck and skill were with this captain and his crew. I saw the ship on its side on the sand banks. I saw carpenters repairing twisted wood. People from the lands were watching. Slowly they approached. Who were these strange white-skinned ghosts? They were starving ignorant fools.

One day the fools set out with a harpoon and they came across dugong and turtles. All were slaughtered and brought back to the ship. When the people of the lands saw what the men had done they were outraged. Female and young turtle and dugong alike were killed. These were greedy, hungry men with no knowledge, who did not care.

In a rampage, the shore was set on fire. The newcomers' tents and possessions were in the path of the flames. The soldiers and crew responded with horror and were quick to take up arms. It was then the warrior was shot.

That night earnest discussions took place in both camps. The old men looked into their campfires. For many nights, they talked. There could have been war, there should have been war.

Some days later in the morning on the beach an old man appeared and walked towards the captain. The old man was rubbing his hands under his armpits and showing his open hands to the captain. "We know you cannot understand our way," the old man was saying, "but let me teach you. Let me show you how the land can recognize your scent and presence." Again and again he wiped his hands under his armpits and tried to show the captain that his mission was peace.

The captain could not and would not understand, but through this brave old leader peace was restored. The captain would not be so lucky in the future. As I looked over the new forests and lands we had come to, I saw that there were many times when there was no peace and understanding - only bloodshed, violence and tragedy ensued. In losing the magic of the land there should have been common ground between the people of Éire and the peoples of the Great South Land. Only after lifetimes of tragedy would understanding emerge.

I saw countless old men walking towards muskets. I saw a little boy dreaming in the sand dunes. He and his brothers were running and hiding without a care in the world on sands that were the colours of the rainbow. It was near the brown snake place on a beach that caught everything drifting across the warm ocean currents. All around them were spirits Wurrey, the tricky fog, Old Lady carpet snake, the Magpie brothers, the giant dingo dog and the outlaw, Arrimi, who delivered mayi (wild food) to those whose spirits were down. I cannot tell you these stories because they are not mine to tell. I have to tell you a story for which I have ownership, responsibility and most of all a direct feeling. Do you understand why? I was being shown this little boy dreaming as a hint. Our two destinies were intertwined but if I tried to tell you his story it would not have the punch or the carry that it should. So many stories lost their meaning because they were told without the permission and ownership of the story tellers. This is something to learn and understand. Over time you will know what I am saying.

DARK MAY TERROR: Inoculated from the poison and death they bore within, the maiyal (strange white ghosts) came like a curse from hell. The pain they caused was beyond the worst nightmares. They brought pestilence, vice and death. A black mist spread across the Great South Land. Ceremonies and the basic chores of life were disrupted. A terrible feeling was in the air. The spirit of the land was lost. There was war, much worse than war! There were profound misunderstandings about water, trees, and air. But worst of all came Mindye - a serpent of death with a head like a bull with a huge mane and a tail like a ring-tailed possum. Ten miles long travelling through the countryside at a blurring speed it left a trail of death dust. It spat gal-gal-la (poison).

It emerged from the holds of ships, from blankets, from breath, from food and from the very presence of the strangers.

The shadow of Great Chief Shingas and his brother Pisqueton and the infected small pox hospital blankets of Fort Pitt now hovered over the new settlement. Was the vile and evil act to be replayed here? Or was the physical presence of the strangers enough to invoke the serpent's poison? Variola major played havoc on the shores of the great Eora homelands. It spread along the banks of the mighty rivers and harbours that had been so peaceful and safe for millennia. Skin crumbled, faces aged and melted, the shock of a child or a husband or a brother or a sister or a wife or a mother becoming a grotesque horror was enough to make one die alive. These white ghosts were truly angels from hell. They had absorbed plagues, pestilence and pox and now this horror spread across the land. A simple nick of the skin with cow pox would have prevented the carnage but this knowledge would come later and these strangers could not know the accumulated terror they wrought. First came burning fever, headaches and back pains, then throats and noses stung. Breathing and talking were restricted and painful. Nothing could be swallowed. Senses screamed for bado, gapu, water. Then the blood was invaded. Pains in bones and limbs. No food could be held down. First the horrible pustulesence attacked the forehead, then the face then the hands and feet, then the trunk. Like a million mosquito bites, boils formed and filled with rank poison. The rash detached the outer layers of skin from the body. The whites of eyes became blood red. Spleen, kidney, muscle, liver, testes, ovaries and bladder began to haemorrhage. Within weeks, sometimes days, death came as a welcome relief. Those who survived bore the 'scales of the Mindye'. You could not see the Mindye but the swathe of death would mark its path. Thousands, perhaps tens of thousands, lay dead.

Mindye was a nightmare from hell in the plain light of day, a holocaust before even one shot was fired or before any point of good could be shared or before even the greatest controversies could be gauged. This mist of death crippled those who could sing and dance the land and knew its secrets. This pain would last for many generations. Nothing, only bitter imagination, could reveal its intensity. So much knowledge and joy was lost. But men and women survived and did the best they could: Arabamoo, the great Barangaroo who lost her husband and two children and found consolation with Bennelong, Gomi, Gnoo-lu-may, Nanberry, Yerrinbe, Boorong, Pemulwuy, Yemmerrwearne, Wilmerding... and many others. This was not the end, just the end of the beginning. Women continued to do their djama. Men disappeared and appeared. Ceremonies continued. Warriors planned guerrilla warfare. Arthur Phillip was adopted as a bäpa, and speared for his crimes in a makarrata of sorts: "We have not yet been able to reconcile with the natives..."[20]

MY THOUGHTS TURNED to the peril of wandering rocks. Beware! Many sailors have foundered on 'a piece of worthless coastline'. But if you can be patient you will be one step closer to the lost paradise on earth. Be attentive, take the images and patterns into your imagination. Graduate from art to life. Stumble and fall - the knowledge is too big for you to carry. Too many questions! Why did they not pay attention to the violent storm and the three water spouts that danced across the ocean when Gulaga first appeared on the horizon? It was an omen for even he who chased a chook all across Australia. And you ask: How is this ancient land magic? You do not have the stamina and patience to really begin to know! The answers are never-ending. This is the wonder and mystery. Do you think that words in a book could tell you? No. Real knowledge must be lived, sung and danced. A whole life of learning and careful study can take you down the road a certain way. Eyes, fingers and brains are enemies. You must feel the way with your heart. Words are just clues. They are bread crumbs. Secrets are passed on life after life. There are no libraries, just buŋgul. Sacred country is a swamp. Here is spring water, places of life and energy. Trapped here is abundance, knowledge, understanding and learning. Birrikidji's special dreaming![21] Why are you so intent on putting these things into a box in a museum or a university? Do you really want people to forget sacred djäma and drive mining trucks? So many things have eluded you - patterns on skin, bark and poles, lines, sand sculptures. You would not have a clue. In your ignorance, you think you are powerful but it is you who smash to pieces every time. It is you who destroy the earth. It has taken so much death, so many fully-lived lives full of mistakes and tragedy to get here, to this point of gentlest touch and first comprehension. Shed your anthropological arrogance and your certainty, begin to see, begin to feel. Let us make a beginning with Djanda lying on the sandbank in the sun, daydreaming. Eyes half-opened she contemplates the clouds on the far horizon. In her mind's eye are great river and salt water estates, sand dunes, swamps, rocks under the sea, animals and new peoples. This was the beginning of a great journey. Or is this just a goanna? Perhaps. There have been so many misunderstandings. Milirbum is Millirrpum: this artist and glorious litigant are one and the same, a lost clue and connection because the mainstream culture can't decide how to spell his name, like thousands of

Yolŋu birth certificates. Ridiculous madness and ignorant simplicity still prevail over knowledge. Is this the way you want it? Here so generously given is a great and undeserved gift - *something special from the mission arts and crafts shop - a pattern usually reserved for skin. You like it on your walls! but once again you fall down.* Djanda, the companion of Djankawu and the sisters Bitjiwurrurru and Madalaig, was there when the whistling trees were planted and he saw the sacred dilly bag with the spirits of the new land. Djanda so old and sacred symbolises so much of what you don't know about the *miwatj* estates and all of the estates and magic of this ancient land. But this *dhäwu* is only partly about Djanda. It is a story of apology and remorse. It is a story for the Yolŋu who are lost between worlds - drifting between the ancient mysteries and Woolworths. It is a story of connection. It is a story of learning and beginning that all of us must do over many generations to come. It is a story of wild dreams and turbulent nights, tragic journeys and heroes, tribulations and ignorance. The most trustworthy friend betrays the most trusting partner causing chaos then calm. In these never-ending travails, wisdom too slowly emerges. Or does it emerge at all? Great minds ponder the criss-crossing, intertwined paths and the universal dawdle through day and night. The terrible cross and crown of thorns progresses up the hill. Precious Praha and the countless confessions, dreamings and perfect blow-jobs. Will the peloothered man's slothful dreams be remembered? Will the fruits of so-called civilisation, rape of the earth, false pride and machines, kava, gambling, alcohol, pornography, electricity, roads, refrigeration and sugar, prevail over the truly learned ones? Will the adolescent fool ever come to maturity? Will the power and tranquillity of millennia ever be appreciated? Will the top of the world come to know the power of the south - the lost paradise? Will the paradise survive the vandals and thieves? Will the earth itself survive? Djanda at the centre of this "religious cult" still watches with amusement. He will prevail over our time, that much is certain. Will there be a happy ending for us? That is for you who are reading to determine.[22]

BABABADALGHARAGHTAKAMMINARRONNKONNBRON
NTONNERRONNTUONNTHUNNT-
ROVARRHOUNAWNSKAWNTOOHOOHOORDENEN-
THURNUK![23] Great forces were being unleashed on the earth. Where did they come from? These were warnings from the earth itself. The year without a summer was an omen of momentous change. It was a premonition. Times of lack and scarcity in turn create their opposite pulses of plenty and excess. I could see my world of Éire and all of the countries of the North being pummelled by these forces. Some had too much, some had too little. It was one extreme or another. Our faery world was overcome by whirring, noisy machines. Great numbers of men, women and children were leaving the countryside to work in factories, towns and cities. Great orders of the world were falling. Feared and powerful kings and queens suddenly seemed absurd. In all this people were losing themselves. The people of the South Land had an intimate sense of connectedness to land, animals, plants, stars, oceans, winds and clouds and all of the world that only we faeries know. But in Éire too, ordinary human beings could feel joy when there was the time to breathe and feel the land. I could sense with a feeling of dread that this feeling for earth and sky was about to change. Life was becoming something to be managed. Great masses of people began to congregate together. They became lost to the land and knew little of its care. Resources were to be plundered and used. Human beings became lost in their own power to change the world. All of this is written in history books. But there is the magical underside which has only been felt and never written down. That is the purpose of these words for you. Can you see now why Ḍilkurrwurru Wataŋgurr had appeared to me?

For he and his people were united with our magical realm in preserving the spirit and magic of our worlds in these times of momentous change. We were united in our hearts and equally threatened by the dramatic forces at work in the world. For the people of the South Land whose law was careful guardianship and management of all of the dimensions. spaces and creatures of the world, distribution of food and resources to all, selfish accumulations of power and the machine-like pursuit of resources and lands was incomprehensible. Wars over land and scarce resources had occurred between the great warriors and clan groups of the South Land. When starvation, misadventure, lack of capacity or enfeeblement prevailed, one group would replace another - sometimes peacefully and sometimes through conquest. But in all eventualities the land, the night sky and the seas existed as living family members. There was no gain in destroying the very fabric of life. The patterns and rhythms of seasons had to be respected, honoured and cultivated. We faeries and wise elders began to talk of a war of worlds. In our homeland of Éire, a war was breaking out between the old and the new, the haves and the have-nots, the country and the city. Most of all, machines had to be fed. In the fascination for production and progress, heat had to be generated, whole forests were consumed, mass crops had to be produced, large populations of ants had to have new housing, water, sewerage systems and roadways. Chaos prevailed and in the chaos people had to fend for themselves. Millions were starving. Boats set off to find new resources, new lands. Laws and rights of ownership were asserted by foreign monarchs on territories and peoples that they could never have imagined. An age-old story of conquests began to unfold, this time it would stretch to the lands of the South.

First came the scouts:

"If you discover the Continent abovementioned either in your Run to the Southward or to the Westward as above directed, You are to employ yourself diligently in exploring as great an Extent of the Coast as you can carefully observing the true situation thereof both in Latitude and Longitude, the Variation of the Needle; bearings of Head Lands Height direction and Course of the Tides and Currents, Depths and Soundings of the Sea, Shoals and and also surveying and making Charts, and taking Views of Such Bays, Harbours and Parts of the Coasts as may be useful to Navigation. You are also carefully to observe the Nature of the Soil, and the Products thereof; the Beasts and Fowls that inhabit or frequent it, the Fishes that are to be found in the Rivers or upon the Coast and in what Plenty and in Case you find any Mines,

Minerals, or valuable Stones you are to bring home Specimens of each, as also such Specimens of the Seeds of the Trees, Fruits and Grains as you may be able to collect, and Transmit them to our Secretary that We may cause proper Examination and Experiments to be made of them. You are likewise to observe the Genius, Temper, Disposition and Number of the Natives, if there be any and endeavour by all proper means to cultivate a Friendship and Alliance with them, making them presents of such Trifles as they may Value inviting them to Traffick, and Shewing them every kind of Civility and Regard; taking Care however not to suffer yourself to be surprized by them, but to be always upon your guard against any Accidents. You are also with the Consent of the Natives to take Possession of Convenient Situations in the Country in the Name of the King of Great Britain: Or: if you find the Country uninhabited take Possession for his Majesty by setting up Proper Marks and Inscriptions, as first discoverers and possessors."*

Then came the occupiers:

"With these Our Instructions, you will receive Our Commission under Our Great seal constituting and appointing you to be Our Captain General and Governor in Chief of Our Territory called New South Wales ... It is therefore Our Will and Pleasure that you do immediately upon your landing after taking Measures for securing Yourself and the people who accompany you, as much as possible from any attacks or Interruptions of the Natives of that Country, as well as for the preservation and safety of the Public Stores, proceed to the Cultivation of the Land, distributing the Convicts for that purpose in such manner, and under such Inspectors or Overseers and under such Regulations as may appear to You to be necessary and best calculated for procuring Supplies of Grain and Ground Provisions.

Then came the war and greed.

The reptile brain knows no feeling. It kills. It shuts off. It disappears into the ether, dirt or forest. When the heart gets in the way or something more complicated than the careful act of killing, then irrationality and emotive violence manifest themselves. This emotional violence is daunting. But most often the eyes simply stare straight ahead and nothing other than the modality of killing occurs. There is no emotion.

All this Dilkurrwurru Wataŋgurr saw. How could there be an explanation for this destruction he thought to himself? Dilkurrwurru threw himself on the ground and began to cry. His tears were rivers and his grief shook the leaves on the trees. The tears attracted small animals and birds that gathered around him. The mokuy and spirit beings found him. They saw in him their own ceremonies of sacred crying. It was here in this place of death and destruction that a new spirit began to emerge. It came to us too. We who were struggling to understand the changes in our world knew that we must be as one with Dilkurrwurru Wataŋgurr and his people. One of the daunting tasks was to preserve the rigour and precision of the ancient ceremonies. The knowledge was placed in great rocks and trees. There it waited for a hundred years if necessary for a kindred spirit to awaken and revive it. But it would take many generations for the world to understand. It would take the greatest minds, philosophers, dancers, athletes and poets to tune in, for all these abilities would be required to bring the spirit of the land back to life. All over the country the old men and women put courage and fortitude into the hearts of those who were to die. Warriors knew how to die bravely. But they became crippled at the thought of women and children falling at the hands of the newcomers. Great gatherings were held in the rainforest to give warriors, women and children the blessings to pass properly into the spirit world. A calm came over the land. It broke the elders' hearts to gather the adornments of everyday life and protect them from the marauding evil. The sacred cloth and string, the baskets, spears, rubbing tools, designs and sea craft would never be lost. These things would be needed by future generations to understand the sacred qualities of day to day life. Dilkurrwurru Wataŋgurr and the network of elders worked with quiet determination, recording, dreaming, registering all. They were there for the future for those who had the heart to claim them again.

Leaders looked for chinks in the firepower of the marauders. Many brave women and men took them on wild goose chases up hill and down dale. But no-one had ever witnessed death and destruction like this. It was astonishing to see warriors simply fall dead hit by a projectile with the enemy well beyond throwing range. What was this evil? Men, women and children died with the knowledge that they would ultimately prevail. This was our spiritual promise and resolve to them. The ancestors of those who killed would cry for an eternity for the crimes that had been committed and the horror they had wrought.

They too would cry and crawl with their hands in the dirt trying to recover what had been destroyed. Countless children would ask their bewildered parents over many generations: what madness was this? It would take much deliberation and a concerted effort by all of the world's first nations and peoples to finally put an end to war and destruction. This great cause of respect and understanding became a long quest over generations. This was the destiny of us faeries and the survivors of the great war of the worlds. Our dreams became fused together as the alien invaders roamed across the great southern continent bringing carnage and tragedy everywhere they went. Would the land ever forgive the newcomers? Could the first peoples ever lose the pain and trauma of these years? Could the newcomers ever forgive their own kind for the sheer bastardry of it all? Great confusion and ignorance prevailed. It is the first reaction of someone who has been treated cruelly to play out that cruelty on someone else. Can you see in this how we faeries and spirits had our role to play? We were there waiting to be asked and consulted. We had to wait for people's heads to be ruled by their hearts and we too had a lot of learning to do.

.

Gapu-dhä-yindi (High Seas)

Yet she goes with footstep wary
Full of earth's old timid grace. [24]

I HAD FLOWN THOUSANDS OF MILES, followed a thousand roads, dreamed of a calico bonnet, watched women and children struggle along muddy byways - this was Éire in the troubled times, when the countryside was changing. Food and resources were being sent away. Families and children were starving. Cruelty prevailed. A hurricane of change was blowing. I could sense the anger of the people all over the countries of the north. Barricades blocked roads, rebellion was in the air. Evicted from their homes, huddled together on commons land with no capacity to live new dreams emerged, new passions were ignited. Pitted against tyranny, autocracy and greed many people began to have a dream of a more perfect society and welfare for all. This dream too would yield up its tyrants. My heart was with the people trying to survive. Armies and police were pitched against those who wanted to challenge authority and those who were hungry alike. If you did not move with the times then you were trampled over. Despite the tumult there were people whose spirit had not been broken. This was what drew me to Honor Hughes. When I first saw her, she was eating oysters and sea urchins with her children and it was a wondrous sight. I fell in love with her from the first moment I saw her. I kissed her instantly and so it began. She was the embodiment of all that was good and courageous as she battled across the muddy roads. Honor could make a broth of dandelion, sorrel, dock and grass delicious for her children. She wore a bracelet made from the golden locks of her first-born child. All these things made me come to this mother of Éire and her children. Honor had her demons but I forgave her for them. I also felt her pain. I would stay with her now for many a year, many an adventure. Creating magic and love within Honor's world became my destiny.

"HERE IS JUST THE THING I WAS LOOKING FOR, this magic pebble will make our soup thick and hearty and our stomachs will be full," Honor told her children. In them I felt Éire's pain. For how could a whole nation be allowed to starve? With each tribulation and cruelty, I could feel Honor hardening up against the world. I knew that I had to stay with her and to sing to her and keep her heart and the hearts of her children open.

Honor still believed in magic but as time went on she became more attuned to practical things, to surviving and to putting one foot in front of the other. She had seen and endured much harshness from men. She had heard of a noble woman who was taking in women and children in the terrible years and had searched for her. She was the hope of Ireland, the only woman with means, who cared for those who did not have enough to eat.

Like so many people of Éire in these troubled times, Honor was evicted from her one-room cottage because she could not pay the rent. With her six children in tow, she was walking from the west to the east in search of shelter, food and the fabled noble woman.

That first night I slept with Honor and her six children in the fields we were at one with the earth. The stars were our sleeping companions. As the sun rose I watched as Honor hitched her skirt up and jumped over a stone fence into a paddock in search of firewood and food. Even by gathering firewood, Honor was breaking the law. What a sight! Honor was a striking woman. She was tall, lean and fit from gathering firewood. Her hair was curly - a place where birds might nest, something wild and gorgeous.

Honor was not to be trifled with. She was a match for any man. Working people respected her greatly for her pride and independence. She was a very beautiful woman but she kept this hidden under her shawl and the warm layers she kept wrapped around her. She thought nothing of her beauty and disliked the attention it attracted. All Honor wanted was respect and the right to pursue her life with her children.

Honor loved the natural world and had no fear of the wildest weather and animals. She had no hesitation in taking her children into the countryside. With her two faithful dogs she was not afraid of anyone. In so many ways the wild was a relief. Apart from anything else it was a relief from paying rent. If anyone could help the children to move on to a better life she could. Her six young ones kept her constantly working. They were very well-disciplined and always supportive of their mother. It was amazing that after all the tribulations the children appeared well-washed and clothed.

Honor spent every waking moment caring for them. Food was whatever she could rustle up of the herbs and grasses in the field. She was strict but loved each child without limit.

Her oldest boy Hector was a tearaway. At only twelve years of age he was already strong and fearless with his mother's courage and purpose. "Who's to know if we stole a lamb mother?" Honor quickly boxed him round the ears and he cowered in fright. "And what would happen if you did that Hector! You would kill us all with grief if you were caught." But Honor knew her children were hungry. "If there's any stealing to be done it'll be me that has to answer for it, Hector." She looked down into the eyes of her faithful dogs who she would die for and who would die for her. They were amazing dogs who would run in the wild at night catching rabbits and faithfully bringing them back to the grateful family. But as so many foraged for food there was barely a hare or rabbit to be had.

After weeks on the road Honor knew the children needed something warm and filling. They too were in danger of starving. Honor had dispatched many a lamb. She knew that the animal needed to be thanked and respected for allowing human beings to create food from its flesh. With her mind made up she had not a moment's hesitation in quickly snaring a young one, creating a fire and cooking it up, carefully using every part of the animal for food.

With few implements, Honor quickly improvised the cooking, she threw the whole animal on the fire coals and the smell of the lanolin and wool wafted across the countryside as she carefully singed it down to the flesh. The flesh was cooked with a slow heat until the joints and the flesh could be pulled apart.

"Let us be thankful for this providence," Honor said. "Forgive me," she said to the lamb silently, but she knew that it was never wrong for a mother to take food for her children. How good the flesh tasted! The glow of the fire and the warmth of the food in their stomachs made the children happy for the first time in weeks. The dogs too were fed and slept contentedly.

Honor looked at how the colour came back into her children's cheeks. "Keep your mouth closed when you chew your food," she said.

I watched all this and was full of admiration for Honor and her capacity to look after her children. But I also saw her heart hardening against men. I knew what I had to do, and from that time on I slept on the shoulders of the youngest child, Mary Hughes, who was just five years old.

Faeries do not have the magic to change things. We cannot be seen or heard except in very special circumstances. But we can put happy thoughts and wondrous ideas into the mind of a child. Faeries especially love to sing and make music. Even at the worst of times, faeries can point to the good and to the true and to the beautiful. They remind children not to follow mean thoughts or violent actions. But just to do good. Even small gestures can make a difference.

As I slept on Mary's shoulder I brought the night's stars into her dreams. Mary was flying through the milky way, happy, dancing and silver. I hummed a beautiful lullaby to the camp and everyone slept soundly.

I hummed *Eddie Kelly's Jig, Mouse in the Mug, Flowing Tide* and *Cooley's Hornpipe,* and for a time the spirit of the great land was at peace.

As morning came I noticed that other faeries had gathered in the camp. Each child had been adopted. It made me happy to think that all over the countryside, faeries were putting sweet dreams into children's' minds in these troubled times. Through Tanaquill my messages of the troubles had travelled the length and breadth of the British Isles and I knew that the same was occurring there.

But soon there was more to worry about. From somewhere in the future the song of a jolly jumbuck came into my mind!

46

Running over the fields came an angry farmer. Honor's dogs were quick to turn him back. But with a terrible curse the farmer howled: "I know you Honor Hughes, you've taken one of my lambs, there'll be all hell to pay for this."

The momentary peace and happiness of the family was now replaced by more stress and turmoil! "Quick children," Honor said, "you all know what you have to do."

SIMON OF CYRENE TAKES THE BURDEN and saves humanity from a complete curse. What was he thinking as he painted for the mission arts and crafts shop? Was it his partnership with the mystery man from the University of Melbourne? Like Simon he was a miracle. Bolŋu appeared on the afternoon of the first day of the great journey. In the middle of the tempest, his ḻarrpan poised, he smiled at the travellers. His presence was immense, his powers were wondrous. A myriad of stories and places were in the mind of the artist and great warrior. Reflecting on the great storm he and his sons had weathered, he painted the drops of rain and heavy rain mixed together beating down on the roof and through onto the bodies of the men. Thunder rocks the sky. Thunder bolts are thrown down. Electricity. Creation. Chaos. A bolt screams down splitting rocks, a thousand eyes on the landscape rising in the air as clouds. Djambuwal heralding the ŋarra calling for the people to come together. The joy of the wet season rain and changing seasons. The rock under the sea. The cod swimming linked to the lightning. Yams growing in the soil nurtured by the rain. This great and fearful being hosting life.[25]

"A fond farewell to the white potatoes, pleasant it was to be in their company, generous and cheerful, laughing at us from the head of the table. They were 'the nurse that kept us amused at meals, day-time and night-time'." [26]

I SAW THE POLICE COMING with the farmer and his dogs. My faery friends and I flew to action. We made the farmers dogs snap and yap and chase their tails. Honor and her six children were masters at giving police the slip. They could run like the wind over the fields. With new sustenance in their bellies they were gone in the wink of an eye. We faeries were overjoyed and laughed at the gormless police but we could not laugh for long...

"Away children away. They will never catch us. For we are one with the rabbits and birds. Let us fly." Honor told her children.

They did not need a second to gather their clothes. All knew that they must run in separate directions and then when their energy waned they were to wait by the biggest trees they could find. Honor had trained them again and again. The blankets flew up and became capes. Little dark clouds streaked across the paddocks as they made their getaway. The two dogs led the way and periodically double backed to see that no-one was following. Hours later the dogs and Honor would find the children one by one in their hiding spots. It was a well-practised routine.

No-one could ever catch them.

Something happened here in the wilds. In escaping the cruelty of Éire at this time Honor and the children found harmony. It was something that Honor would return to again and again in her life. She could turn away from town and village life and be happy in the wild. The children were hungry but there were so many delights. A tiny bird flew onto Honor's shoulder. Yes of course it was me playing tricks. The children laughed. Honor turned with a stern look in her eye. This is not a playground she said with her gestures. But she too grinned to herself. Without a house or a kitchen Honor and the children became tuned into the land. By firelight they could look up at the stars and go to sleep in the warm light and wake up with the dawn. Honor knew that despite the lack of home comforts this was a special time. Animals, plants, wind, cloud, rain became familiar friends. This feeling which Ḍilkurrwurru Wataŋgurr had called wäṉa was looming in my mind. Every dimension of life from the stars in the sky to the grains of sand on the beach was related and had its place in the family order of things. It amazed me that human beings could feel this oneness with the world. I thought that only faeries could have these feelings. But as I lived with Honor and the children in the wild places of Éire I started to understand that slowly and surely the human world would evolve and learn. Something was awakening in this hardship that would tie the fates of Ḍilkurrwurru Wataŋgurr and his people with ours. Wäŋa! True deep feelings of being at home in the world. This was something we could never forget from our times running from the authorities in the wilds.

In love and in tune with the wilds Honor and her children would never have been caught, but these were troubled times. Families were desperate for food. If strangers appeared there was a great temptation to report them to the police and to claim a pittance for food. Honor knew this and never questioned the ethics of a mother who, like her, was desperate to support her family. She avoided towns and villages and houses. She and the children had come to prefer the wild places where only us faeries dwelled.

In the night, I noticed young Hector would wait until his mother was asleep and then he would steal away. Honor knew that Hector was up and about and thought nothing of it. Hector was a tearaway. He could run for miles over the moonlit fields and paddocks. He had fallen head over heels for Sinead Keogh, a lovely girl his age, youngest of ten. At night, he would run miles to be with her. He threw pebbles against her window. Down she would climb and the two would talk and sleep until the hours before the dawn. One night Sinead forgot to go back to her room and her stern father found her sleeping in the barnyard hay. "What nonsense is this?" old man Keogh said in her ear. "Back to bed for you, missy, and watch out if I ever catch you sleeping out here again." He suspected nothing but Hector was cutting a little too close to the wind. If his mother had known of his night-time visits she would have admonished him and that would have been the end of the matter.

It was probably Hector's scent that the police dogs followed one moonlit night and as the morning light emerged, the policemen surrounded our little camp. It was not Hector's fault. He could never have known of the presence of so many police and soldiers in the countryside. Things were changing in Éire.

Hunger and famine were inspiring the people to stand up openly against the authorities.

"We have done nothing wrong," cried Honor as she stood ready to fight and flee. "It is a god-given right for a mother to feed her children. The crime belongs to you who would not grant haven to those in need." How my heart heaved as I heard these words. For it was the truth. It was Éire's lowest hour and we faeries knew that somehow, some way we would try to right the injustice of these troubled times. We loved Honor and her spirit and her children dearly. Whatever happened we would follow them to the last. But the hardening of the heart is a terrible thing and I could see in Honor's eyes something unforgiving, revengeful and bitter. This would take a long time to heal. The reverberations of the non-magic world were hurting so many people like Honor who were becoming locked in their own thoughts of revenge and justice. Stone-heart would be matched by stone-heart.

It was impossible to get away this time. There were over a dozen police and dogs. They were searching not for Honor, or even Hector, but for the signs of insurrection and rebellion in the countryside.

Honor and the children were tied together and walked into the town of Ballyncarrigy by police.

This was the beginning of a long period of waiting.

Along with the beloved dogs, Honor and the children were first held in the small-town stockade. For many weeks, here they lived on oatmeal, potato shavings and water. It was in some ways a better diet than they had lived on in the countryside. At each meal Honor would do something that would ensure that the children ate their food without complaint and gratitude. But then it came time for the dogs to go. Honor managed to send word to her family members. Everyone wanted the staffie hunting dogs that were so well-trained. But how they howled, and how Honor cried, when it came time to separate. She loved those dogs more than life itself. But now she had to think of the children.

Mary stayed with her mother. Each night I sang to Honor and the children. I sang so many songs and hummed so many tunes

The Mug of Brown Ale, Fred Finns, Music in the Glen, Shoemakers Daughter, Dinkie's Reel. I loved to see the children's smiles as they danced and sang in their dreams.

Finally, Honor appeared in court. At that time, the penalty for stealing a sheep was very harsh. The misguided landlords and farmers thought that if they imposed the harshest penalties it would stop the hungry people from stealing food. But nothing can stop a mother wanting to look after her children! Hardness begat hardness!!

The human world was moving from one system of power and authority to another. The authorities were realizing that even if they imposed the worst penalties, instead of submitting, people would rise up together. So, a new solution was coming forward in the minds of the magistrates and officials of government and power – send the people away as far as possible, impose monotonous routines and work.

Honor's lawyers stood and barely mumbled: "Petitioner begs most humbly to state that Honor Hughes was left a widow with six fatherless children who have been dependent on the charity of a humane and charitable public for support. Hardship alone induced her, and the tears of her wretched orphans compelled her, to do what she had to do to feed her children."

But the magistrate didn't even look up. I flew up to the magistrate as he sentenced Honor to imprisonment in Van Diemen's Land. I looked into his eyes. They were eyes of molten blackness. "Please sir what of my children?" cried Honor.

The magistrate looked down on her and then looked away.

The court clerk said coldly "You may take one child with you but there is no room aboard the convict ship for more than one."

Tears streamed down my eyes as I watched Honor step sorrowfully down the court aisles, carrying Mary in her arms.

At that instant, I started to understand the meaning of my dream. Where was this place? So, this was the reason why there were frequent trips between the prison and the ships in the harbor? I knew that somehow the loss of magic occurring across the countryside would be re-born and re-emerge in a new world. I knew also that we of the spirit world had found allies at the bottom of the world. People who believed in magic and spirits and who nurtured their dreams and contact with the spirits. One day they and we would combine to help the world understand that man could not be the centre of the universe or play God. We would teach the world to listen to their hearts and to sense the spirits in the land. Magic would ensure that families lived with kindness and generosity all the days of their lives.

In that most desolate hour of sorrow I knew that I needed to go with Honor and Mary to this new world and that the fate of Éire and the world itself would depend on what I learned there.

Honor did not cry, but she was desperate and determined for her children. She sent word out to her family and they organised for Hector, Patrick and their smaller siblings to be taken away from the stockade.

With tears flowing, Honor told her children to be strong. "Always remember I love you more than life itself. We must all find our own paths, but no matter how we are separated I will always be with you in spirit and mind." The children hugged their mother. She knew she had taught them all well and that they would live life fully and strongly. This was a very special woman and these were extraordinary people from an extraordinary time and they carried with them a spirit that was unconquerable. But if you asked Honor she would scornfully say: "I am always alright. What other choice is there but to survive?"

293 Bathurst 536 Narromine 860 Bourke 1408 Cunnamulla 1496 Tambo (Swim) 1806 Longreach 1937 Crawford Creek 1937 Kyuna 2144 Caamoweal 2626 Barkly Homestead 2935 Three Ways Roadhouse 3064 Dunmora 3386 Katherine 3732 Stuart Hwy turnoff 3747 Lookout 3914 (167) Goyder River Bridge 4165 Rocky Bottom Creek 4196 Maypuru 4244 Gapuwiyak 4267 Lahynapuy 4301 Baniyala 4310 Gurrumurru 4322 Wandawuy 4325 Bobby Beasley Creek 4332 Microwave Tower 4340 Garrathala 4359 Water sign 4364 Cattle Station 4367 Buymarr

4369 Dhaniya 4378 Mata Mata 4479 Manymak dhuwala waŋa nhina.

GENTLE VERONICA SAVES HUMANITY FROM ITS WORST. Underneath the lilies swim baḏaltja in the fresh water. What a presence they have. Sometimes they make the mistake of lumbering along a path or track and are easy prey. But here they are safe in their own realm. The lumbering clumsy one becomes majestic, swimming deep below the surface. How are they linked to parrot fish swimming in the salt water? These are questions to be asked on the proper occasions. Perhaps you will be lucky and hear a story that will inform you. The big lily yulgu roots are sacred, prized food. At Gudaidj-bingaru the ground is stained with ochre in the water. The sand covers the yulgu roots.

All this coloured ground is mixed up like paint on the ground. In the brackish water, life forms and moves into the active world from the nursery. These places are also symbols for leaders to plan their worlds and estates and to make allowances for family over many generations. Colours on skin forms the connection between the human world and the greater family of the world - baḏaltja little grandfather![27]

I'll penance do with farts and groans
Kneeling upon my marrowbones.[28]

MARIA WAS MORE THAN A CONVICT SHIP. It was a magic ship. Its voyages reverberated across time and through the generations. Great, great grandchildren would sing of a wind called *Maria* with Mr O'Hara playing his fiddle and wonder in reverie about what the words really meant. The wind blew their very life force to them.

Later they came to learn of the sacred winds of the north: Luŋgurrma, Djänu, Djoparra, Bulunu, Dharratarra, Garramiṉḏl, Maḏirri, Djalitaŋ, Galabala', Bärra' and Lirra-ŋa'ka. Winds can talk, make you feel, make you dream. They bring people, trade and things - sometimes good, sometimes bad. That first cold Irish night on the tip of the mast I heard a vibration, it was long and sonorous, a sound I had never heard before. It was coming from the future and the past. It was faint and strong and came from a very long way away. It was a healing sound bringing with it a healing wind. Like the breath of a giant creature, it gently touched me and I fell into a long dream... Once again, I saw the strange land at the bottom of the world and the ever-appearing beautiful woman anxious to help everyone. Her large family loved her and always wanted her to be around them. She made everyone laugh and sing. She had great dreams and plans. In the morning hours before dawn, this beautiful woman would talk of the biggest yams, the warmest possum skin coats and the most delectable oysters. She lived life to the fullest and she allowed her moods and activities to determine the course of her own travels. In the early morning as the sailors came climbing up the rigging I wondered: Who was this mysterious and wonderful woman? Only much later would I understand. The Galpu clan with their healing yidaki sounds had come to me to ease our passage into the future. One day we would create a grand alliance to heal the evils of the world. Nothing is ever easy, good things take time was the message that soothed and washed over me.

THE AGONY OF THE CLIMB and the burden so great. Folk climbing the Reek in Mayo stumbling trying to find in the cold mist some purity, some semblance of the sacrifice that might make things right, thinking of the million who starved, the troubles of the serpent and the tree and the worthless foolishness of men and women. Falling in the mud again, the weight so great and yet with this humiliation and weakness is something greater and more powerful. Wititj at Garimala billabong, rainbows form where the rain hits the surface of the water. Wititj brings the thunder and lightning of the wet season. Water lilies are in flower. Djaykuŋ can be seen swimming, its body swollen with eggs. The growth and fertility of the wet season emanating from wititj. Vibrating, shimmers, colours of the rainbow, glistening water. Great spirit of the earth.[29]

IT WAS A DREADFUL, SAD DAY when Honor, Mary and I were rowed out to the *Maria*. I looked out at the vessel and its rigging and I sensed something. I noticed its masts, tall, straight and strong. The timbers were corked and nailed. This would be our home for nine long months at sea.

The *Maria* lay moored for weeks but gradually more and more men and women came on board. One day to Honor's amazement the women and children were called onto the deck. There before them was the woman she had been searching for: the noble Cathleen. She was a beautiful sight and she carried with her stacks of books, new bonnets, tunics, small bags of cotton and needles and carefully cut pieces of cloth.

"Irish women!" Cathleen exclaimed, "You are strong and you will survive. Please accept these gifts for your voyage ahead. You are well to be sailing away from the tribulations here at home, but never forget the magic of your homeland. Good luck and good fortune come to those with pure love in their heart."

Honor was revived by the message of hope. She did not need to be told that she was stronger than anyone could imagine. But Cathleen formed an ideal for her of what a strong, good and kind noble woman should be like. It remained with her all her life. *'You lived by actions not words.'* Those that promised much, the politicians and the officials, paled in contrast to this noble woman who knew that she had an obligation to act with dignity and generosity to all – no matter what the cost. The Countess Cathleen followed her sense of justice wherever it would take her and it became for Honor a code of living that she would take to the new land. Over future generations this credo became a family trait.

THE CHILDREN ON SHORE did not know when their mother and sister's journey would begin and whether they would be able to say a final goodbye. They would come down to the harbor to see if *Maria* was still at its mooring. They would stand for a few minutes waving out at the gunnels of the ship. Each day they came until one day the mooring was empty and the *Maria* had begun its journey. It was 23 July 1849, just over a year since our adventures in the wilds had begun. "I love you my children. I love you my dogs," Honor murmured quietly as she hugged Mary. I transmitted the message over the winds and into the hearts of Hector and the others. There was no greater grief a mother could have. Yet Honor had a belief and knowledge in what she had taught every child. She knew that whatever happened to her, she had equipped her children well.

In Honor's mind she saw children running across the countryside free. Every child had a faery that would stay with them for the rest of their lives. Even at this worst of times, we put good thoughts into the minds of the children. I began to whisper in Honor's ear. A better life would, somehow, one day come of the journey to the strange land so far away. She did not want to hear but I would never stop trying and I too hoped that one day we might see the children again. But for Honor and so many others it was the last she would ever see of her homeland and of the children that remained. It was only in death that she would finally re-unite with them. Has this pain of separation ever gone away? Maybe it should never be forgotten. And yet in the years to come so many other children would be taken away from their parents for some reason that no-one could understand. When will people learn?

That night I sang a lullaby to Mary as the waves rocked against the bow of the boat. It was a beautiful Irish song – *Mist Covered Mountain*. I planted the images of Éire into their souls. They would never forget their origins and the fundamental right of a mother trying to look after her children. All pain was catalysing into hate in Honor. She was numb with the loss of her children and dogs. She dreamed of a rising tide, of land by the waterside. Thank god she still had Mary. Other women, who had lost much more, accompanied Honor and Mary on the great voyage, only this recognition and compassion for those even more unfortunate gave Honor some sense of equilibrium in her emotions and feelings.

That night we felt new strains and creaks within the internal timbers of *Maria*. Honor and Mary had only a small cot to themselves but it was enough. They were heading into the open sea and the rolling of the swell now created a steady rock. In a habit that was to last her lifetime, Honor took out the small needles given to her by Cathleen and carefully began to sew. At first it was tentative, but then Honor started to apply her legendary concentration.

Each tiny stitch was carefully made. Nothing would compare with the high quality of Honor's embroidery. There was never a stitch out of place. The little needle kit and pieces of cloth became magic in themselves. It was here that Honor weaved her spirit and hopes. In later times people who saw the quilts the convict women made wondered at the spirit and magic of the courageous women. There were some things that money could not buy and some spirits that could never be broken. In the future weaving would be a means of communication between the newcomers and the people of the land. Weaving would join people and land. It would join women across all experience. The sacred djäma of women across the world would come together. The great weaver of Mata Mata came to me again and again. Knots united peoples. Dyes from the roots of the land. Pandanus harvested and split. So many hours of quiet contemplation and thought.

After a week at sea... there was no wind. We were in what they called the doldrums. Neither coming nor going, it was the worst of times. I looked into the future and I heard songs of divers returning home from a place of red sand and blue seas. I could see women from the desert with no fear diving deeper than any man in the sea. 'These lugger sails are moving too slowly.' [30] I hummed these songs of eventual homecoming. Something seemed to stir. The women and children were only rarely allowed out on the open deck. When they emerged into the sunlight the open sea was a wonder for them to behold. It was as if a wind was blowing with my dreams and songs of the future. Slowly the ship began to move again. First the sails flapped, soon they grew tight.

Along the coast of Africa we sailed and then we came to the Cape of Good Hope and the *Maria* pulled into port. Honor looked up to see a flat mountain. The ship took on plants, animals and grains. Honor wondered at the sights of unfamiliar trees and the wild lands. "One day I would like to come back to this place with my children and my dogs," she thought to herself.

As the *Maria* pressed ever south we faeries sensed a new kind of energy around us. It was wild and stormy but amongst the waves were sea creatures and birds and beings that played in the waves. The faeries sensed a new world of animals and spirits and stories of the stars, moon and sun. Into this new world sailed Honor and Mary. They were leaving the land they loved but I realised too that there had been many centuries of pain for the women and children of Éire. Could there be a new beginning?

As the *Maria* sailed I sensed my old world of natural spirits leaving us. In the night, meteor showers lit up the sea. Every evening on the horizon I saw large clouds, then lightning and thunder. These clouds symbolised the changing seasons of the Great South Land.

As our journey progressed I could again hear the sonorous vibration from far away. It was once again the sound of the peoples of the North of Australia playing the yidaki. When the great masters played the vibration would travel over great distances, over mountain ranges, across seas and over islands and then back. All these things were signs that we were crossing ancient pathways and songlines.

As I looked across the dimensions of time and space, I knew we were coming to a new natural world. But so too did Honor and Mary. Night was becoming day. Winter was becoming summer. The seasons were becoming shorter and more subtle. Instead of four seasons, many more subtle changes in the weather were occurring. Winds brought changes from different directions. Hot came from the North, cold from the South.

At a certain point in our journey the *Maria* crossed the ancestral path of the spirit beings that created the clans and territories of the peoples of the South. I could feel wisps of wind on my face - one day in the future I would learn this was the breath of the great serpent *wititj*. The spirit beings recognized the sacred qualities of faeries and sent them messages and signs of the land and its spirits.

One day the faeries watched in amazement as a water spout appeared from the ocean. It spiralled hundreds of feet into the sky. In its midst they could see something that they had never seen before. It was Bol'ŋgu, Thunder Man, Controller of the Seasons. He too sensed the new spirit beings from the Northern Hemisphere. Suddenly rain fell from the heavens in great buckets. This was sacred water. The fresh water would form in the clouds, fall as rain on to the earth, sea and into the rivers then merge again with the sea. It was cleansing, sacred rain and the faeries recognised it as a blessing.

Human beings in their tall ships had been seen in Southern waters before, but the faeries were something different. Bol'ŋu brought the water spout closer and closer to their ship. He wanted to show them how he carried with him the seasons and change. He pointed his larrpan (spear) to the heavens showing his powers. His lighting and thunder bolts symbolised new life and growth.

On board the captain, crew and the men, women and children making their journey to a new land were scared and then mesmerized by the events of nature and they too knew that they were moving into a new sphere of life and magic. But, with the dislocation occurring from their own lands and nature, it would take a very long time before those on this journey to their new world would really understand its nature and the natural forces and spirits all around them.

Faeries are never frightened. They knew that they needed to acknowledge Bol'ŋu',[31] so up they flew. Around the mast and up into the sky they flew, a thousand faery lights. Bol'ŋu was satisfied at their tribute, the water spiral moved closer, spraying the ship with foam and rain and then passed away until it disappeared over the horizon. It was the first time Bol'ŋu had seen the tall ships acknowledge his presence with respect and knowledge.

I came to believe that we were on a journey for the children and the generations to come. The rain revived our spirits and I dared to hope that the future would be brighter than the past. I was starting to see that one day a friendship would be formed between Honor and Mary's descendants and the people of the land. I saw that one day descendants of these Irish convicts would wear white mud on their faces symbolising their oneness with the people of the land. As I dreamed all this I heard the vibration of the yidaki in the far distance.

Bubbles in the water... the great Galpu song man teaches the old white man like a baby... just learn in your heart... just hear in your soul... sound it out, make your wrong pronunciations... and spellings... aaagh learn to split your tongue... will you ever learn? Wadrayin, Bunbarrnmi, Djarimirri, Dimitmi, Bulkaninmi, Gurranbarrmi, Gapu, Walmanin, Ningarrwaruptunnin, Ningarr Walmanin, Bapiwong, Maymangnuwong, Garnwanawong, Nuwarrumbawong, Dangu gapu, Woonakawuy, Dumanawuy, Dawawinainyawuy, Dawnmarmapiwong, Marnapiwuy, Darrannicoyanawuy, Warranawuy, Woorangama, Gapu, Dwanna, Walmanyiri, Djarrimirri, Wanakuy. Gapu. Galmuklipthimum, Minburrawuna, Dolonuru, Gandyapi, Gakirimanga, Marjitpa, Nyulawannayin, Mukrichwarnmanwuru, Walmanyin, Gapu, Djarrimirri, Gurumbalami, Ya, Bapawarigal, Ya, Buruwala, Binyipimi, Djulauradi, Gunapunbun, Buruwala wananin, Warigul, Warigul, Warigul, Warigul lurrayinin, Nokuy Bumbiluwuy, Bunbiriuwuy, Bunbirriwuy, Nolahuwuy, Madayin, Madayin, Linga, Walmanin.

DOWN INTO THE HOLE IN THE SAND SHE FELT. Elbows, shoulders and then half her body went into the opening. Yes, there were precious eggs that would make a feast for all. She gave a little yell and this was met with other excited cries. Instantly she felt happy knowing that tonight a great feast would be held. This was the first time I saw Lalla Bakitju Gunda. She was a luminous presence. "I have eggs!" she cried. Yells of approval followed from up and down the shoreline.

Far to the south of Ḏilkurrwurru Wataŋgurr, the family groups had encountered boats and sailors who came to catch the seals and mutton birds. These were barbaric men who did not understand the laws of nature and did not know the rules of hunting. They killed females and young alike and they wanted more and more pelts and bodies, much more than they needed to feed themselves.

I saw that Lalla knew that the newcomers were dangerous and tried to keep her distance. But she and her women elders and relatives also knew they had to find out more.

All the young warriors loved Lalla but she was promised to Woorady of her mother's clan group. The two became great friends and they often found secret places to talk and dream about the lives they had in front of them.

As Lalla grew up, she saw more and more Europeans pass down sea lanes along her homeland shores.

One day Lalla had a dream of a wandering star. I entered a dream within a dream. It was Ḏilkurrwurru Wataŋgurr calling her. That morning Lalla told her extended family of what she had seen. Together in the Milky Way, Ḏilkurrwurru and Lalla had talked and showed each other the disease, war and terror that had come to the South East of Australia. Ḏilkurrwurru told Lalla of the survival escape of his own clan. To survive the invading monsters would require much planning and strategy. Lalla would walk between worlds - the most dangerous of all ground.

Ḏilkurrwurru saw the faery magic of the British Isles was fading and under threat. Equally the heritage of his own and Lalla's worlds were facing their greatest challenges. Those in the spiritual realm needed to come together if the evil and harm that was all around them was to come to an end. But how? And when?

In the turbulent year that saw Honor and her children locked up in an Irish gaol, death crept across the Great South Land and Van Diemen's Land. Eight great Aboriginal clan leaders sent a petition to the Queen of the British Isles, Victoria. They wrote that the peace treaty to which they had agreed had been violated and that they were being treated as prisoners. They wanted no more gaolers and dishonest men.

Lalla knew that it would be impossible for the far queen to understand what was going on so far away. She saw that the best chance of weathering the storms that came with the new settlers was to flee their beloved forests and journey to the islands. This was a desperate quest, one even more troubled than Honor's had been.

I awoke once again with a start and wondered at the land of the south, of the future, and saw now that the unique magic of Ḏilkurrwurru Wataŋgurr and Lalla offered hope to my own land and the revival of the magic of the world. This is now a quest for all, I thought. The carnage and ignorance was too much, too great and yet a tiny glimmer of hope, a spirit of resistance and a resilience was emerging even beyond death.

WHAT WAS IT ABOUT THIS SHIP? As the timbers creaked words seemed to be uttered. Then I knew. The timbers were from the forests of Éire. Have you ever listened to trees talking? "Sheee" is what you hear first. It is the sound of the wind in the leaves... but after a long time if you are very tuned-in you can hear the timbers themselves crying "Sheeee." Then if you listen very carefully you can hear conversations taking place. I could feel in the timbers the sounds of the forests back home. But there were other things - red sawdust was everywhere. The timbers were talking of ancient forests and of trees with red flowers. From all this I knew that this tiny vessel would carry us safely to our destination. Despite all the cruelty of the crew with their jibs and whistles, they could not touch Honor and Mary. Deep inside the ship was a cocoon of life which spoke of trees and gardens and animals and birds. I planted this understanding deep within Honor and Mary and they would tune in and carry this feeling of the wild, all their days. I reminded them day after day of the magic of the world and somehow I knew that there was something big ahead, something that would set the world straight again.

Sheeee - the timbers creaked and moaned. "We miss our leaves and bark!... Cold!... Hold strong!" – they were saying. I flew down to the depths of the ship and picked up some red sawdust in my hands and threw it up in in the air. Sheee – "Ancient lands and forests," "Sacred lands," I heard from within the creaking mass. Then I saw in my mind's eye the beautiful red cedar trees of the Great South Land. A cargo of convicts was coming to the South Land and a cargo of beautiful red timbers and planks for the finest furniture was coming back to Éire and the British Isles.

"Oh no!" I cried as I saw giant monsters of the ancient forests being felled with axes and saws. "No, can't you hear the land," I cried out. These ancient trees held the very fabric of the earth, and through that, the world. All the cycles of nature would be disrupted. Without them the beautiful understory and delicate, park-like qualities of the forests would be gone for generations. The newcomers could not see. I saw the people of the South Land running like the wind beneath the ancient trees and then the wasteland that was created after the trees were chopped down. I saw the soft, cool fires that were lit by the peoples of the land. They burned small areas and cleaned up the fast-growing saplings and preserved the ancient trees. When the cedars were gone the soil became dry and barren and fast-growing eucalypts and other weeds took over from the slow-growing red trees. The forests themselves were changed and people would forget and never know what the ancient forests looked like. Hot, wild fires without the stewardship of the people of the land would burn the country to moonscape, killing animals, plants and everything in their path. And even worse, a million feral animals and plants would invade the Great South Land turning the paradise into a muddy, desolate wasteland.

"Sheee..." the timbers creaked and moaned. I saw in the fine cabinetry of palaces and fine houses the cry of the cedars and ancient forests.

That cry would haunt those houses for generations to come. And deep within the wood lay ancient knowledge and messages waiting for those with the right intuition and understanding to reveal them. "One day we will return! One day the ancient peoples' knowledges will return," the timbers were telling me.

But for now the horror of the ancient forests' desecration was foremost in my mind. I wanted to plant within Honor and Mary's minds a deep secret - a time in the future when the secrets of the forests would emerge.

TO HOLD A LIFE WITHIN is a special power of women. It provides untold strength and endurance and a special wisdom. Honor and the convict women were tested to the limits by their gaolers and captors but all of them found ways to put the cruelty and ignorance of their sentences behind them.

Life went on. For over one hundred days the women on the ship huddled together and endured the rolling and rocking of the holds deep within. The holds were their special fortress. They held pantomimes and dances and told stories that carried on for days. Many of these stories were of the magic of Éire. A special comraderiy of women grew up and a suspicion of all men. First it was cold then it was hot and humid in their small compartments below the deck. Oh how the women relished their time above deck when the wind and salt would kiss their faces. But it was here too that they had to endure the glances and pinches and insults of the crew and the soldiers.

Below deck they sewed quilts and clothes and tried not to let the constant rocking of the boat make them sea sick. Their food was always hard tack - biscuits that could easily break your teeth. Each day the women were given a piece of bread. Honor would share it with Mary. As she ate, Honor wondered about her other children. Her mind drifted back to the green hills of Ireland. I would sing jigs and reels.

The women would quietly hum their favourites. We faeries would come and go as we pleased. But most often we chose to stay with the women and children. When we were up on deck at night we noticed mysterious *milika* (cat fish)[32] come to the surface and *warrawada* (milk fish)[33] bathing in the moonlight. Once we caught sight of *mana* (the shark) on his journey hunting across the ocean.

With the new animals, islands and seascapes, even we faeries with our great insight could only wonder at the dimensions of a new land and its peoples.

But as was our way, we knew that we needed to talk to the spirits and to ask for their help. We knew we had to be in tune with the new lands and seas. We knew nothing of the new world but we knew that respect was a basic first step and that friendship took time and effort from all. I frequently went flying out over the horizon to lure the flying fish to shoot up onto the decks near Honor where she could catch them. With Mary, she dried out the fish and this new fare became an important supplement to their diet. Every time they ate they thanked the spirits of the land. Honor and Mary also thanked Cathleen for their safety and asked for guidance.

I wondered about the other faeries that had stayed behind with the other children and how they were going back home. Honor too would look off into the distance thinking of Hector and the children so far away at home. Each day Honor broke up her daily rations for Mary. They shared the best they could.

I also believed in the spirit of Cathleen - it was a spirit of a new and better age. Men and women are good in themselves and no matter how bad their so-called crimes, there was honesty, love and beauty in everyone. It just needed to be discovered, brought out and nurtured. But it was not just the women, the men had suffered greatly. Many of them too were fighting for what they believed was right, and many of them were simply taking food for their families' survival. This was no crime. But these were dark and painful days. Many men and women suppressed their feelings and simply survived on instinct and intelligence. They didn't dare cry because they would never stop. After cruelty and suppression it was hard to love and be loved. You had to learn again to turn on your feelings of affection and learn to trust someone. Feelings were buried deep in the unconscious.

It was the little things that mattered. Mary had discovered a little friend. He was not a rat but a marsupial mouse that had come aboard with the cargo of cedar in the last voyage to the Great South Land.

Honor knew of the little creature too, at first she thought of eating him, but Maisie the eastern chestnut marsupial mouse was a distraction. The little animal was a symbol of their desire to one day have their own home, garden and domestic animals. These things could not be expressed in words but only in the unsaid care of a little creature and the sharing of their meagre rations of food and water. It was desperate below decks but there was also a capacity for commitment and comradery. The toughest of the women like Honor outwardly cared for no-one but their children, but in Honor's relations with Maisie and at odd moments with other women, she opened her heart. It gave me hope that cruelty would not beget cruelty and that our great tribulations could be overcome. In this constant struggle just to survive, no-one dared to think much about the future, and yet a special spirit was born in these women and their children. New life would come. New hope would arise. A chance to heal the great suffering and to build something better would emerge.

WHEN THE OLD TRIANGLE WAS ERECTED above decks the mood aboard *Maria* changed. As rope bound hands and legs and whips flailed skin, power shifted. The dreaded punishment was supposed to summon up fear and compliance but it began to create an atmosphere of disgust, followed by anger and then internal rebellion. At each of the blows, hearts stopped. 'I was thinking of so many things he didn't know of...' was the common, primordial thought in each of the women's minds. At first there was a low murmur, then women moved slightly with each flay of the cat o' nine tails. The first officer whispered in the captain's ear. The men on board noticed it too. The captain knew immediately that he had made a great error. He had hoped to set an example to thieves but he had created something that he now could not control. The women stared into the bloody flesh and lost sight of the feckless individual. A feeling of empathy and light emerged. It aroused the men. It made those in the triangle arch their back and the women murmured slightly louder. Realising his mistake the captain ordered the women below decks. But even there they could hear each blow and the audible sounds of the women became louder. The blood was flowing on the decks. The disciplinarians wanted to erase any possible feeling of sympathy. They responded with even greater severity. But what had arisen was more than the revolutionary hatred of the authorities and landed gentry - it was devil-may-care solidarity with blood, flesh and death. Through it all they came to recognise the blessings of the other. It brought the men towards the women and the women towards the men. This wave of feeling was building with every day on the voyage. A desire for something new and different now became palpable. No words were yet spoken but there was a stirring of spirits. 'What have we got to lose?' Some began to think of life in a new place without the old rules of order. The claustrophobia of the cities and towns and the rule of police and gaolers was producing new desires, new dreams and unexpected ideas and feelings. The sovereign might take some time to die but her power was lost and she was surely doomed. Insurrection against oppression and cruelty swept the world and the desire for something better than servitude stayed with these new convict emigrants to the far shore.

FEMININE CREATIVE FORCE forms the backbone and structure for all things. It was our original knowledge. There was no fall from grace. There was no apple. Yet something was stolen. Let them take it. We will guard the sacred ground, make the preparations, lament the child who has turned into an adult. Without us nothing can proceed. Who is more powerful? What a question you ask. We celebrate our wisdom and age. We do not lament the loss of our beauty. For this time is the best of times. We recognise the great burden you carry for us on the great hill. Take these stars, this garak, it is wondrous and beyond our minds. We must dream and feel to contemplate its richness and wonder.[34]

YOU CAN GET THEM DOWN THAT LITTLE street, oysters, the best of the best, win the prize every year, so good with a little fresh bread, bottled ones, fish them out, down there on the sand dunes that's where we will go... he brought me flowers, I like that, kissed me first time he saw me it was nice and then our picnic and we lay there feeling our way excited by new skin touch looking up at the clouds in a heaven of oysters and bread don't tell my brother that I would go so far but who knows when or how neither of us was going to let the opportunity pass no-one there in the park and then we found a room in that place right on the beach the full joy anticipation of it all I make a lot of noise we must move farther away oh thin walls got to get out of this shed with its rat droppings and spider webs impossible to clean I long for my own room with a big window with brick walls my own private place sighs and groans it is part of it in the afternoon sun on the sand yes I like that and in the night bodies lit up by flashes of lightning oh god in heaven there is nothing like nature the wild mountains the waves moving this force so strong and powerful riding it his heavy frame upon me and oh yes the shivers ran through me never get sick of it oh yes liquid flowing I felt him pulsate and groan and I kicked him off so hard he hit his head on a tree and stood upright whiteness into the moon light cross eyed and drunk all weak-kneed panting and wheezing I wiped him with my handkerchief and then pulled him down again satisfy me completely birds I love them they come to me even the wild ones sit upon my shoulder and keep me company when I am gardening his head in my pelvis if you can't do that then its a deal breaker was it why she left him no complaints here oh yes keep going like that oh feathers and down sweet jesus more more fire sweat yes he's not stopping yes you machine bastard holy mother yes there don't stop oh it hurts so well you good thing oh its been so long divine splashing nothing beats it again and again oh this is good never had it so good can he do it again he can I will be sore spinning worlds mullet coming down the passage dolphins diving through the waves riding them chasing each other playing weaving wind blowing the spray in the air birds wheeling coming down diving on me landing on my head being with me green backed turtle swimming around the rock beneath the sea safe peaceful quiet exhausted content where was I what world did something touch was I resonating in some other place and time am I here again this tide so high so wide so strong can see the crinkles on the water dreaming longing dying and coming again and again looking at my fingers shaking feeling glorious hair running through it running along the shore no father go away swimming he was so cruel not going there breeze goose bumps falling deeply will this one last? for a bit at least I've told him he knows what he is in for but perhaps too much never told anyone that much never again perhaps one day I might break my rule and we might talk again hatred mingles with pleasure cant settle it one way or another better to shut it all out birds yes birds in my garden... lovely... alone on my balcony inspired by that north wind again... when that old triangle jingle jangles the north wind will heal me... for a little while at a time... enough relief and there's always another one to entertain too short that is a worry that is a worry thank god for the birds children oh children dogs come close...

THE CEREMONY carried on into the moonlight. I knew these rites of life. It was natural and good. But I had seen nothing like what unfolded before me. The people and the spirits knew that I was there looking on. For it was me and the newcomers who were also being sung with powerful forces. All celebrating the force of fecundity, of life and change. The force itself was something to be celebrated, acknowledged and used. Losing every taboo the snake full of lust greedily ate the sisters and their baby. But as the other great snakes stood on their tails to spray life into the world they noticed the bulge in her belly. "You have jeopardised our future." And you must pay dearly for this break with law and culture, this source of fecundity of the world and the land. At that the giant serpent fell to earth with a thud vomiting out all that had been eaten. The great power of fecundity and life reverberated across the lands through the great snakes. The rain come down in great sheets of force that etched the land with new channels. The land flooded. The ceremony subsided and the lightning snakes lit up the sky in great displays of force and being. All were satisfied. All were spent.

Guku (Honey)

"I go swimming in my mind, another place, another time..."[35]

WHAT WAS THE NATURE OF THE spirits I had been dreaming about? I could not know who was speaking to me or why. I could not know where they came from. It would take a thousand years to know the answers. It was a familiar dilemma. Spirits of the northern world were bandied together as "faeries". There were hundreds of different spirit worlds: *sheoques, merrows, leprechauns, cluricans, ganconaghs, pookies, dullahan, leanham shees, far darig, imps, far sidhes, far gorta* and *banshees* and many more not known to human beings. My own family was the *daoine sidhe*, if family is the right word to describe a large rollicking band of spirits who could change shapes and see through time and space.

I was discovering that the people of the South Land were also wildly diverse, independent, and there were many spirit realms. It was astonishing even for me. Was this the last wild magic in the world? Certainly it was the oldest magic I had ever known. There were hundreds of peoples whose ceremonies and knowledge had existed continuously since before time was recorded. Let me mention their names because a little piece of magic comes with the name of an ancient people. Can you say these words aloud? I want you to do this because one of these words will reverberate in your mind, this word will be the name for the people who lived where you now live. Their spirit will come to you.

You will feel their magic. If you are lucky they will adopt you and you will see our world with new eyes. Say the words slowly and when you feel the vibration close your eyes and imagine that you too are running and hunting in the ancient forests! Aiabakan, Ajabatha, Alawa, Alura, Alyawarre, Amangu, Amarak Amijangal, Anaiwan, Andakerebina, Andinyin, Adnyamathanha, Anguthimri, Ankamuti, Anmatyerre, Antakirinja, Araba, Arabana, Arakwal, Arrernte, Arnga, Atjinuri, Awabakal, Awarai, Awawawawa, Awinmul,

Awngthim, Baada, Badjalang, Badjiri, Baiali, Baijungu, Bailgu, Bakanambia, Balardong, Banbai, Bandjigali, Bandjin, Barada, Baranbinja, Barapa Barapa, Barbaram, Barimaia, Barindji, Barkindji, Barna, Barunggam, Barungguan, Batjala, Beriguruk, Bidawal, Bidia, Bidjigal, Bigambul, Bilingara, Binbinga, Bindal, Bindjali, Bingongina, Binigura, Biria, Birpai, Bitjara, Brabralung, Braiakaulung, Bratauolung, Bugulmara, Bukurnidja, Buluwai, Bunganditj, Bundjalung, Bunurong, Burarra, Byfieldt, Bwgcolman, Daii, Dainggati, Dalabon, Dalla, Dangbon, Danggali, Dangu, Darambal, Darkinjang, Darug, Dharawal, Diakui, Dieri, Djabugandji, Djabugay, Djaberadjabera, Djagaraga, Djakunda, Djalakuru, Djamindjung, Djangu, Djankun, Djargurd Wurrung, Djaru, Dja Dja Wurrung, Djaui, Djerait, Djerimanga, Djilamatang, Djinang, Djinba, Djirbalngan, Djiru, Djirubal, Djiwali, Djowei, Djugun, Doolboong, Duduroa, Duulngari, Dungati, Duwal, Duwala, Eora, Erawirung, Ewamin, Gaari, Gadjalivia, Gambalang, Gandangar, Geawegal, Gia, Giabal, Gkuthaarn, Goeng, Goreng goreng, Gudjal, Gugu-Badhun, Gulidjan, Gulngai, Gunai, Gunavidji, Gunditjmara, Gungorogone, Gubi Gubi, Gunwinggu, Guugu-Yimidhirr, Idindji, Ilba, Ildawongga, Inawongga, Indindji, Indjibandi, Indjilandji, Inggarda, Ingura, Iningai, Irukandji, Ithu, Iwaidja, Jaadwa, Jaako, Jaara, Jaburara, Jadira, Jadliaura, Jagalingu, Jagara, Jaitmathang, Jalanga, Jambina, Janda, Jandruwanta, Jangaa, Jangga, Janggal, Jangkundjara, Jangman, Janjula, Jardwadjali, Jarijari, Jarildekald, Jaroinga, Jarowair, Jathaikana, Jaudjibaia, Jauraworka, Jawoyn, Jawuru, Jeidji, Jeithi, Jeljendi, Jeteneru, Jetimarala, Jiegara, Jilngali, Jiman, Jinigudira, Jinwum, Jirandali, Jirjoront, Jitajita, Jokula, Juat, Juipera, Jukambal, Jukambe, Jukul, Julaolinja, Jumu, Junggor, Jungkurara, Jupagalk, Jupangati, Juru, Kaantju, Kabalbara, Kabikabi, Kadjerong, Kaiabara, Kaiadilt, Kairi, Kaititja, Kakadu, Kalaako, Kalali, Kalamaia, Kalibal, Kalibamu, Kalka-dunga, Kambure, Kambuwal, Kamilaroi, Kamor, Kandju, Kaneang, Kangulu, Kanolu, Karadjari, Karaman, Karangpurru, Karanguru, Karanja, Karawa, Kareldi, Karendala, Karenggapa, Kariara, Karingbal, Kartudjara, Karuwali, Katubanut, Kaurareg, Kaurna, Kawadji, Kawam-barai, Kayimai, Kaytetye, Keiadjara,

Keinjan, Keramai, Kirrae, Kitabal, Kitja, Koa, Koamu, Koara, Koenpal, Koinjmal, Kokangol, Kokatha, Kokatja, Koknar, Koko, Kokobididji, Kokobujundji, Kokoimudji, Kokojawa, Kokojelandji, Kokokulunggur, Kokomini, Kokonjekodi, Kokopatun, Kokopera, Kokowalandja, Kokowara, Kolakngat, Konbudj, Konejandi, Kongabula, Kongkandji, Koreng, Korenggoreng, Korindji, Kotandji, Krauatungalung, Kujani, Kukatja, Kukatja, Kuku Yulanji, Kula, Kulumali, Kumbainggiri, Kunapa people, Kundjey'mi, Kungadutji, Kungarakan, Kunggara, Kunggari, Kungkalenja, Kun-indiri, Kunja, Kurrama, Kureinji, Kuringgai, Kurnai, Kurung, Kutjal, Kutjala, Kuuku-ya'u, Kuungkari, Kuwema, Kwantari, Kwarandji, Kwatkwat, Kwiambal, Kwini, Laia, Lairmairrener, Lamalama, Lanima, Larrakia, Lardiil, Latjilatji, Lotiga, Lutnigh, Madjandji, Madngela, Madoitja, Maduwongga, Magatige, Maya, Maiawali, Maijabi, Maiku-dunu, Maikulan, Maithakari, Malak Malak, Malantji, Malgana, Mal- garu, Maljangapa, Malngin, Malpa, Mamu, Manbarra, Mandandanji, Mandara, Manthi, Mandjildjara, Mandjindja, Mangarla, Mangarai, Marra, Maranganji, Maranunggu, Maraura, Marditjali, Mardudunera, Maria-mo, Maridan, Maridjabin, Marijedi, Marimanindji, Maringar, Marinunggo, Marithiel, Mariu, Marrago, Martu, Marulta, Matuntara, Maung, Maya, Mbewum, Mbukarla, Meintangk, Menthajangal, Meru, Mian, Milpulo, Mimungkum, Minang, Mingin, Minjambuta, Minjungbal, Miriwung, Mirning, Mitaka, Mitjamba, Miwa, Morowari, Mpalit-janh, Muluridji, Muragan, Murinbata, Muringura, Murngin, Murunitja, Muthimuthi, Mutjati, Mutpura, Mutumui, Nakako, Nakara, Nana, Nanda, Nangah, Nangatadjara, Nangatara, Nanggikorongo, Nanggumiri, Nango, Narangga, Narinari, Naualko, Nauo, Nawagi, Ngadadjara, Ngadjunmaia, Ngadjuri, Ngaiawang, Ngaiawongga, Ngaku, Ngalakan, Ngalea, Ngalia, Ngaliwuru, Ngaluma, Ngamba, Ngameni, Ngandangara, Ngandi, Ngan'gikurunggurr, Nganguruku, Ngarabal, Ngaralta, Ngardi, Ngardok, Ngarigo , Ngarinjin, Ngarin-man, Ngarkat, Ngarla, Ngarlawongga, Ngarrindjeri, Ngaro, Ngathokudi, Ngatjan, Ngaun, Ngawait, Ngewin, Nggamadi, Ngintait, Ngoborindi, Ngolibardu, Ngolokwangga, Ngombal, Ngormbur, Ngugi,

Ngulungbara, Ngunawal, Ngundjan, Ngurawola, Ngurelban, Nguri, Ngurlu, Ngurunta, Niabali, Nimanburu, Ninanu, Njakinjaki, Njamal, Njangamarda, Njikena, Njulnjul, Njunga, Njuwathai, Noala, Nokaan, Noongar, Norweilemil, Nuenonne, Nukunu, Nunggubuju, Nunukul, Oitbi, Ola, Olkolo, Ombila, Ongkarango, Ongkomi, Otati, Pakadji, Pandjima, Pangerang, Pangkala, Paredarerme, Parundji, Paiyungu, Peerapper, Peramangk, Pibelmen, Pilatapa, Pindiini, Pindjarup, Pini, Pintupi, Pitapita, Pitjantjatjara, Pitjara, Pongaponga, Pontunj, Portau-lun, Potaruwutj, Potidjara, Punaba, Puneitja, Punthamara, Pyem-mairre, Rakkaia, Ramindjeri, Rembarunga, Ringaringa, Rungarun-gawa, Spinifex people, Tagalag, Tagoman, Taior, Talandiji, Tanganekald, Targari, Taribelang, Tatitati, Tatungalung, Taungurong, Tedei, Tenma, Tepiti, Teppathiggi, Tharawal, Thaua, Thereila, Thiin, Tirari, Tjalkadjara, Tjapukai, Tjapwurong, Tjeraridjal, Tjial, Tjingili, Tjongkandji, Tjupany, Tjuroro, Tommeginne, Toogee, Totj, Tulua, Tunuvivi, Tyerremotepanner, Ualarai, Ualayai, Umbindhamu, Umede, Umpila, Undanbi, Unjadi, Uutaalnganu, Wadere, Wadikali, Wadja, Wadjabangai, Wadjalang, Wadjari, Wagiman, Wailpi, Wakabunga, Wakaja, Wakaman, Wakara, Wakawaka, Walangama, Walbanga, Walgalu, Waljen, Walmadjari, Walmbaria, Walpiri, Walu, Waluwara, Wambaia, Wanamara, Wandandian, Wandarang, Wandjira, Wangaay-buwan, Wangan, Wangkathaa, Wanji, Wanjiwalku, Wanjuru, Wanman, Warakamai, Waramanga, Wardal, Wardaman, Wardandi, Wargamay-gan, Wariangga, Warkawarka, Warki, Warlmanpa, Warray, Warungu, Warwa, Wathaurung, Watiwati, Watta, Waveroo, Wawula, Wayilwan, Wembawemba, Wenamba, Wenambal, Weraerai, Whadjuk, Widi, Widjabal, Wiilman, Wik, Wikampama, Wikapatja, Wikatinda, Wikepa, Wikianji, Wik-kalkan, Wikmean, Wikmunkan, Wiknantjara, Wikna-tanja, Wilawila, Wilingura, Wiljakali, Winduwinda, Wiradjuri, Wirangu, Wirdinja, Wiri, Wirngir, Wodiwodi, Wogait, Wooptang, Wongaibon, Wongkadjera, Wongkamala, Wongkanguru, Wongku-mara, Wonnarua, Worimi, Worora, Wotjobaluk, Wudjari, Wulguruk-aba, Wulili, Wulpura, Wulwulam, Wunambal, Wuningargk, Wurango, Wurundjeri, Wuthathi, Yamaji, Yuguurtuu,

Yadhaykenu, Yanyuwa, Yarra Yarra, Yiman, Yolŋu, Bangerang, Jotijota, Yotayota, Yoorta, Gunbowers, Gunbowerooranditchgoole, Loddon, Ngarrimouro, Arramouro, Woollathura, Echuca tribe, Yota Yota, Bangerang, Kailthe-ban, Wollithiga, Moira, Ulupna, Kwat Kwat, Yalaba Yalaba, Nguaria-iiliam-wurrung, Yuggera, Yuin and Yulparitja.

These sacred names entranced me. As I mouthed them I felt their power. Do you? The pain of losing so many is unbearable.

The newcomers saw only one culture and one set of people. They failed to understand the majesty of small territories and lands. They saw only a mirror of their own world. They wanted one king or queen who served only their law. They believed that their culture of clothes, paper, books, buildings and the law of the courts was civilized and superior. The people of the oldest land had magic in the way they lived. The newcomers could only vaguely understand the oneness of people with the universe of insects, plants, animals, spirits, stars, earth, clouds, rain and dreams.

A THIRD TIME HE FALLS.   The burden is beyond comprehension. The load cannot be carried. Elders struggling between two worlds trying to hold the magic and the djäma together. Yet in this impossible challenge lies the future paradise. Could anything be worse than the voyage to Van Diemen's Land? And yet like the tragic procession, this journey would eventually lead to this point of shimmering knowledge - bir'yun. Storms surge around Dhambaliya. In the midst of the tumult Djambuwal makes the waterspout between the clouds and sky. He holds his larrpan high, it flies like a shooting star across the sky at night. It is the vibrations of the larrpan that makes thunder. It speeds over a clear night sky to tell mourners that a deceased person is travelling safely to Baralku. The waterspout forms a theatre of danger, a special life force, a vortex that mixes salt water and rain together in a chaos that later settles and calms. New life thrives within the water. It is energised and charged up by the electricity of the air and sky. After the dry season the land becomes fertile and green. These cycles of life make the people strong.

Djambuwal is welcomed each year. Deeper knowledge comes to those who meditate on the tribulations and moods of the earth. The theatre of the sky is greater than any man-made power - its natural wildness makes the earth clean, and washes away clutter and debris. This is a time to look with awe at the universe and to see pathways to other realms and dimensions.[36]

"...the chart was considered as little better than a representation of fairy-land..." [37]

IN THE DARKEST TIMES you have to take pleasure in small things like sewing, putting fingers in paint, making circles in the sand, tying your shoes or slowly drinking gapu. You progress from there. These were dark times. Within the gloom though there were little pieces of light. It was mid-winter when we emerged from a mist and I saw for the first time the rugged coastline of Van Diemen's Land. Voices in my ear whispered a beautiful name Raagapyarranne - an ancient river surrounded by dense forests. Just like the Cape there was a mountain above us – Unghbanyahletta. It was not flat and there was snow at its peak. This land was wild and beautiful.

But with landfall came new trials and tribulations for us. Honor had to brace herself for another shock. Mary had the beautiful wild locks of her mother. She was also learning to appreciate her mother's love of the wild and of nature. With me on her shoulder most of the time Mary had a wonderful imagination. She was also a stickler for detail. "My name is Mary not Marie," she told all and sundry proudly. She loved to tell tales of her brothers and of their adventures. Her older brothers and sisters were her lifelong heroes.

Honor realized that a prison was no place for a young girl. No matter how painful it would be Honor knew that she may be separated from Mary. She tried to tell herself that this would be for the good. It would not be a world away, just a comparatively small distance that separated her. But it was still hard to bear. It just made her more determined to survive anything that was thrown at her. Each night on the *Maria* Honor would coach Mary.

"There will be a time when we will be together and we will have our own house and furniture and our own little piece of land," Honor would tell Mary.

"We just have to endure. They will take you away from me but wherever you are I will find you and you will find me. We will never give up, until we have built our house together my darling."

Those first steps off the ship were hard for the women. Honor and Mary's legs turned to rubber. A shipload of women drew men to the wharves. How Honor dreaded this. But she knew how to handle men. She knew that she could cut them cold and she knew how to manipulate their egos. Honor held her head high as she and Mary paraded up muddy Macquarie Street. Up a long hill we marched. Some women were pregnant. Some had lost children on the voyage. In all of this the women were glad to feel the wind and the air of the land.

We marched past the court house and a church. The church would become a regular part of the routine of a prisoner. In the onlookers along the route Honor noticed that there were settlers looking at the women as workers and house attendants. She also noticed well-built brick cottages with neatly kept gardens. She smelt the scent of new plants and trees and flowers. Perhaps there was some good here, but she dared not get her hopes up too high.

By the time they passed the stockade where discipline and hangings were carried out in the new colony, there was still two miles up a long hill to what was called Cascades, a factory for the imprisonment 'and improvement' of convict women. Eventually the women came to a large wooden gate. A gatekeeper unlatched the mighty door and into a new bleak environment walked Honor and Mary. Inside was a woman with a white bonnet, the Matron. She was no Countess Cathleen. All of the women were taken into a room, they washed with cold water and were given coarse grey shifts. Honor and Mary were issued with two shifts, two aprons, two caps, two handkerchiefs and two sets of socks.

The rules of the *Cascades* were written on the walls: "Female convicts must observe the utmost cleanliness, the greatest quietness – perfect regularity and entire submission. If these be observed... patient industry will appear and reformation of character must result."

If these were the ideals, the realities of life for the women at the Cascades and on the *Maria* were very different. Women like Honor Hughes conformed when they had to, but they knew that they had done nothing wrong, they knew their own minds and each tribulation just created a burning quest in their hearts for justice and life.

It was at this point that the most painful part of the process began. "Honor Hughes, your daughter Mary is to be assigned to the orphanage. With good behaviour you may see her every month. Say your good-byes now and be quick about it."

No matter how she prepared for it, losing the right to look after her youngest child turned Honor's heart to stone. Her face turned to granite. She looked at Mary and kissed her on the cheek.

"There you go," she said and, with that, Mary and I were gone. Mary did not cry. She knew she had to be strong for her mother.

"I will see you again mother," she said in such a brave way that made tears come to my eyes.

For a while I flew between mother and child comforting both. Luckily there was much to do in these early days of life in the new land. Mary remembered what her mother had told her brothers and sisters. She would be strong and they would always be together in heart and mind. Mary was taken away to the Queen's Orphanage with other girls from the ship. How Honor looked forward each month to that one day when she could be with Mary.

In all of this I was as busy as ever. I sensed much more than Honor and Mary could about the new land. There was a wonderland of nature all around. I winced when I saw the insensitivity of the newcomers to the special qualities of the land and its environment. They were going to make the same mistakes all over again.

The attempts to curb the spirit of the women would also fail. There was no possible way that the freedom and feeling of Honor could be put in a box for long. If you tamed her, it was only for a short time. She would bow her head but then look up with the wildest grin. Whatever space she could make for herself would be filled with the greatest quests and ideals. Honor knew that if she went along with the gaolers and matrons she would get her chance at freedom before long. She could see that she could get out of the Cascades and into the world.

Many of the Irish women had created a new feeling in the colony. Far from being kowtowed and broken, they were a flash mob, the pantomimes performed below decks on the ships became shows performed in taverns. The skills learned in sewing and weaving, would become exquisite quilts and gowns. Even in the toughest times, these convict women wanted to experience the passion of life, and the seeming futility of the situation infused them with an unconquerable spirit.

Through all her tribulations Honor was finding her power. Every day there were more trials, more petty rules to observe and more prying eyes to escape. Honor suffered many indignities and torments. The worst she suffered were those created in her own mind. Honor loved the spirit of the women. She would see a flash in another woman's eyes and a special spark of energy would go through her. She was capable of remarkable things. But there was a hardness growing deep within her. She began to distrust the world and to think only of her and Mary's immediate needs. Nothing else mattered. Many of the women talked of injustices and of the evils of the time.

"There will be no politics for me," Honor would say. "Leave me out of your thoughts and calculations."

If there was a song or a laugh Honor would be there but if the subject turned to politics and injustice she would turn inwards.

"We make our own fate," she thought inwardly.

I could not blame her, but I wanted her to enjoy the joy of unconstrained expression and life. Honor was turning off the parts of herself that were too painful to bear. She blamed herself for the loss of the children. The pain was unbearable. The problem was that as she turned herself off she made herself numb. Her subconscious feelings were still there untrammelled. Without knowing it Honor would punch or lash out if she felt restricted. She unknowingly took pleasure in the pain of her adversaries. She distrusted all men and could only relate to those who, like herself, had endured great suffering.

If she could not heal herself, she could heal others. There were many women who had been damaged by all that had happened. Honor had a way of talking and working with those whom the world wanted to forget. She alone could bring women back from the pain of the world. When someone would not eat Honor would simply place a morsel of food that she had prepared nearby. If it was ignored she would not even bat an eyelid. At the next meal time the process would begin again. Honor never gave up and soon the hollow eyes of a sad woman would look up at her with gratitude. It was the same with animals. The wild birds of the cascades would be tame in Honor's hands. They would perch on her head and shoulders.

Honor was defining a set of values that she had already found in the Countess Cathleen. Nobility of spirit was what mattered. It was something though that she could still not embody when it came to the world of men. She muttered the most demonic curses and imagined the most horrific tortures for those that were cruel to women and animals. There was a disconnect in her mind between her ideal and the cruel realities of the Cascades. Most of all Honor wanted a simple life and the freedom to walk in the wilds and to have her own safe home where she and her children could be safe and self-contained.

Mary was growing up. She moved out of the infants' section of the orphanage and began to follow the strict regime of the older children. Every day she woke very early and was thrown into a routine that took her from the vegetable garden, to the wash house, to the kitchen, to the sewing room to the dormitories and back again.

Mary was being trained as a servant. If she was well-behaved, she might leave the orphanage and obtain work with a family or farm.

Each month when they met each other, Honor would plan a future life together with Mary. Honor was working hard to obtain a pardon, a ticket of leave, and on every occasion she could, she petitioned the Governor for the chance to live freely with her daughter again.

I began planning too. I started to place images of the islands off the coast into Honor and Mary's dreams each night. There was much in Honor and Mary's lives that prevented them from seeing and feeling the qualities of their new land, its spirit beings and people. I noticed that the loveliest of spirit beings of the land would not come near the brick structures of the female factory and the Queen's orphanage. They sensed the emptiness and cruelty of the gaolers and guards. Little mischievous creatures that played tricks and games appeared near these cruel men and women and made them twitch and scratch and gave them nightmares.

In Ireland these mysterious beings are called imps. They loved to play cruel tricks. Here too there were gulkas that rewarded cruelty with cruelty and created a cycle where often guards would wake up miles away from where they went to sleep with wet shoes and clothes. They then faced a freezing walk home. The guards would be chastised by their mates for drinking too much rum.

Mary was growing up interested in everything and everyone. She formed a loyal group of friends in the orphanage. Like Mary many of the children left brothers and sisters. Many had lost their parents. Such children grew up very quickly. At eight or nine they could work as hard as an adult, they were quick and agile and learned everything fast. Without exception the children had a vision of freedom in their hearts. No matter what torment they faced, they were quick to each other's side.

They knew they could build a better life if only they could get out of their penitentiary.

"In the future children will not be allowed to starve," they silently told themselves.

Mary was growing tall and beautiful like her mother. When she saw Mary on her monthly visits Honor would chastise Mary about her looks. "Conceal your hair and good looks Mary. Be aware of prying eyes. Keep your head down." The time was fast approaching when Mary would be outside the walls of the orphanage, already she was spending many days working in shops and stalls as instructed by the matron.

She had become a talented dressmaker in her own right. Honor talked earnestly with Mary about the importance of winning a position as a servant in a good household.

My focus had been on Honor and Mary but there were many beautiful souls from Éire. There was the blood of rebellion flowing in their veins. Many young men had been sent to Van Diemen's Land because they were vigorous and strong and had stood up against injustice. They wanted equal rights for men and women regardless of their religion or creed. Out of this tumult would come new ways of thinking and life.

But my pressing concern was magic, the laugh and the spring and the skip, the dew falling and the mist and the rain, in all these things were little spirits and magic, and despite all the troubles I wanted the joy of feeling these things to come back into the world. I wanted Honor and her friends to feel them again.

So it was one fine autumn day that Christopher Martin came strolling past the Cascades. Honor, washing the entrance stones, heard his whistle. Christopher was a ribbon man. His crime was to challenge the authority of an oppressive establishment - the landlords of the Irish countryside - in order to restore shelter (a cottage) to evicted neighbours. His friend had been hung and he had narrowly escaped the noose but Christopher's whistle was that of a man of troubled mind and yet of good conscience and inner happiness. If ever there was a hero for Honor and Mary then it was Christopher. But Honor remained suspicious of any man. She put her faith in good women, if there were revered men in her heart they were not of this earth.

When she heard his whistle she somehow knew that this man would feature in her life. She watched his loping gait and his gangly, stringy stride with a quiet detachment. Christopher had been sent on an errand, a rare privilege to be able to move freely through the town.

Soon he was gone, but as he carried the flour over this shoulder he looked down at the older woman's form and muttered, "Pity be."

To this Honor whispered curtly, "No need to pity me young man." To which he replied, "You did not take my meaning, this plight we share is wrong. " And with that he was gone. It was rare for a man to be so polite and respectful. Her outward appearance hardened but she felt a little lighter at the thought of young Christopher Martin.

It was on Davey Street, Hobart Town, that Christopher first saw Mary. Her curly hair was tied back but as she flicked her head, her hair-band slid down and the wild curls tumbled down. From the first time he saw her Christopher was enchanted. Mary turned and saw him too and she could not disguise a little jump in her heart and she smiled knowingly at him. Honor had schooled Mary not to acknowledge the advances of any young man. But she knew this one was special. Like Honor, Mary knew that her curly hair would weave a snare that would catch Christopher Martin. It was certain and it was easy.

But all this was yet to be. For faeries, love is like blood. It is the source of life and hope. I treasured the moments of contact between Mary and Christopher. It made the world seem right for a little while. The sandstone cliffs and caves along the river had been places of refuge and for sharing food for thousands of years. It was here that, as they were granted greater leave, Christopher and Mary would leave messages for each other and, on rare occasions, meet. In the caves Mary and Christopher would sit reading a note savouring the thought of each other's presence. As they sat they also started to notice the black of fires on the walls and the mounds of shells. Mary would sometimes climb a tree near the foreshore and hidden from view she would hear the conversations of those who passed below.

I prayed for the land to accept these two young ones. Sometimes Mary would watch Christopher come and go and then she would take his message to read high in the limbs of the tree. There she would dream of a future life.

Christopher had the same burning passion as Honor in his soul. He was afraid of no-one. He regretted none of the actions that had brought him to Van Diemen's Land. One moonlight night he told Mary the story of how a young family had been thrown out of their house because they could not pay their rent. When the news came to Christopher and his friends they were incensed. The town soon heard of the furore and as the rumours circulated the local police force also began to become alarmed. Christopher was determined to restore the family to their house. The men had passed around a hat and raised the rent money that was required. In the late afternoon they walked to the farmhouse. A new tenant manager was moving in. Christopher yelled out

"Take back your goods and chattels, sir, we have the rent to restore the house to its rightful residents."

"And who would that be?" the surly manager replied.

"You know exactly who we are talking about, the O'Bryne's have lived here for generations. We have here the rent that is owed. So kindly move on."

"It is far too late now," the manager replied. "Get off the land or it will you who will be sorry."

At this the crowd exploded and the manager and all his possessions were thrown into the street. Christopher ran to find the O'Brynes who had departed with all their furniture on a horse and dray. As he did a line of constables were filing down the road. As Christopher came back with the O'Byrnes they could hear the crowd yelling. Christopher jumped from the dray and ran towards the house. The constables were picking up the manager's furniture and placing it back in the house.

With that it was on for young and old. Soon shots could be heard, several young men were wounded and one was killed. By nightfall Christopher and seven of his mates were in irons. Six months later they were bound for Van Diemen's Land.

But far from breaking Christopher, it only made him more determined. Aboard the ship the talks each night turned to politics. There would come a day when Éire would be free, and all men and women would be treated with dignity. It was this spirit of freedom and rebellion that brought Christopher to the Great South Land, little did he know that this feeling and spirit would come to define the new land and its people. I knew that one day in the far future it would also become the basis for a deep understanding between the traditional peoples and the newcomers.

The magic of the earth was all around us. But it took even me a long time to see and feel it. The people and the spirits were very patient. The same pain and fear that had swept over my land like a dark mist was here also. Midst the turmoil, how, I wondered, could Lalla and her people ever trust any of the newcomers and how could they possibly accept me? It is hard to describe the brutality she had witnessed. Honor had lost her children but Lalla's beloved Paraweena was murdered, her sister kidnapped and her uncle shot by a soldier. So many of her friends were never seen again. But this is not the end, for you may kill the flesh but you cannot so easily kill the spirit and the magic.

Lalla Bakitju Gunda and Ḏilkurrwurru Wataŋgurr were seers. They gazed beyond their own lifetimes. Deep in the essence of the world their magic would endure through all the pain and cruelty that could be inflicted upon them and their people. For their lands were unique. They had created a paradise that had lasted far beyond the kingdoms and epochs of my own land. Even when the very earth itself was blasted by ice they had survived. They knew that the spirit of place would come back like a tiny green shoot emanating from a seed. Lalla knew that the magic of the world needed to be placed in the hearts of the newcomers and from there it needed to return to their birth places and sacred places in Éire. Over time the Aboriginal men and women would teach the music, ceremony and dance to the newcomers so they too could feel the true spirit of the land. Only then would the colonists understand the meaning of dispossession - more than ownership - the land lost its guardians and spirits. No matter title deeds! No matter bricks and mortar! The land owned the people, not the other way around. When this deep and intimate relationship was severed the world became a darker, empty, meaningless place.

As Mary and Christopher became closer, the spirit of the trees and the place also came to them. From their union and relationship good things would come. The dynamics of the world cannot be taught or told, they have to be felt. Such things cannot be taught in classrooms or written in books. Life has to be lived. These feelings could not come all at once, they had to be learned over many generations. Seasons had to pass. Plants and animals had to be observed. Storms and tempests had to flood the land, planets and stars had to revolve through the night sky. Pain had to be endured.

"Human beings still have much to learn about nature, but first they must find and see in operation the spirit element at work."[38]

STRIPPED BARE, laid on the dharpa, naked and bound, exposing the cruelty of the world and the madness of men. We need a fence to keep the buffalo out of the sacred ground. They are wandering willy-nilly destroying everything. The name is yiŋapuŋu, place of the dead. Can you see Yikuyanga and Murnimiya with their spears up against the tree? The marks of sand crabs and people. After food, the sand crabs and worms strip the scraps clean. Close relatives sit around the holes where they light their fires and eat. Those who prepare the body must stay with the fish. Yikuyanga catches parrot fish. Marlwiya make the decisions about the organisation of the people. They mark the places for the fires. Guwak men, those hunters, straighten out the family relations. At the finish two clouds tell the story. They say that someone from home has died. The spirit is passing from the ground to the cloud. The marks in the cloud are the blood of the people mourning. Nyapililŋu is crying as she sees the clouds. Her special embroidery in the form of a girdle across her shoulders and chest symbolises her presence. She brings blood hitting her head with her digging stick.

Land is burned purifying the country. The soul rises to the clouds and falls to the land as rain. Spirits enter the rain and the rain falls on the people. Spirits enter the people. The cycle of life goes on. All this is perilous. Be respectful and thoughtful. Nature takes care of its own, that is the philosophy: nature's recycling and dreaming. Stripped by maggots and crabs, bones are placed in the sacred poles and bark. Everything is a metamorphosis, even a piece of plastic thrown from a fishing boat.

Garbage trucks, crematoriums and man-made compost heaps make no sense. Our garbage and our bodies await the crabs, maggots and worms. 'You white fellas are funny, you place all your garbage and rubbish in one place."[39]

"She was a wild thing amidst classical furniture."[40]

NOW WAS THE WORST OF TIMES I THOUGHT AS I looked at the cruelty and bleakness of the orphanage and the stony fortress of the Cascades. I was worried about Honor. How much cruelty had she endured at the hands of men? Any sign of spirit or spark and she immediately drew the catcalls and often a blow or a slap and worse. Yet often it was one in, all in amongst the Irish women. So many times I saw strong men withdraw from the ferocity of the women below decks. The women won many victories and commanded a great deal of respect. But I could also feel Honor's heart hardening and her distrust of men growing. Now I was also feeling the pain of the people of Van Diemen's Land who were dealing with all the tribulations that Ḍilkurrwurru Wataŋgurr had predicted. Disease and concerted violence were raging across the countryside. In so many ways Honor and Lalla were in common cause. They were negotiating the most terrible situation.

Lalla Bakitju Gunda and her people performed ceremonies to protect the land. Don't you realize? It was how people could link up with us on other planes. It was how people could become one with the magic of the world. If my people of Éire and the peoples of the world could feel the spirit of the land then they too could feel the special harmony of the world.

The world could become magical again and there would be no wars, no prisons, no hate. This was what the world needed to understand. The people of the south had maintained a paradise, a land of pristine beauty, for thousands of years... they could show us peace and law that would protect us all. If we could only learn and listen.

Don't get me wrong, there are tyrants and villains in all worlds. But this ancient law was attuned to a spiritual and moral code beyond my comprehension and well beyond the newcomers'. It was attuned and speaking with the natural world in a way I had never seen before.

"... bees, wasps and ants do not simply remove something from nature... they also give nature the possibility to continue living and thriving."[41]

BUZZ, BUZZ, BUZZ, FOLLOW ME, FOLLOW ME... Honor looked up from her cell. "Oh if only I could," thought Honor. "If only I could follow you, strange little bee, if only I could be in the wilds again and follow you to your sweet honey."

The bee was a messenger of the people of the South Land. For they were following the bee. The bee had led them to me. A hive had formed in one of the crevices of the stone walls.

I could see the people gathering out of sight of the guards. That night they came with long sticks and expertly pried the hive away from the walls of the Cascades. At midnight they feasted on the sweet honey. It flowed like water and could be drunk like wine.

When the hive fell honeycomb fell through Honor's cell window. In the morning she feasted on the sweet waxy honey.

"Oh, thank you, little bee, you have revived my spirits. I will be free one day soon and I will work as hard as you to build a new life."

It takes a million flights of bees to make a bucket of honey. The bees must travel many miles. The people of the South Land too were thanking the sacred bees for the food and energy they had given them.

The people had survived the darkest time of the newcomers. Like bees they had swiftly traversed and weaved through the forests and the newcomers had not even seen them. Can you follow a bee flying in the air? It is quite a challenge. The people of the South Land have come to know the land, the trees and flowers by following the bees - it gives them a special knowledge of the land. Following bees also teaches a secret about how to appear and disappear at will in the countryside. This is why Lalla and her people prevailed through all the attempts to capture them and to harm them. But the costs of even this evasion were terrible.

Over many weeks soldiers and men with guns and dogs had walked in long lines across Van Diemen's Land to hunt down the people of the South Land. What a folly. With their knowledge of the land how easily the men and women of the land avoided the hunt. But the intention was cruel and evil and I knew that the pain of Éire had come to the South. How could this evil be stopped? I was transported to hundreds of creeks and mangrove swamps where people were slaughtered. I saw the crescent scars and tattoos on warriors chests. I saw the eyes of those who survived. I saw them over generations repay the cruelty and horror with a determination to lead. Yiman! History is told by the victors but time holds no barriers for survivors. Revenge is a curse and a promise and an obligation. In the end all want peace and consolation. When will it come? In long lines, I see them, police black and white, farmers, settlers, warriors, waiting for forgiveness and peace. Sins of the fathers and grandfathers, rainbow water finally bringing peace.

This too was what the people of the South Land asked themselves. They watched as soldiers returned to their barracks. Now they could return to the forests for a time. But the cattle, sheep and axes continued to destroy the fabric of the land.

Revived by the honey, Lalla Bakitju Gunda's people were determined. They too like, Dilkurrwurru Waṯaŋgurr on the mainland, would need to plant their knowledge for the long term. They too would have to live to fight another day. Some began to plan their passage to the mainland, others to the islands, others to pockets of forest deep within the interior and along the wild coasts. Ceremony would begin to protect the future. Even in this time when the moieties and clan structures had been challenged, when great battles with the newcomers had reduced the numbers of men, women and children, the people knew how to survive and to preserve their culture.

The spirits were wild. The newcomers would undergo great hardships. Insects and vipers would attack them. They would grow crops at the wrong times and feel uncomfortable in everything they did until they started to understand the patterns of nature guarded by Lalla's people. Over time this would lead them to the philosophy of the first peoples. Their time would come again.

From her prison cell Honor knew of injustice. Even she, so foreign to the people of the land, began to understand as she ate the precious honey that there was something beautiful and wonderful about this land and its people. I would nurture that hope in her heart and in Mary's heart and in her children and her children's children. One day the newcomers would celebrate the ceremony, dance, music and knowledge of the first peoples and understand its importance. One day they would understand that to live well in this new land meant making the first people's philosophy part of the way every person interacted in the world. Only then would safety, love, security and prosperity return to all.

OH TONGUE OF THE FIRE[42] can you ever now be replaced? How we miss you already? Reciting and memorizing everything, teaching us the names of every headland and bay, every river and knoll, every hill and valley, every blade of grass, tree, insect, bird, animal and living thing. Are you already sailing in the stars looking down at the bugul imploring the young people to work harder? How we miss you Ḏilkurrwarra? The fire at Rocky Bottom Creek igniting on the island to greet us. It was you, we know this now. Thank you, wise man and leader.

Nails hammered into wrists and through feet – a heartless and cruel act that is a measure of all that is wrong in the world.

The horrible spectacle of Garray hoist aloft high on the hill for the huddled masses to see. Tourists walk up to the sightseeing tower at the top of the park oblivious of the centuries of worship and reflection. But perhaps some here do reflect well as they walk. Survivors of the communist terror and brutality meeting in bars, smoking like chimneys, reflecting and proud of their new profligacy.

New lovers, and old partners who have grown into each other, find their way. Most cannot see that the very structure of the fortress and monastery exists to protect this vision. So much concrete and carving, so many bricks, so much toil and so much blood was spilt here. In this city of soul and sin, the blood of the saviour and the gypsy are now mixed. Free apples and the calling of the bells to mass are all that is left. Survivors of the communist terror and brutality meeting in bars, smoking like chimneys, reflecting and gazing at one another as if it were a miracle to be alive. Velvet revolutionaries all. Sacred paintings sold through the mission arts and crafts shop supplement the scarce funds of this church. The sweet irony of it all! Bright sun, too hot, shone causing the travellers to question their journey. This image stored in the minds of the great painters, generation after generation since time began, memorised and repeated, practised in song and dance, has outlasted the stone and paint of the great cities. Djauwaldalwu - home of the lindaridj parakeets - belonging to the ancient sisters, flying like little coloured comets across the sky. Catch the lindaridj, catch the meaning, takes time and effort for us foreigners and falsely proud and superior balanda, it has taken so many generations and so many mistakes over many years to reach these cursory beginnings. [43]

ON MARY'S FIFTEENTH BIRTHDAY she received news that she was to leave the orphanage. I had been hard at work coaxing good thoughts in the minds of Mary's matrons, and then in the colony's officials. Mary was to work on a little farm on Bruny Island off the mainland. It was here that Lalla Bakitju Gunda and her family had also come to escape the harsh world of the new colony.

I had planted a slow-growing seed to be respectful and patient and to listen with their hearts. At night time I placed images of Lalla and her people into Honor's dreams. She was a woman like Lalla who had learned to live in the wilds. The two had a lot in common. Mary would collect mussels and pippies and bring them up to Honor and Lalla knowing that they had the powers of life and longevity. Lalla was like us, she did not like talking, she shared feelings and ways of doing through her presence, rather than words.

Life was still tough for everyone. It was only on rare occasions that Mary could escape her domestic duties and roam free.

Christopher too had been anxious to be near Mary. He had won a ticket of leave on a Hobart farm and worked his way to be near her. Finally Honor too worked her way towards Bruny. All of them were good workers and they found ways to win favour. Like a spider slowly weaving strands for a web they found ways to be together. On the windswept island these children from an oppressed world found themselves alongside Lalla who has seen the ceremonies of her lands halted and so many of her people killed. These survivors of two genocides had much to think about and many burdens and cruelties to overcome. It was as if someone had planned for them to be together at this time of deep sadness. Their dreams were immortal and I too began to think of my own existence merging with their pain and the wilds.

Honor and Mary dared to think of a new life. Honor too won a ticket of leave but she could not get to Bruny at first. She worked in Hobart for a farmer's wife for another year before she gained permission to finally join her daughter. It was many long years before mother and daughter could finally be together. By the firelight at night how happy they were at last with Christopher.

Lalla could not be so easily cheered. She had eluded her capturers in the early days and sailed over the strait between the mainland and the island. There were many encounters and betrayals. Slowly Lalla was fading away to the spirit world but I knew that her descendants had been safely taken to the islands. I also knew that Lalla had planted a spark in Mary's mind that would grow in understanding through her life and her children. Honor too was growing tired of the material world. She had worked so hard to ensure that Mary was safe. She had endured so much.

Honor was cautious for Mary. She dreamed and wondered how she could ensure that her life would be a good one. She wanted most of all for Mary to erase all hints of her convict heritage.

"You must go to the mainland and pretend that I am not related to you and hide Christopher's crimes," she would say.

It was this desire for safety and freedom that brought Honor into conflict with Christopher. She knew that he was a good and honourable man, deep down. She shared his love of freedom. But for Honor it was the old nobility in which she placed her trust. Her first instinct was to fly at the signs of danger. Whereas Christopher, despite all that had happened, would still not shy from a fight.

"It is not just you that we must think of, Christopher Martin." But he was also quick to respond.

"You know that is not what motivates me to fight. If we don't stand together we lose."

"I do not care for your grand schemes, young man. I care only that Mary is safe, that she has a roof over her head and that whatever children you two have, god help them, grow up without the pain we have endured."

"I will never endanger her, you know that."

"You must use your brains, Christopher. Your words are careless. Vain ideals are dangerous. No man can anticipate the twists and turns of life.

"A chance event, a bended ear can throw you back in prison or even to the gallows. We are ordinary people we cannot get involved in the affairs of police or officials. It is not our place".

"It is we ordinary people that must lead the world to a better place. We cannot allow the troubles we have come from to define our lives here. We must work to ensure our children do not have to endure the pain we have suffered. You of all should know this, Honor Hughes!"

"Watch your tongue, young man, you talk nonsense. There is no risk worth taking that would endanger Mary. I have left five children to the mercy of their fate. I would die before Mary had to endure another prison. We must forget our past and learn to live again simply and purely."

"I cannot forget! For all the pain that I and my fellows have suffered would come to nought."

At this Christopher stormed away. He knew that Honor was stronger than he was. She would never play unless she won. Part of the reason she argued was to show the tenacity and fierceness of her spirit. She could not be ignored. She would never change her mind. There had been enough martyrs and senseless losses. It was time to surrender and live. There was a great deal of work to be done.

Yet as he walked away Honor's words had the effect of crystalizing something new in his mind. This remote and strange place, so far from his homeland, would become a political homeland. A place where Jack was as good as his master. It would become a place in the world where the oppressed might seek refuge. It would become a lighthouse. Suddenly for a moment it all seemed to make sense to Christopher Martin. Nothing had been in vain. And I too started to think that with Lalla's spirit with us, something new in the world might emerge. It was a glimpse, a spark amongst dark times, a little burning coal of possibilities.

Lalla Bakitju Gunda was walking up the cliff face from the beach. She had been collecting tiny shells. Slowly and expertly she had weaved the small shells into a necklace. She sensed Honor's discomfort and slowly she placed the shells around her neck.

"Queen," she said and laughed. Honor looked at her with her wild and flashy smile. At this moment the world changed a little. A shooting star raced over the horizon in the early night sky. The ancestors of Éire and the Southern land were recognising each other for the first time. A feeling of great warmth came over us. The world seemed right for the first time in a very long time.

MOSQUITO THRUST his great probiscus into the ground. The mound is there for all to see. Can you imagine him as a persistent and annoying man? He lived long ago at Djawalaŋu and then travelled to Millingimbi and the paper bark swamp at Darbilla. Adversary of Birgudaŋbaŋgitj, he was a formidable foe. His law is very clear. He created rules of guardianship and relations with the land. Great waves of the tiny flying biting creatures protect the land from invaders. At the end of the wet season when yams were ready, young stingrays were prolific and fish were fatty, mosquito was also active. It takes great understanding to live with mosquito. He tests you. He wants to know: do you really want to stay on my country? How are you related to me? Do you know? "Along with borrutj I will bite you and bite you. The waves of pain will sweep your body and when you have the will to resist, it will be like a rush of fever through your body and mind. I will welcome you then. For you will have shown that you are ready for my country. No you won't get sick. I will protect you with the land. But be careful, once you have endured me you will always come back to these lands. You will see, hear, touch all around you in a different way."

In my world there are limits too. Magic is something that everyone must feel for. If you stop believing, there will be no magic. How I loved Honor. I tried to tell her how beautiful she was but she did not want to hear. I was losing her. When she remembered tough times she fought with the land and her own being. I knew, by looking back through the tides of time, of the little girl's essence, how innocent she was. I saw a little girl seeking her father's affections, who could not understand the roughness and harshness of the world. I saw how cruelty begat cruelty and I wanted her to stand back and also see this. But most of all Honor felt the pain. I saw her harden and become tougher than any man. This was how Honor, for all her pride and independence, was closing up.

She shut herself away for fear of the fierce attacks of mosquito. But when she shut herself off from the world she also shut herself off from love. How I tried to turn her. I asked myself why could she not open herself up to understanding and love?

Don't fight mosquito, it's impossible to win. You have to figure him out. It was because Honor felt the need to fight fire with fire that she had advised Christopher not to endanger Mary with idle rebelliousness. But when it came to herself she wanted revenge and to inflict pain on those that had hurt her. She felt repelled and attracted to people who were as hard as she had become. Was it because she needed someone who was equal to her in endurance? Or was it just that she was tired of being pushed around by people over whom she had no control or influence? Did she need a protector? Or someone who had as much reason to lick their wounds as she did? Was it inevitable that she would make those close to her suffer as much as she had? I could not alter her course. There were some things I could not change. There were some things I could not repair.

GARRAY IS SPEARED AND DEAD. The human agony of the great one is over. Countless painters and sculptors and a million sermons and outpourings of grief capture this moment. But this dhäwu is but a pup in time. The wangarr ancestors' journey is far older. It tells us not of the sins of man but of the origins of life and land. It tells us how we belong and are part of the ground. Our family are the mosquitoes and yams.

All this has been lost in the written down words of gold books and the idolatry of churches. The radical Islamist are correct to lament the falsity of words and statues. Their bitterness is not warranted or justified. Hatred begets hatred. Destruction is not the right way. We must simply learn. Even Allah, Yotchin, is captured in the stories of the land. They left Donydji, the wise ones, on their sacred journey. Like the kings of old following a new star in the sky, they camped each night and contemplated the world. Guwak would sit on top of the cashew tree eating its fruit. Possum studied the spider spinning its web in the high branches. He saw the spider web at dawn when the dew glistened in the silky sinews. A low cloud hung on the horizon. In this way the possum learned to spin burrkun - the sacred string that holds ceremonies, people and land together. From their vantage point on the ground marlwija witnessed all these events and became the guardians and organisers of ceremonies of the Manggalili people. Guwak would watch possum spinning the burrkun. Different lengths of the sacred string were attached to the lands and people the wise ones visited on their way to Djarrakpi and beyond.[44]

ALL AROUND THE ISLAND THE SPIRITS DANCED. But the newcomers were locked into their own pain and suffering. At times the little birds would fly onto Honor's head trying to tell her that life was about loving and giving. She found the little birds and animals better company than most human beings. But her pain had locked her up. She could not hear the ceremonies. She simply turned off her feelings when she had to. She would look at the world and see trouble and unconsciously hit out. She knew she had to control these feelings and looked to create her own refuge. It was this that drew William Jones to her. He was a strong man. He was a good carpenter and sawyer. He could build a house and that was what Honor needed. She had stopped dreaming of things that she could not control and looked to earthly prizes and the means to achieve them. It was the marks of the floggings on William's back that drew her to him. Honor's physical scars were hidden. When I first saw William's back it took my breath away but worse were the emotional scars etched in Honor's soul. She would never tell anyone but me of her feelings. In the moonlight she would talk to me and tell me of the wonders and love she had felt as a little girl. But silence and endurance of pain was something that was more natural to her, it was something she understood. She wondered at William's physical signs of pain and how anybody could endure them and was drawn to him.

William had deserted his regiment and was sentenced to fifteen years hard labour in Van Diemen's Land. It meant that he would never see his mother, wife and family of five children again. Such a penalty would break any man. It was meant to be a lesson to other soldiers but if William had the chance he would have deserted again and again. He could not see why he should follow a trumped-up officer's commands and he had no intention of laying down his life for a cause he little understood or even recognized. William was by no means a model prisoner. He just did not care for himself or for anyone or any time in a dark hole that put the fear of god into the toughest man. He had endured four months hard labour on the Tasman Peninsula – enough to kill any man. But he had survived. Somewhere at his darkest moment he found the will and the reason to live. The letter 'D' was branded on his left side. He had a long scar under his chin where some ne'er do well had tried to cut his throat. Honor knew who he was and how he had endured. She saw in him something that no-one else could. She had seen herself in his pain.

Like the scars, the 'D' etched so deeply drew Honor to William. Normally she would never speak to a man. But she saw, as he worked in the sun, the scars and the great tattoo. At first she was repelled and thought him ugly. She saw also that where other men cut timber roughly, William, with no effort, produced perfect planks of the beautiful blonde Huon pine. On many occasions Honor had tamed wild dogs. She saw in their wildness their great strengths that could be moulded to her benefit. Dogs were protectors and so were wild men. I wanted to tell her that protection was no salvation but she and William both longed for safety and just minimal consolation. A small shack and garden on the Snug River was their great aspiration. You have to understand how enormous a prize this seemed for both of them. It was almost too much to hope for. It was a place to hide.

It took William fourteen years to win his ticket of leave. For all this time he was under the control of cruel gaolers and mindless regulations and darkness. In the year 1854 he obtained his freedom. Honor had already planned the site of the house. William was just grateful to have a job to do. Honor did not want dependency on any man, William would build a house on her terms or none. The timber was of the highest quality and with few tools they created a comfortable cottage and a working farm. They did not own the land, they were squatters

- neither had ever known anything but paying rent or camping on somebody else's property. It was enough.

Building the shack was a shift for both of them. It was an escape, a luxury, a refuge. William had left a wife and five children in Liverpool. Honor found it too painful to think about the children she had left behind in Éire. At night with alcohol fermented from potato peelings, the pain in both their lives was dulled. Their senses were shaken so nothing mattered any more. They did not want to chase the memories that had been lost. My enduring grief was that the spark was lost in Honor. My job could never be done with the dull and stupefied mind that cursed alcohol brought about. This was an affliction that cursed Éire and cursed the people of the South Land. It was a short circuit that left them stalled in a place where there was no physical or emotional pain. They could not go on to understand the dimensions of life that brought real ongoing happiness and love. I kept trying to revive Honor. But she kept moving back into the battle with William, they would rather fight in their minds against all that had been done to them than walk through the pain to peace. I prayed for rain to clean up the land and to free Honor and William again.

The spark of life never goes out. It just goes out for a time - usually due to misunderstanding. It would take two hundred years to soothe Honor's pain and to understand the healing power of gamunungu.

Honor and William were living at a place where the deep colours of the earth were mixed up like paint on the ground. They were living in a no man's land - not part of the culture of Éire, not part of the culture of the South Land with no ability to recognise what was good and what was bad. The same fate befalls people of all kinds after a war and great cruelty. It was necessary to apply the white clay again and again until the pain and the torment left them. A time would come.

Honor's wild spark transferred to Mary and Christopher. Honor's drift into oblivion made me even more determined to find a way forward. Lalla Bakitju Gunda had by this time also moved away from Oyster Bay and Bruny Island. She captured the hearts of all who came to know her. If there could be such a thing as an Aboriginal queen she was it. She, like Honor, had seen the heart of darkness but she would never succumb to it. The land would always speak to her. She moved into Hobart town when she became too frail to walk down the cliffs to collect oysters.

In the evenings she would look up at Unghbanyahletta and dream. In her mind she would place the knowledge of the universe there for the coming children to learn and understand. A time would come.

Family became Mary's quest. She missed her lost brothers and sisters and threw herself into motherhood. First came Edward in 1855, then Michael in 1863, then Martin in 1865, then came the twins Elizabeth and Susanna in 1867, then William in 1870, then Alfred in 1872, then Alice in 1874 and then finally Emily in 1876. It was the most comforting thing of all to have ten children – they were future protectors and benefactors but most of all they were her symbols of survival. Lalla and her people also over the coming generations came to see a similar importance in mothers and children. They would build the future and recover much of the magic of the past. The feminine force of creativity was in their very essence, it was their destiny. All of the spirits of the land willed it to be so. They waited patiently to join with the new children and to make new camps and to start new adventures. We faeries waited for the moments when we too could bring magic into the minds of the young ones. And so, dear children, you too are part of this destiny.

Honor's grandchildren were a great gift and every time she saw them it took her out of herself. For a few minutes, for a few hours the wild life would return to her eyes. "Come children we must run with the wind," and throw her shawl out in a great whirl of magic that would bring Mary and Christopher running to see the excitement. All of the children had their father's spirit of justice and their mother's love of nature and the wild. In his later years Christopher had learned to curb his tongue. He looked at William and so many of his countrymen and he knew that what Honor had taught him was right. You had to win and not lose. You had to pick your fights and live to fight another day. Christopher was building a foundation in his children's hearts. Every man and woman that came to his house was welcome and treated with respect. No-one was ever turned away from a meal. No man or woman under Christopher and Mary's watch would ever go hungry.

Perhaps it was this spirit that made young Michael grow so tall, perhaps it was because the sunlight and spirit of the land had entered his soul or perhaps for the first time in two generations there was plenty to eat and the bounty of the land was plentiful. Soon there were no boots that could fit him. At first Mary began to make shoes for his huge feet but these would soon fall apart. In his trips to Hobart town no cobbler had ever made a size 13 shoe. So it was that over the generations Michael would always be remembered as the giant of the family. I saw in this gentle giant something that would bloom and develop. I began to spend more time with this man who was also a target for the gaolers... they saw his size and it caught their eye.

Christopher knew that he had to prepare Michael for a life in which he would attract attention from friend and foe alike. The problem with Van Diemen's Land was that the gaolers and police were always looking to bring someone down. Christopher had seen how a great man could be singled out. He would talk quietly at night of the mainland where Michael might not stand out so much from the crowd. Mary would watch over them as they talked. I could see in these conversations how Michael carried the life of his grandmother and a touch of the spirit of Lalla within him. How I came to love this great man. I came to spend more time with him, once again I knew our destinies would be intertwined.

FAERIES RECORD in their ethereal form and spirit all those things that words and documents cannot convey. We are the wild ideas and excess that can only be experienced and felt in the heart not the head. Sometimes a photograph captures pain and greatness.

But it is we faeries who hold all the laughs and winks and heartfelt crying and craziness of the world in our being. Official writings and history do not comprehend the past because they miss what we see and feel in our very being. Faeries see the misunderstandings and we laugh heartily when things come out upside down. In the encounters and tragedy of Honor's time there were many times to laugh at times when the normal response was to cry or get angry. This ironical laughter came to be a trademark of the new community spurned from Éire as well as Lalla Bakitju Gunda's people who were under attack on their own homelands. Upside down views and misunderstandings about the precious environment and the rights of man made us laugh. Laughter was the only medicine that could heal the pain. From this laughter, understanding and knowledge beyond books came. The words Djadjawurrong, Mallegoondeet and Wathaawurrong do not come easily to rigid tongues. It would take more than two hundred years for hard tongues to loosen and flex. The way seasons, flowers, animals, stars, the moon and maggots have their place in the great cycle of fertility would long remain a mystery to the newcomers. The visitors to the new world might even view acts of friendship as acts of hostility and vice versa. Proud requests for kinship rights of food, clothing and technology were viewed as begging. Hard work was regarded as sloth. Meanwhile the people of the South Land carried on their lives wondering at the new technical products of the newcomers, the circuses, the music, the wanton destruction of lands and the gardens of the earth.

So it was that "King Billy" of the Wathaawurong strolled past the tents of the Ballarat gold fields naked but for a tall, black top hat. Giant Michael Martin saw him with a knowledge and recognition that came from standing out in a world of cruelty and oppression. Michael recognised the ridiculous madness that had taken shape in Billy's mind and in his heart. He had seen it in his grandmother Honor - how she said one thing and meant another, spurned people she should have loved and lived in a fantasy of alcohol and distractions. Michael could see into the future for a second. He could see the madness causing others to move on determinedly and powerfully. In his daydream he saw the great Kangushot organising a great walk-off of pastoral stations in the red desert country, he saw the world consume mountains of iron ore and of so many more struggles for justice and understanding. He would see a football team of champions paving the way for the enlightenment of many generations of people. It was from chance encounters of incredulity and wonder that alliances, friendships and thoughts grew. Over many generations Michael Martin's family would live here near the great quarry of precious metals known by the Wathaawurong for millennia and readily shared with the newcomers. There was no thanks or acknowledgement for the world's most plentiful and easily accessible gold mine. The newcomers just took greedily. Travelling salesman from the Wathaawurrong had traded green jade and stone across the nation since the beginning of time. Thus King Billy resonated in Michael's very being. Over generations, descendants of the Martin family came slowly to understand that mud was as precious as the gold, that the land must be treated softly and with respect, that it was not a good thing to change the flow of rivers and that imbalancing soils might poison all. This understanding that began to form as Michael shared his meagre possessions with King Billy was a very long time coming. So now you see a little more of how we faeries work! Spreading our magic! We moved over all the colonies of Australia. The natural spirits of the land welcomed us as friends. We, in turn, could feel the wonder of Australia and its first peoples. We did everything we could to encourage the imagination of the people who came to settle in Australia. It was a long and difficult journey. It took us some time too. Sometimes we would cry in frustration as we tried to bring people to understand nature and the spirit of the land. Every generation of children came a bit farther in their understanding and feeling. Often little children did see. They recognised faces in trees, faery rings and our brightly coloured toadstool houses. For many years Australian newspapers would publish children's stories and verse about faeries.

Little sparks lived on in each generation. But something bigger, even harder, was coming. I could feel it in my being.

A MAN WITH SIZE 13 SHOES IS AN ICON. He is a target. Christopher had taken to bringing young Michael with him to the Hobart town markets to help with the produce sales. He stood out like a sore thumb. It was there that news came that gold had been discovered on the mainland. Father and son looked each other and knew that Michael needed to seek his fortune there. They had heard how in only a week 800 men had journeyed to the towns of Clunes and Ballarat. In the hubbub of the gold rush Michael might have a chance. To remain in Van Diemen's Land was to forever bear the convict mark and to attract the attention of the police. That night, as they returned home down the channel, they joked of striking it rich. Most of all though they dreamed of a new life of freedom. The next day Michael began to make preparations for the long journey to Melbourne town.

The assiduous warfare and hostility of the Van Diemen's Land police and settlers was averted by hiding, eluding and moving to safer ground. Lalla Bakitju Gunda's people could easily do this. But many prepared to die rather than see the great natural cathedrals of nature pillaged. They simply threw themselves knowingly at the firearms. Others allowed themselves to be found and executed by cruel and merciless soldiers, police and settlers. Tribal rivals were often recruited to track the secret pathways and they used their discretion to decide who would live and who would die. This was a time in the world when a person could be killed, exiled or flogged mercilessly for stealing a morsel of food. In Éire, tens of thousands of men, women and children had starved to death. Violence begat violence, cruelty begat cruelty. It was a disease of pain. But no violent regime is sustainable. A war machine eventually breaks down. Events conspire to create peace, even when heads are hot and hearts are cold. There is no long-term enterprise from the business of death. The pain must give way to love, the lion must lie down with the lamb.

Honor and Lalla, two wise women, craved solitude, quiet and peace to wait out the storm. They were haunted by demons. But the thought of the demons brought a quiet determination. Ceremony and songs were the essence of life in this new country. In the future no man would be allowed to starve. Honor had an outwardly hard exterior and a propensity for violence and aggression but beneath her shell was overwhelming kindness and goodness. The remnant survivors would never turn away a stranger who was hungry or a family who suffered misfortune or accident. Honor knew beyond anyone how to help someone who had been badly hurt. These became the unwritten laws of the bush and the South Land. Every small moment of happiness and laughter was to be prized at a time when life was cheap and short. Often those who seemed most rough were disguising their own inner kind and gentle nature.

Michael was not alone amongst the descendants of those who had been transported to Australia in his quest for a new life free of the old tyrannies. Many of the Van Diemen's Land convicts were victims of injustice and they were passionate about making things right. I watched a spirit of independence emerge from the men. They would kowtow to no-one. Many detested the police and former gaolers.

Michael was keen to strike it rich. He arrived on the goldfields in the heat of summer. There were many police and soldiers journeying with him that day. I knew that something was up.

As he arrived on the goldfields he was quickly drawn to a beautiful aroma of food cooking on an open fire in a dry river bed. A man was hunched over a saucepan cursing.

"That is a fine brew you are stewing there, I would gladly pay you for a bite to eat," said Christopher.

The man looked up from his fire and smiled.

"Lay your bedroll down here. Come and eat with me I would be glad of your company. This meal may be my last," the man said turning quickly... "You are welcome. I have no rosemary and thyme to flavour my stew."

Michael who had learned a little of bush herbs from Honor grabbed at some wattle seeds.

"Sir, try these native peppers. They will add flavour to your stew. But what do you mean that this meal may be your last?"

"I am Rafaello. I have come to make my fortune and yet these English bastards want to tax us when we have not even found a speck of gold. We will not bow down to them."

"Tomorrow we will make a stand. We have sworn our allegiance to the Southern Cross. I will not live in a land where the authorities tax us and do not give us a vote or a say in the affairs of state."

"Sir, I would gladly share your company and I share your sentiments. My parents were transported to this southern land from Ireland for having similar views."

That night Michael and Rafaello talked into the early hours. Much rum was consumed. Michael resolved too that he would make a stand with Rafaello and the others. But when he woke Rafaello was gone.

In the distance he heard gunfire. He was soon on his feet. He ran towards a hill in the distance where he could see a frenzy of activity. "Michael, here!" he heard from the trees. It was Rafaello.

"Many men have been killed. Help me to escape!"

Michael quickly was at his side in the bush. He noticed others and helped them hide in camp tents. There was a feeling of shock and later Michael heard twenty of the miners had been killed along with five soldiers. The soldiers were revengeful and angry. Some of them were trackers who had lost their own sense of humanity and simply did the bidding of the tyrants who took their lead from Éire and England. It was the ultimate irony. The authorities proclaimed that the revolt of Rafaello and the others was over and that order had prevailed but again injustice had been sown in the minds of the men. They would never forget and out of the pain of the revolt and its suppression was born a new determination to end the bloody ways of the old world and to create a new world in which taxation without representation could not occur and the rights of all men and woman to vote for their representatives was sacrosanct. The old order was changing and I thanked God that I had sung Michael into a deep sleep that morning.

I was glad that Michael was safe, I could not have answered to Honor or Mary or Christopher. Many others were not so lucky. But something had been sown in Michael's survival. In Melbourne Rafaello and others were charged with high treason. It made no sense. Michael attended the trials every day he could and every day he saw the absurdity of the situation. He was as determined as ever to work for a new life and a new world.

The words of his grandmother Honor burned in Michael's ears. "Do not get yourself killed or put in jail. We have lost too many years and too many lives. Survive!"

After the revolt there was no place for a man of Michael's size and beliefs on the goldfields. Reluctantly he wrote to his father. "There would be no lucky nugget!" The docks were a world where Michael might lose himself and find steady work. It was here that Michael first saw Annie Kewley. Did I play Cupid? Well, in a way. I could see their future daughter Ivy running like the wind bowling balls like a demon. I could see again two great families intertwining and building a new spirit of the land. I could see a Russian silversmith. I could see teachers. I could see the world turning.

Many newcomers were simply greedy for themselves but on Bruny Island a special seed had been planted. It would take many generations to emerge and it would take many years for the catastrophe of the coming of the white ghosts to be overcome by the people of the southern land. But slowly, slowly, it would emerge. The songlines and ceremonies would reconnect. The white ghosts would understand that without the people of the land there could be no real substance to the new world. I dreamed of the time when the philosophies that I had learned would flow back to Éire.

I could see that the magic of this Great South Land needed to flow back into northern worlds. I could see that the paintings, stories and the stewardship of lands needed to return their meanings and messages to Éire. I knew that the magic of a skip, a wink and quick step, a laugh and a jest and a challenge would once again emerge. Most of all I saw how the world would learn to look after the wonders of nature with new care and understanding, thanks to all that I learned from Lalla Bakitju Gunda and Dilkurrwurru Wataŋgurr. I saw that one day we would all look up at the Milky Way with a new wonder and new possibilities would emerge in this world. New lives would bring new creativity and wonder. It would bring this message to you.

But storm clouds were again brewing. The journey never finishes. It continues. You have to have this spring in your step. When something bad happens, use it to do something good. Let a wellspring of desire emerge in your soul. That was what was about to happen. Dilkurrwurru's grandchildren were starting to stir. Honor's grandchildren were coming to bring a new vibration of love and understanding forward. I could see them. Stories of vagabonds and shiralees were coming. From gloom came hope.

WINDS JOINED THE SETTLEMENT with Europe and the thriving American colonies. The further south, the wilder the trip to the Great South Land. At 40 degrees latitude there were the famous Roaring Forties, at 50 degrees latitude were the Furious Fifties and most perilous of all was the Shrieking Sixties at 60 degrees latitude. To sail in the Southern Ocean with these winds was called 'running the easting down'. The ideals and aspirations of the hunted and oppressed that had been transported to the colonies began to emerge through all this. As more and more ships came to our tiny island I was dreaming again deep in the forests of the Huon Valley. It is important that you know of this time and these possibilities. For me it was just like at the beginning of this story. The past, present and future came together for a moment. Now I can see all the way through time to you who are reading these words. My problem now is when to stop. Looking back and forward, we magical beings started to understand: Embrace the spirits of the land and be attuned, like the first peoples, to vibrations of land and sea. Talk, like the first peoples do, to the ancestors and spirit beings, ask for their guidance and they will protect and show you the land in which you live. Most of all understand that the people of this land will show you many dimensions of life that have been lost. They are people to respect, to listen to and to know as friends. There are so many things I could still tell you, a thousand pages would not be enough. I speak to you now not of how I came to this land, but of your place and time. When I came to this land two peoples who suffered great cruelty and pain were thrown together. In what I have said already I have told you enough. I want to tell you now of what has happened since then, of what must be done now. I think you are beginning to know. It is time now to talk of how the magic of the world needs to be restored and treasured... and how you can help. These final chapters of my story are patches from a giant quilt... You will have to put the whole fabric together from the glimpses I can give you. This world is for you to make. You can do anything. The past is simply a story. The future is something to create, something to give your heart to. Let me now try to pick up from where we were... it is impossible to tell of all... but let me try to pick out some important things that will help you.

WHALES ARE REVERED by the people of the South Land. When they beached themselves elders would coat themselves with whale oil. It was the old people coming back home. The grease would ease creaking joints and bring a rejuvenation of spirit and life. It was a fearful sight to see the old men and women smeared from head to foot with oil and blood emerging from the stomach of the great beings. But the life sources of the great beings were in themselves a kind of magic.

The people were celebrating, dancing, becoming one with the life of the whale. This special creature had a special magic of its own. When newcomers saw the old people and the feasting they were disgusted. How could they understand? Would it be two hundred years before the newcomers would learn of the world beyond and the great sea to which the whale soul now swam and the gift of grace and lightness he gave to the people smeared with his life essence.

The newcomers understood only one thing, the great whirring machines and wheels required oil. When they took the life of a whale they did not understand or celebrate the life essence of the whale. In their hunting ships, men from America and Europe pursued whales as never before. They were hunted across the great oceans. The world became a smaller place as captains of the great hunting ships followed the wild winds at the bottom of the world. Time after time, conflict after conflict came about because of the greed and disrespect of the newcomers. These battles have become invisible but I tell you of them now so that you too can know the special qualities of the whale and how its holds the world together.

The hunting of whales brought newcomers by the score with great tales of wars, revolutions, pirates, treasures and wealth. The little convict town became a place of news from the Americas, Africa and the centres of the new world. Even the captains of the ships from Éire and Europe were finding the winds at the bottom of the world and making fast passages that were never possible before. Bruny Island, Van Diemen's land, Hobart town, what is now known as Tasmania, were small settlements but they were now part of a new world.

The news from the colonies of the Americas often arrived in Hobart town well before it made it back to London and the capital cities of Europe. Ships also came bringing passengers: engineers, carpenters, merchants... Back in Scotland, Wales, Ireland and England, times were tough and many came now seeking their fortune attracted by grants of land and jobs that were scarce back home. In all of this, Honor, Mary and Christopher were making their way, eking out a living and searching for the precious independence of spirit that had been denied them in Éire. It was here that after the darkest of hours some light began to shine through little cracks of the convict walls.

For some years Mary had collected little tubers in the pockets of her dress. Honor would have chastised her severely had she known. At the height of the great potato blight and famine in Éire it was a crime punishable by imprisonment and exile to steal potatoes. Following the spirit of her powerful mother, Mary knew though that it could never be a crime to nurture and enjoy the fruits of the land.

At night Mary would go to sleep dreaming of placing them in the ground so that she could grow her own food. The ultimate freedom was a garden of her own. It, more than anything, would lift her spirits. On Bruny Island she had her chance. She carefully prepared her ground. It was barren and stony. But slowly she turned over the soil until at last she was able to place the small tubers into the ground. When the leafy vines emerged from the ground Mary's tears flowed freely. Here at the bottom of the world she knew there was a new life and new hope. Every day she spent more and more time in her garden. She gathered seaweed from the beach, dried it and broke it up and worked it into the soil. She collected precious seeds and soon she had such a diversity of food that she was astonished and delighted. Pumpkins, potatoes, cabbages, brussel sprouts, broccoli and tomatoes grew in abundance. Soon there was excess to be sold and traded.

Christopher too had begun to work the barren, stony soils. He too had success. Working with a small group of traders up and down the coast, he began to harvest produce with the Hobart market in mind. Lalla looked on with amusement at the activities of the family. 'Yams and food are all around,' she thought. But she knew it was too much to tell these things to the newcomers. Only in the future would the knowledge freely be shared by people learning about more than just food. They would have to understand the full philosophy and law of the land. Meanwhile little England and Ireland began to emerge over the pain of the first peoples. Lalla Bakitju Gunda looked off into the distance not knowing whether to laugh or cry. But she was glad to see Honor's children doing well even when her own children and family were lost in the mad oblivion of the colonial invasion. When she moved to Hobart she would come regularly to Christopher's stall and he would give her the staple food she had learned to eat. For this midst the barbarity she was grateful. He was the only man who could make her smile.

Each week Christopher would set sail on a small dinghy and bring the farm produce for sale. On a blustery January afternoon, Mary came down to see him off. The Dentrecastreaux Channel was a notorious strait which ran between the island and the mainland. An impetuous captain had wrecked a great ship underestimating its twists and snares in bad weather.

"Do you think you should wait until morning? The swell is high and the wind is picking up."

"Don't worry, I will shelter in the coves if necessary. I can't wait until tomorrow. I have to reach the markets in a couple of hours. I promised. Don't worry, I will get through and see you tomorrow night."

With that he pushed off and the sail was soon set. But Mary was right to warn him. No sooner had he pulled out from the lee of the land, a great buster tore through the tiny craft's sails. Christopher struggled to bring the boat under control. But he had seen it all before and using sacks of potatoes as ballast. he managed to ride out the squall with just a small jib.

At dusk he arrived on the wharves of Salamanca Place at Hobart town. It was a pitiful sight. The mast of the small craft had cracked and the sails were torn to pieces. Christopher had no time to contemplate what had happened. He soon had the bags of produce onto wheel barrows and began moving them up to the square. It was a hard slog and when he finished he simply threw himself down into the torn sails that lay on the hull of the little craft and went to sleep.

As daylight came, Christopher heard a cough and then a young man's voice.

"What a wretched sight! You will need some repairs." Christopher looked up to the wharf and saw a man about five foot six in height, slight in build. He looked unwell.

"Yes," said Christopher, "I am not looking forward to the job of re-splicing the mast and sewing up these sails. But that cough doesn't sound too good either."

"I am perpetually warding off this cold. It's not that bad," said the voice of the young man. "If you row your boat round to my father's yards our men will re-splice your mast. That will give you a chance to sew up these sails. It was a fair blow yesterday."

Unaccustomed to the generosity of strangers, Christopher quickly jumped to the wharf.

"Sir, how can I thank you and pay you? My name is Christopher Martin."

"I am Andrew Inglis Clark, shipwright, I would be glad of your business and for payment simply bring me some of your produce. We will come to some agreement. Tonight please come to our family table and you are welcome to sleep in the yards."

It had been a long time since Christopher had been treated with such courtesy. He recognised in the man a kinsman in the best spirit of the countryside.

Mary and Christopher were now technically free to live their lives as they wanted, but their gaolers and administrators still thought of them as convicts and felons. Yet here was a young man who simply treated Christopher as a free man. That night Christopher listened as the remarkable family talked. It had been a long time since he had heard such a free exchange of views.

At the head of the table was Andrew's father Alexander. As guests, there were several visitors including captains of Boston whaling ships that were being repaired. Christopher listened as the family asked of the progress of a great internal war in the American colonies. How passionately the family inquired of the progress of the war. It was a war to end slavery. In the middle of the meal Andrew rose and spoke with a passion Christopher had only heard in the gatherings he had attended in the Irish countryside. Andrew decried slavery in all its forms from Rome, Greece to the new world. He went on to argue that the transportation of convicts to Van Diemen's Land was also a form of slavery which must also be stopped. There were inherent rights that every human being must be entitled to. These rights could not be abused by those who owned property. Christopher listened as the talk turned to the great union leader Lincoln. Slowly Christopher found himself rising to his feet.

"My name is Christopher Martin." At first no-one paid attention.

Then someone cried: "The courageous mariner of the Dentrecastreaux Channel. He survived that blow that would have sunk many! Hear him out." The room hushed.

"Gentlemen... I am sure your weekly incomes could pay the ransom of me and my entire family. It would free us from our salt-encrusted prison. I am not worthy to speak on this stage as your equal but I beg your indulgence. I was transported here because I dared to fight the English suppression of my people in Éire. Thousands of my countrymen have died of starvation because potatoes and grain were exported back to England. I have seen these things first hand. Nothing was left to feed our own people, even though we had adequate crops to feed our countrymen at the height of the great failure of our staple crop, potatoes. English landlords used the opportunity to evict our people from homes where they have lived for generations. I have now been in these colonies for ten years and I have faced the worst pain and the cruellest punishments, but I will never bow down to tyranny. I applaud your speech,s gentlemen, and I thank you for your invitation that allows me to share the bounty of your table."

At that Christopher sat back down in his chair. He lacked the eloquence of the Clarks but his few words had an impact. The American whaling captains looked intently at Christopher. They explained that an increasing number of Irishmen who had emigrated to the United States were joining the union cause. There was a round of applause for Christopher from his new friends. Andrew looked admiringly at Christopher.

As he went to sleep that night Christopher's mind ran at a hundred miles an hour. The pain of Ireland and Scotland and the pain of convicts like him who had been victims of injustice might come to something in this land. The fights of the Irish homeland might not have been in vain.

As he sailed back home to Bruny, Christopher's hopes and dreams were enlivened. Unlike his stormy journey to Hobart town, now moonlight glittered on the channel like teardrops rolling in the waves. He could not wait to tell Mary of his adventures. Over the coming months Christopher would stay regularly with the Clarks at their house *Rosebank*. He, like many in Hobart town, came to rely on Andrew for news, information and ideas. Andrew invited him to come to a new debating society - the Minerva Club. Passionate speakers debated the rights of man, the abolition of capital punishment, the vote for women, the need for democracy in Van Diemen's Land and the need to end transportation. Minerva was at the cutting edge of democratic thinking which would have been a welcome development in any of the major cities of the world.

At one of the meetings Andrew began a passionate speech.

"Many of the evils and inconsistencies attending government in the Colonies arise from the absence of a written Constitution defining the powers and privileges of every institution and every officer in the State."

"But how can you write down what is right and wrong for all time?" a young woman asked.

"Every man and woman, at every time, must make their own interpretation of right and wrong using the wisdom of their ancestors as guide. What is written is malleable. Each generation must mould it to its own purpose and have that responsibility."

When I heard these words, I could hear D̲ilkurrwurru Wataŋgurr: "Our law never changes. The law of these newcomers changes all the time. How are we to deal with these newcomers." But I could feel in my heart something coming together. The ancient law of the land could never change. But the laws that govern people in their communities needed to ensure that famine and war never came to the land again. Every generation had to own the laws and to adjust them to ensure that they were working well. Could ancient law and modern law work together? I wondered these things.

But this idea of democracy and of ordinary people having a say in the rules that applied to them was radical. All over Europe and the Americas, older orders of kings and queens were collapsing. The caring nobility of Countess Cathleen was a rarity. A murmur went through the room, for it became clear that Andrew was planting a vision and a quest to build a new and better way of life that built on the dreams of people like Christopher Martin who wanted a world free of tyranny.

In Van Diemen's Land and across the colonies the idea of gaolers and appointed governors making all the decisions was something that no-one except the self-interested wanted.

Minerva was a light in the darkness. For Christopher, it symbolized all that was not possible at home. A family might be free to own and work their own land. There would be no taxation that flowed to an authoritarian government or foreign power. There would be representation for men and for women. There would be 'freedom under the wattle trees' of the South Land.

Christopher remained a stout friend of the sickly Andrew. As years went by he watched him move into politics. He encouraged him in his design of a system of universal suffrage or voting that ensured that all of the thoughts and beliefs of people would have to be represented and respected. This became a benchmark of Tasmania and of this period when men and women sought a new kind of freedom.

One morning Christopher was on the docks and he saw Andrew disembarking from an American whaler. It had been months since he saw him, now he knew why.

"Come, Christopher, I must tell you the news."

Christopher knew that Andrew would be referring to the great war in the American colonies but there was something more.

"I have visited Boston and visited a great man of law. I have a plan for the unification of the Australian colonies. We will have a great Federation, Christopher. Our children and our great grandchildren will be free to make their own destiny." He talked excitedly of a great meeting to be held in Sydney town and of the invitations that had been sent to all the colonies and to New Zealand.

At the heart of the great Constitution that Andrew had drafted was the notion that words must not be locked in stone. It is up to each generation to make their history and to learn the lessons of the past. It was a great and just philosophy. But there would be many twists and turns and it would take a lot for ordinary men to understand the nature of the great Constitution in Andrew's leather satchel. In a land of gaolers, where men were accustomed to receiving orders from the governments of the kings and queens of England, it would take a long time for people to stand on their own two feet.

Andrew would make a trip to Sydney town where all the secretaries of the colonial state had assembled with their plans. They would link all the colonies together. They would form a new country, Australia. But it would take another century before the Minerva Club's ideas and the great vision of Andrew Inglis Clark would mean anything. He was a great man of law and a friend to common men like Christopher Martin. In the short-term Andrew's ideas would be overrun by ignorance; the law would become the stuff of the narrow, hard gaolers and of men who wanted to protect their own power. In all this the new nation would be created on a great flaw of ignorance about the original ownership and stewardship of the land.

For the people of the great wet and dry seasons in the north of the country the new artificial nation and its boundaries meant the end of a fruitful 800-year-old trade with their friends the Macassans who would come to gather trepang from the ocean floor. The Miwatj people had already joined the world spice trade and had been trading with China for generation after generation. No longer would cloth, steel, tobacco and rupiah be plentiful. It was a disaster and more than any time, even in the midst of the great challenges to Ḏilkurrwurru Wataŋgurr and his peoples, this was the worst of times. The first peoples were once ignored, misunderstood and treated wickedly. When would it end.

Men can be full of their own fluff and bubble. Even Christopher and Andrew, like so many others, were so entranced in their own dreams of the rights and wrongs of the world that they could not see or understand the full implications of the tragedy that had occurred all around them.

They and all of the newcomers enjoyed the fruits of thousands of years of careful stewardship of the lands and animals. They did not understand they had greedily destroyed the fabric of productivity that had been carefully built up over such a long time. They could not feel or understand the great persecution of land and people that had occurred all around them. The cruelties of home had been exported abroad and the first peoples of the land were the victims.

Of all people, it was Honor who felt Lalla's pain and the pain of the land; she absorbed it in her very being. But she could not speak or articulate it. I spent my days dreaming. I looked into the future and heard a million conversations. It heartened me to read the poems of little children who sensed our faery presence. Yet I watched a cycle of ignorance perpetuate itself again and again. I knew it would take lifetimes for things to change. I had to place Honor's feelings into the very marrow of a child's being. In time, we would break the cycle of ignorance. The spirit and ancestral beings merged into the trees and lands waiting too. One day the special magic of the Great South Land would become part of the framework and laws that governed men and women again. At this time, in the future, the world would spin well again.

Waniulŋa (Sacred Dog)

Following the trail of the dogs we made our way to the old man's grave to pay homage and restore the world...

A CAULDRON OF MANY PEOPLES was bubbling over. Rivers were breaking their banks. The backbones of warriors over a myriad of time were lost and would have to be discovered again. The Garden of Eden could not be recognised. Fruits of wonder rotted on the ground as men fell down starving. Blind were leading the blind. For those who endured the Ice Age in warm havens beneath the ground, survival was a long-held instinct. This swarming empire of war-like technologists would give way. How much damage would they do? A lot! The tough task was to figure out how this swarm of fools could be incorporated with the law below the top soil. Could they be reconciled to it? Or would they, and did they, just deserve to die as lonely and futile fools? In the great troupe of heroes, the descendants of Monyu, Arrimi, Pigeon and other great warriors were taking up the quest for their peoples. On the shoulders of the visionaries walked new leaders. In every community the struggle was renewing: resistance fighters like Tjandamurra, political statesmen like William Cooper, William Harris, William Barak and his friend Annie Bom, Jack Patten, Doug Nicholls, Eric and William Onus and fighters for basic rights like Norman Baird and Louisa Briggs, all these men and women, and hundreds of others, took up the cause and inched forward.

Unsurprisingly as time went on they showed themselves to be above and beyond their adversaries. This time they were equal in strength and resources as their foes. They were not outnumbered, they had the firepower and they could show what they were made of. This ethic carried on through the country boxing rings and into the modern era of knowledge, innovation, sport, one-on-one the new warriors reminded each other of their strength and character.

Times of comfort after suffering are times for doubting, of not believing in magic, only the children followed us. Most of all the world squandered its resources. There were some who still did believe in magic and who understood the majesty of the land. Who were they? Ha! They were asleep in the fruit boxes of markets, earning a living picking crops and many were still roaming the lands. To know of these things, I have to tell you of another great journey I made. I am allowed to tell because it unleashes a secret. The secret that brought this story to you. Are you ready to hear it?

WE SPIRIT BEINGS HAVE A HAND IN TURNING the tide of what is remembered and what is not. I am not talking about official history. I am talking about what matters in people's hearts. We place the spirit of grandfathers and grandmothers into their sons, daughters, grandchildren, great grandchildren, great great grandchildren. We help them remember and we turn up the important things that are never included in the official histories and written words. I must tell you a story. I can hear Honor in my ear saying "No!"

But it is time for you to hear it. The story is about rebellion and of new beginnings. It is about a new feeling that came to flourish. It was about the pain of Éire and a spirit of something new. It is also a story about the persistence of mistakes that people make when they have too much self-importance. The seat of a king or the hat of a policeman can lead a person astray. People lose touch with the way nature sits. The lessons of the poor and the maltreated were still to be learned, but slowly a calm resistance was emerging amongst the newcomers and the people of the South Land. Rough men and roaming cattle churned up the land. The spirit of Dilkurrwurru Wataŋgurr was linking to the spirit of freedom. Emerging from the toughest of conditions the new citizens were creating their own value system and ideas. The secret messages and communiques of the old prisoners were legendary.

In Van Diemen's Land, Christopher knew of John Kelly from Tipperary.

He had been transported for stealing two pigs. As Honor had said so often, it is no crime for a man to steal food when a whole country is starving. But she would not have a bar of John. Once burned never forgotten. Christopher thought differently. He thought highly of John and had encouraged him, like Michael, to seek his fortune away from Van Diemen's Land. Now news came of his death in Victoria. John left a wife and family and as is the way of the Irish, Christopher sent word to young Michael to inquire as to the wellbeing of John's wife Ellen, her five daughters and three sons.

OLD MAN FOG CAME BACK TO ME because our paths crossed, our meanings and our stories were intertwined. There were so many spirit beings like this misty man influencing the lives of the newcomers.

I saw the mighty Dungala, snap back and forward in time did I go. I saw steamboats eating up the cathedrals. Rivers being poisoned and dammed. Voracious insects and animals in plagues. Lalla Bakitju Gunda came to me. She was silently weeping for Tunnerminnerwait and Maulboyhenner. Brave warriors, they had killed two of the cruel whalers who had persecuted and murdered Aboriginal men, women and children. I saw Broger. I saw Wonngu. Planobeena, Pyteruner and Lalla were there in a court meditating on the destruction of Tasmanian and Victorian lands. These images came back and forward to me.

Fog showed me the new brutality and killings. Driving and hunting men, women and children into the mangroves near the law ground. After sixty years of settlement newcomers devised terrible ways to eliminate strong culture and ownership of lands. Worst of all, it is the epitome of evil for a people to be turned against itself. That is what the newcomers unleashed. For fifty long years a vicious campaign using teams of countrymen took place. Countless men, women and children were killed. Flour was poisoned and left for unsuspecting camps. Men, women and children were shot. Elimination squads were deployed anywhere on request. A million tears were shed on the Palmer River. On the 25th October 1873, a town was formed by miners. There had been one hundred years of peace since the first conflict with *Endeavour* and its crew. Now, like lightning, all the pain and suffering that Lalla

Bakitju Gunda and Ḏilkurrwurru Wataŋgurr had endured in the South had come to the rainforests of the North. Now the conflict and greed came over the rivers and streams like an evil curse. In their search for gold, men destroyed the ancient fish traps and stopped the flow of rivers and streams. These newcomers were men who could not be reasoned with. A guerrilla campaign began. A state of open warfare prevailed. Rifles and horses were deadly enemies. Warriors killed 133 horses on the Palmer River road from Cooktown. At first the Guugu Yimidhirr and their extended families and regional allies had the advantage. But with gold comes terror. The ascendancy was gained by the police. Armed with rifles and with their own horses they cut a path from Balabay and all resistance was overcome. They were soldier, police, prosecutor, judge, jury and executioner. Vengeful miners also had no hesitation in taking the law into their own hands. Hundreds of men, women and children perished over a thirty-year period. In this time white evil prevailed.

At Battle Camp, I watched so many brave warriors die. I saw their hope and their fear and I heard their curses of the greedy vandals and thieves who had invaded their lands, but who in the end won this desolate battle. I flew into the future and I saw a birthday party for an old man. Music was played. Food was shared. Hundreds turned up to honour the old man and to celebrate him. I saw them honour in greater numbers than the foremost dignitaries. I saw the little snake that made the old ladies jump. He, laughing to see the old ones move so fast. Even the greatest evil can be overcome. But it takes a long time.

The truth must be told. The demons must be faced. If not, the evil still flies. It can take over and cause a vehicle to fly into a crowd. A man can become an animal with a reptile brain. The brain has to connect with the heart. A determined love must confront a determined hate.

After the ruthless death and destruction of Battle Camp I saw wise elders who had survived the carnage talking about their children.

Many people had become lost. They found themselves at the mercy of the poisons of Cooktown - a wild place of gold and seafarers, pirates and ne'er-do-wells. A refuge had been created at Elim. It was here that a little boy's fate was determined. Newcomers had come with a mission from the one they called God. The little boy looked up at this German man of God and was so frightened of his walarr that he bounded away. His father could not make him stay. Each time I saw his father so heavy of heart bringing the little boy back. It was finally a pussy cat that made the little boy overcome his fear. Only slowly did he overcome his loneliness and longing for his family. Like so many little boys and girls it would be the last time he saw his parents. He was the last of his clan. More children came into the mission for food and shelter.

They endured and survived. On their shoulders, the future walked. This madness of pain and grief travelled North and across the Gulf as it had in the South and the West. Only the big rivers that bounded Arnhem Land in the wet season offered some hope and protection.

Midst the greed and the terror something was also uniting the people who had endured endless pain and suffering. The scaffold, the pain, the poisoned flour and the cruelty and evil united the oppressed. A feeling of contempt for authority was evolving, welling up. There was a need for a place where victories could be won, where the scales were equal and rifles, poison and flour were not allowed.

"In the parkland... stand three old and ghost-like gum trees..." [45]

IRISH MEN BEGAN TO PLAY A GAME amongst the old man eucalyptus trees of the mighty Dungala river. A common need was uniting the survivors of the Irish genocide and the Australian Aboriginal genocide.

There was a joy to be had running at full stretch and kicking a ball, dodging and weaving, disappearing down gullies and across creeks. Women, men, children caught a ball and with a twinkle in the eye disappeared, then appeared, urging the chase. I saw a rainbow and a mighty team where old and young congregated and people were happy even when times were tough. For days and weeks, the game of kicking and throwing a possum-skin ball would continue. Where the ball fell it would be picked up the following day. These were joyous occasions when time and worry stopped. Barefoot boys and girls would dash and dart between the trees. Old men and women would outwit their younger peers with cunning and guile.

Irish children grew up playing their own games. Soon they too played with the Yorta Yorta families. It was the time before fences. The Irish families came to adapt the spirit and freedom to their own kicking games with a leather ball. A game would evolve. It would become immortal and its sacred ground would form on a ceremonial site of the Woiwurung people. We spirit beings worked in concert with the friendly murup and ngamat beings. There would be magic here for generations to come. The games were magic. They came to be revered and witnessed by hundreds, then thousands and then millions. Men and women would run with winged feet. Young ones would fly through the air and great feats would be performed. Slowly men and women would come to understand the magic of place and land through these things. All these good things were occurring. I looked into the future and saw a great man peer deeply into a collective mind-set as he kicked a ball through the goal posts. As he danced he was saying to the masses of newcomers: *Never, never again will you bend us to your will and your world, now you will hear us and see us in all our wisdom and capacity*.

But the story I have to tell you now was again of my old world. It is a story of my Arrimi, an outlaw, who like old man fog was a liar and a man of truth and justice. He was a killer and a lover at the same time.

He was a profound being for grandchildren to debate and talk about with their grandparents. Because this man like a mist was a spirit come to earth

Michael was now working on the docks in Melbourne town. These docks had great resonance over many generations. I saw that Michael's great great grandson would also work here and gain wisdom that would help him on his life journey. I saw Michael's daughters and sons leave the shores of the Great

South Land on a great pilgrimage. I saw a great old man waving in the mist of Port Melbourne to this family and I saw a son torn because he knew he had to leave, knowing it would be the last glimpse of his father. I saw the ship leaving the dock and later I saw him crying at his loss and rising to greatness as a result. Like others of Éire he had to forge in the smithy of his soul the uncreated conscience of the future. This was also the linkage to the little boy in the sand dune. He too would have to leave his father to make a journey in the world that would deprive him of precious time with the ones he loved so much.

It was a journey that had to be.

Michael often had opportunities to travel on the great bullock drays that delivered and received produce from the country areas. He knew that Ellen had settled at Mile Creek and when the opportunity arose he travelled to see her.

Having been cajoled by the fearful Honor and counselled by his father, Michael would not easily enter an affray. The gentle giant would turn the other cheek under the most trying circumstances. But the tyranny of ex-gaolers and police who thought they could carry on with their cruelty lasted many years. It was always on for young and old when a young boy of Irish or Scottish origins encountered a local tyrant. Of course there were also demons. Of course there were also those for whom cruelty and violence became ends in themselves. But there was also this new spirit. For the injustices of the old world would be settled here and a new philosophy that combined the wisdom of the people of the land and a new model of ethics and justice would be forged here in this new, old world.

I accompanied Michael knowing that my presence would console the grieving widow and family. As soon as we arrived I knew that all was not well. As we were walking down the track to the homestead a policeman on a horse passed us. Every Irishman of the time would think: "Oh no, I have been here before." I remembered the day that Honor and her children had been arrested and I shuddered.

We could hear Ellen's withering shouts carrying into the bush "You ugly fat-necked wombat-headed big-bellied magpie-legged son of an Irish bailiff - get off my land!" The policeman saw the powerful Michael walking towards the homestead and as he turned to look at us Ellen hit him with a shovel. The constable drew his revolver. At this Michael sprinted and just managed to catch the policeman in a tackle, a shot was fired and the bullet passed through the constable's hand as he fell from his horse. The shot might have killed him. "One word of this Constable Fitzpatrick and I will make you wish your mammy had never delivered you into this world" Ellen cried after him. The constable's face turned white. Michael had his revolver. At this. with dust on his uniform, and looking a motley sight, the constable mounted his horse and was away back to town.

Michael grinned and turned to Ellen.

"Warm and gentle greetings from the Martins to you, my dear Ellen. It looks to me like we are up a crocodile river on a moonless night!" At this he laughed out loud.

"The fate of Irish men in this district!" Ellen spat back signalling her contempt at the fleeing constable. It was a funny sight to see him go. Soon Michael, Ellen and daughter Kate were also doubled over with laughter. The women knew that the gentle giant had saved them and were grateful.

That night plans were made. Michael must not be drawn into what was looming as a war between the police and the Irish families of the area. Kate was a wonderful horsewoman. We stayed with the family long enough and then in the dead of night, Michael and Kate made the long ride back to the bullock dray routes that would take him home.

The police reports mentioned a mysterious Irish giant but this was soon forgotten as the fight became even more bitter and intense. There was another big man that the police now sought to bring down. It was Ellen's oldest son Edward. From this banal incident against helpless women a modern tragedy would emerge. Ellen was sentenced to three years imprisonment for the affray. Michael felt a great pain when he heard the news. But whatever he felt was nothing to that of Edward, who had been away during the whole incident. The children of the convict stock were a breed apart. They were fearless and tough. This was not to be Éire over again. Something stirred within the hearts of those that wanted something better: freedom and peace.

In words that would resonate through the ages he proclaimed "I am a widow's son... outlawed."

Edward, his brother, Dan and several like-minded friends escaped to the Darby Ranges where they had played the great game with their Aboriginal friends. They learned how to duck and weave and disappear. Edward and his brothers might have just been ordinary boys caught in a crossfire but I could feel the tremors of their hearts and they knew no fear. I kissed Edward's head and was with him at his demise. We sang songs together and observed a little garden as he walked calmly to his death. This young boy become a sort of spiritual icon for the newcomers and someone respected by the first peoples - who had endured far more pain than the Kellys. I added a tiny pinch of magic and put in his mind the tradition of the great Irish heroes. It was not just the young man who was remembered two hundred years later, it was the tribulations of all those who came from so far away and were so cruelly treated that reverberated so much.

Some may be surprised by the eloquence of the young man; such people know nothing of the magic of the Irish spiritual world. Ten years later Jandemarra also felt Edward's words "...what business an honest man would have in the Police...?" He led the Bunaba resistance and he too became a hero like a thousand nameless warriors of the first peoples. Like old man Fog and the spirit of Arrimi, who also knew how to appear and disappear and was never caught, these men of flesh and blood were to become spiritual figures who did wrong but did right.

At this time of riotous conduct in the South the rivers and creeks of bama land were being invaded. The same fight of the Kellys and Jandemarra and Lalla Bakitju Gunda was occurring.

Something was crossing over for the first time in the spirits of the first peoples and the newcomers. It became a great attribute of these Australians, to stand up against empty authority, to grow up believing that every man was as strong and knowledgeable as a king or queen. Even those who had no sympathy with outlaws began to share their table with a stranger who had met hard times, to revel in the wilds and to make a palace out of the most modest of homes. Something good was coming from something bad. It had to be. We faeries and spirits worked and worked to make it so.

This little boy hiding in the sand dunes would have something of this spirit. One day he would take up the spirit of his kin, of old man fog. He too would change the world. The paths of the Martins would cross his path. There would be many descendants of the fighters of the great tribulations of the world of the famine in Éire and the military and cultural assault on the Great South Land that would intermingle and whose names would become linked. It was good and it was bad. It was clear and it was mist. All these things were things for people of great wisdom to ponder.

Honor's survival instinct preserved Michael from harm. But he stood on that cold morning of November 11, 1880 pondering the past and the future. He, like the new citizenry of this land at the end of the world, began to think differently. Edward sensed this too, he knew that in his rebellion and sacrifice a spirit had been born that would never die. "Such is Life," he said and he remembered riding across the King River Ranges as the trapdoor fell away. A new nation began to form. This would be a republic of pick and shovel aspiration. In Europe, the average man was conditioned to feel inferior. In the United States, democratic men and women, having broken imperial ties and taxes and proclaimed themselves free, felt superior. In this new land men and women wanted the right to own their own land, to grow their own food and to be able to speak and be heard without fear or favour.

Michael and Edward wanted to build their own house and have their own potato patch. This new land was speaking to them and expanding their minds. "You cannot own the land," I whispered. "The land is me," said Lalla. "Mosquitoes are my grandmothers. Trees are my fathers. West Wind is my mother. East Wind is my father. North Wind is my yapa. South Wind is my gurruŋ. Bees are my cousins. When will you understand?" "Gutjarra ŋali birayun nyirana." Tunnerminnerwait and

Maulboyheener had stood where Edward had stood. Had fallen where he had fallen. In the North and the West out of the desolation would come new wisdom. After these sparks of resistance came grinding poverty and famine again.

For twenty years the land drove the new settlers into the ground. It was angry at the destruction of its forests. It was angry that its sensitive caretakers and fire farmers had been thwarted, attacked by ignorant fools of men. These men would starve when food was all around them. They had no idea.

And yet a new ethic was emerging. It was being forged from hardship and pain. Verses and articles were appearing. Not great tombs or works of art, but singing rhymes that could be recited in a pub or a shearing shed. By these things new vibrations were coming forth. New possibilities emerged and people would stand together to oppose what they saw and felt was wrong.

By right of birth in southern land I send my warning forth.
I see my country ruined by the wrongs that damned the North.
And shall I stand with fireless eyes and still and silent mouth
While Mammon builds his Londons on the fair fields of the
South? [46]

Gradually the learning would flow. Most of all I saw the baby sharks. How silly to think the power of the ancestral shark could be caught in a fish trap? In losing so comprehensively, great learning comes.

Brilliant baby sharks playing pianos... taking over the world. The great one dying a lonely death in Darwin. Unrecognised, he had sung in Carnegie Hall but they recognized him only as a drunk so many times. A Charlie Parker genius with feet of clay in a world that did not deserve either of them. Coming to schools in Sydney, confounding us all. Out of the mist would come Eva Annie Cawley. She was the daughter of a sea captain and the mother of Michael's children. I smiled as I saw her come with peace and security. Out of the mist would come a Scotsman whose blood would intermingle with that of bingadji. Dabu and Wallar the scrub and forest bees would reignite once again. Babies would be born.

Battles would be fought. It would take many generations for the mist to clear and for good to be recognised in bad. There was, once more, still so much to learn.

THROUGH TIME AND SPACE through forests we ran. Wuŋgan, Waniyulŋa, Argos, Cerberos - running on all fours faster than ever before. Tiger-dingo-dinosaur of the North, hungry and strong, hairy, smelling, sensing, bounding rivers and hills, following the pee-mail across the Charles Bridge, hunting for guku, searching for mushrooms... Seeing back to ancient times, rejoicing in the freedom of the dog spirit, finding my way back to this dhäwu, remembering the road kill of the drought, lost in my mind, spinning, taking me back to other dry times, lost and found, wandering, lonely, with family and without... These were years of a great dry spell and great dust storms that brought misery across the land. These bleak revolutionaries did not understand that the land needed the wet and dry. This was the cycle of life. White, broken men *shattered idols out along the dusty track,*[47] and woke in fright with big dreams alien to the land. Free from the chains of the past at Barcaldine and shearing sheds across the land, ordinary men and women dreamed of living with freedom. But what did it mean to have a secure house and land and food? The deep messages of the land were still lost on the dreamers.

Bosses and masters made their plans, a great Federation of colonies emerged crassly and coarsely over ancient lines and communities. Nyorŋ'nyurŋdhun! Bi`bi`thun! Lightning between workers, bosses and lawmakers. Bi`bi`thun! All built on a bed of sand and dust. A great swirl of ignorance and arrogance enveloped the land. Crossing great snow-covered mountains, feasting on the bogong, sacred ceremonies of the night, a spirit running wild in the great forest that touches the salt water at Tathra. Reedy Swamp - two little boys trying hard to go to the balanda school. The great Ann petitioning the King. Running to Wallaga and the sacred mountain and up the dividing range to the eastern most point of the Great Southern land. Bundjalong preparing themselves for the long war that would keep their language and culture strong, weeping as their forest cathedrals were pillaged. Teenage girl on the beach in the future, learning and understanding this desecration.

Place something here for the comfort of those who felt that they had nothing: love for themselves. Find it here in this place on this beach. All around the coast running with little spirit children hiding at Red Rocks. Writers and musicians and actors, great friendships and marriages, people communing with the land without acknowledging or embracing the spirits around them. So many years and generations for these newcomers to understand. Go north! Go north! Go north! Follow `ungomarr! Run on to places of misery and places of joy. Why running north? Following dog tracks of course, songlines linking people and land. Re-tracking the dingo tiger who ran away from his land and his people to connect the people of the south with the people of the north. Dog tracks becoming clearer and clearer. At night dreams of a hundred years, a thousand thousand years, waking up old in the dry river beds and savannahs of the Gulf of Carpentaria. Clouds with plants and animals in them floating by. Dilkurrwurru, bigger and bigger, see his white hair and his gentle smile. Willing forward. Dreams of ochre designs placed through dreams. Sold to the mission arts and crafts shop - a thousand dreams across all the lands and peoples - designs to study, learn and understand. Too many dreams, a hundred lifetimes full of dreams and stories. Learn them, remember them hear the stories. These stories they will save the world. Many things will become clear. Walk happily on this blessed land.

Re-uniting the brother and sister dogs on the Arafura Sea. They gave many messages. Dogs pissed on the rocks polluting the water. Thirsty Macassans drank the water, got sick and died. "What was wrong with that water?" "That's dogs' piss. You should have asked us!" "No wonder your people have been poisoned!" Look! Dogs coming from nowhere out of the bush at dawn. Howling! Escorting these stories and protecting them in the journey from me to you and onwards.

White ghosts at Sydney Cove were not the first intruders. Others came to the north. Uninvited - they were torn to pieces by dogs and stung by bees. Traders tried to seduce the dogs and

131

bees. At Djilliwrri they promised houses but a swarm of bees forced them away. Newcomers approached wäwa Djuraindjura with matches, blankets and houses. Bribes and beads! Like they offered Bennelong and Lalla and so many others. Djuraindjura became angry. Joint command of my own land? "No!" "What need have I of these things?" "Fire burns in the homelands, it is I who control it." "My blankets and houses are the greatest on earth." "Why should I share my land and my command with you?" Through the power of the dog nothing was lost. It was because of Djuraindjura that the culture and language of the South would return. Feel these things and they will reveal themselves to you. Nothing has been lost. Fierce, sacred dogs overcome the strongest armies.[48]

> *I swim along slowly*
> *(Wakalam ngarra marrtji)*
> *I see with my eye as my head turns from side to side*
> *(Wanthun ngarra marrtji wanthuna)*
> *The big shark called Garakara Bukumilan*
> *(Yindi Garakara Buku-milanbuy)*
> *These are my names Gululwänga Gadulkirri Wadulnyikpa*
> *(Galuluwänga, Gadulkirri, Wadulnyikpa)*[49]

GARRAY TAKEN DOWN FROM THE CROSS. Precaution, tenderness, love and reverence for the sacred body. All were looking up; no word was uttered. As the nails were removed Mary and Magdalene felt fresh grief. As the body was lowered, his Mother's arms were stretched out to receive it. Ceremonies had gone on for many days. Songs of the journey of mana across the waters echoed across the island. Yä - humming, making the places and connecting the djambarrpuyngu people as she travelled. Through the muddy waters tossing her head from side to side. Her fin was a sharp spear showing her presence beneath the muddy waters. Remembering our beloved one, thinking and dreaming of maja becoming as one with her. Singing the country, freshwater eyes, neck, following the creeks coming to the point where salt and freshwater mix, the chest of the beloved one now travelling and intertwined in the waters. Ancestors now too with us as we sing and dance. There is no time and space. We move between the present and the past. The noise of the waves, flowing cross currents, waves breaking on the shore line, calm waters lapping against the mangrove trees. I will sleep with dhuway near his grave, comforted by all of the images and places of his life. Purified by ceremony and at one with all.[50]

QUEEN BAYINI, BEAUTIFUL AND ALLURING, laden with perfume and jewellery, was loved by Yolŋu and her own people alike. Something of her existed in all strong women: freedom and independence. She could weave a web around a man that would leave him dazzled, confused and immediately in love. Djuraindjura, fierce dog, loyal friend, fighter and lover lived on his own eschewing the comforts of the extended family. He attacked and retreated never losing fights, his pride and capacity for resistance were revered. Djuraindjura's cunning and strength, brought about the great era of diplomacy and understanding in which Yolŋu and fair-skinned Bayini people lived together. Bukulatjpi began to dance the partnership of the Bayini people and Yolŋu in ceremonies that continue through time to this day. Dancing long knives, symbols of the Bayini deity, moving arms and legs, crying out to Islamic worlds from afar bringing into alignment the world views of ancient peoples. There behind the Warrimirri house on the beach is Excalibur. In this time houses, pottery and metals were made in the Northern islands.

A prosperous empire existed in which Yolŋu lived as equals with their mentors and traders cooking rice and using ceramics with their trading partners. Treading the coastline, Djuraindjura, watching black and white men living together harmoniously making pots and swords. The bounty of the land and sea was shared with people of good heart. Then came a time of confusion very much like the time of the white ghosts. It was a time of the Portuguese and Dutch domination of the sea lanes of the world. In one terrible summer, disease and death came to the land of milk and honey. Bayini, the diplomat and muse, was blamed unfairly for the catastrophe. She was punished wrongly when it was she that was trying to save the world. I saw in Honor and Lalla something of this restless, beautiful being. The spirit and mystery of Bayini is in all strong and beautiful women. She is here and she is there. No-one can properly understand her. She is something and she is not. She will trick you and she will love you. In all this she will really know your heart.

Bayini still moves around the countryside reminding Yolŋu people of the halcyon times of the past, that such times are fragile, that they will come again and next time the prosperity must last. I saw the beautiful one sing of Bayini around the world, her spirit was reaching out and slowly once again prosperity and hope was coming. Djuraindjura slept many nights at Bayini's campfire. He would repel those of bad heart and embrace those who would respect the soul of the Yolŋu.

Djuraindjura released his grip and power and Yolŋu became captive to less cultured trading partners. These traders had no desire to stay in the homelands of the Yolŋu. New traders gave linen, axes and tobacco in return for buṉapi so prized by the visitors from Sulawesi for its trade with China. This trade flourished for hundreds of years and countless generations. Luŋgumarr would bring the traders and maḏirri would send them home. When luŋgumarr began to blow, flags would be erected on the beaches - black for Warrimirri, red for dha`waŋu, yellow for Gumatj, green for Wangurri, blue and white for maḏarrpa, and blue for Birrkili. The perahus would come to their established partners, gather trepang and return home. Sometimes women would be kidnapped never to return to their homelands. Doris' ŋandi! Some made the journey to Macassar voluntarily and great charts in the shrines and temples would guide the buṉggawa on their journey. This model of trade when ceremonies are exchanged and families come together across South East Asia was, in turn, destroyed by the white ghosts of the south who barely knew of the centuries-long northern trade. Only now can they see it.

AS I LOOKED INTO THE FUTURE I COULD SEE lines like veins branching out in time, interconnecting, forming junctions, unions, possibilities good and bad. These were the lines of the families that came after Honor and Lalla Bakitju Gunda. In so many junctures there are dogs. They see us spirit beings very clearly. Human beings don't understand very much sometimes. As I looked out in time I saw Anker and Ray Ray at Mata Mata, the beautiful golden retriever called Spinner guarding a family until her last breath. I saw a little dog called Dingo chase a woman down a street. I saw a young boy run out after his beloved dog only to be hit by a car. I saw his shoe fly up in the air. I saw his little sister hiding behind a fence. I was there with this little boy feeling the gurtha on his skin, making him strong. Yes he was emerging through Honor, Mary, Christopher, Ivy and Daedelus - the sixth life. I saw two hunting dogs buried in my beloved Tathra forest. I saw a dog that had just learned the ways of the bush bitten by a snake. I saw Honor's dogs in Éire. I saw Rocky the great boxer of Doncaster. I saw Kingy sniffing jellyfish. Then there was Keela who ran and ran and was always there. She is with me now, snoring, as I dream. I saw the great ancestral pack of dogs that protected Batumbil and slept with her in the wild. I saw them transfer their power and strength to her when her beloved died and soothe her through all tribulations. I saw the dogs crying and imploring the great man of Mata Mata not to journey into the long grass. But he did not hear them. I saw the ancestral dogs run down the continent to Byron Bay and then to Bega and on over the Snowy Mountains. I had followed their tracks north. They had led me home.

Everything must come to an end, at these ends people either learn or they don't. When all else fails the dogs are there. They always forgive us for our mistakes and shortcomings. They watch over us all, they look after you across dimensions of life and time that most people do not understand. No matter what happens the dogs are there.

I was chasing dogs through time. It was a wild journey with many unexpected turns. Christopher and Mary produced so many beautiful children. Then came a great slew of grandchildren. I cannot tell you how many there were. I was so happy. I saw too that Lalla Bakitju Gunda's community was also on the rise. In the north, in the west, in the east and the south. The elders were preparing for a new future, a bran neu dae. Now it was their time to penetrate this new world of officials, police and administrators who had no idea of where they were or the spirit of this land. Elders and balanda of goodwill too were finding the footsteps of the dogs.

But the world that was being created through politics and money was tough, unforgiving and ignorant. The modern times and the first days of this artificial Federation called Australia were even tougher than the days of the coming of the ghosts. Now a mad idea of superiority possessed the white ghosts. They had no concept of what was all about them. They wanted to eradicate all traces of the past. They were scared of the future. They wanted to make everything the same. They wanted to erase all traces of rebellion. They hated the idea of a land created by criminals and convicts. They hated the land and all its dimensions as family. This was a time when children were taken away from their Aboriginal mothers. It was a time when Aboriginal people of the greatest ability were forced to disguise their identity. It was time when the greatest acrobat on earth, the Wiradjuri wizard, called himself Con Colleano and performed on the greatest stages of the world, to hide his true identity. It was a time of untold sadness. Old man Sims tracked his children to Bomaderry but was not able to talk to them. He left two shillings on a rock and signalled to them each time he came to watch them from the fence. A hundred thousand hearts were broken. Ignorance and destruction prevailed and yet, once again, out of this period of tribulation came strength, purpose and knowledge. For having endured so much this new spirit that was arising could never be broken.

MARY HAD TAKEN HONOR'S ADVICE AND changed her name back to Honor's maiden name Finnigan. Each birth was a new beginning. The records would not track them back to the hulks and orphanages and prisons of Van Diemen's Land. The children were free. More and more the philosophy that "Jack was good as his master" filled the talk and ideas of young men and women. Sunlight, hard work and honest toil were producing a blonde-haired, broad-chested, generation as bold and brave as Edward! "I will try anything once" became their slogan. But older minds like Christopher's were less brazen.

Older minds knew that some things should not be covered up. In the struggle, in the pain, was the knowledge of common destinies and friendships.

I saw a dog with a postcard in his mouth. He ran up to Christopher's son Patrick. The card was from grandson Cyril: *To Dad from "Bully Beef Cottage."* Christopher and I read the words over Patrick's shoulder. "Hunkered down, half way to heaven or hell. We did not know, we could not move, we were caught in a murderous crossfire. There was no dinner bell when we scrounged for food, only the sound of machine guns and bombs. It seemed as if the end of the world had come. A one-legged man with a three-legged horse hobbled through the trenches. The cold that comes from living in watery mud goes right through to the bones. I thank you for your prayers father I am proud to be your son."

Patrick was quick to hide the postcard... But Christopher and I had seen it and we cried and cried together for a long time. Why? Why? Why? How did these men and women whose parents symbolised so much of the struggles of Éire come to be in this hell, fighting meaningless battles for authorities whom they should have held in contempt? These were questions that many would ask themselves into the future. Every year I would pray to end war.

Could something good come of any of this? The power to make things *en masse*, the desperate search for new resources to supply the machines and mouths of those who worked them, the ability to move people from one end of the earth to the other, the capacity to search every land mass and even the ocean for more and more, brought arrogance and a lack of respect for human life. There had to be a way to stop the carnage and stupidity, the war and blood. It occurred to me that in the great contrasts and cruelty thrown up by Honor and Lalla Bakitju Gunda's experience something good and wise was emerging.

137

I talk to you now with Lalla's wisdom of a thousand, thousand campfires. Be strong and be courageous but above all else be wise about what I tell you. Others have tried. Two great story tellers dressed the story of war and evil conflict into a story of rings and ogres and wizards. But I must tell you the plain truth. Why did the adults not tell you of these things? It is probably because they are still numb and in shock even after all these years. They cannot fathom the depth of the pain that occurred. It is because they wanted to preserve the innocence of childhood. When pain and suffering came over the world, children were sent to play with us faeries. We were a little fantasy for you to have that would protect you from the world. But you see there really is magic in the world. There is magic to change the world. There is the magic of love. There is the joy of life in magic. There are spirits in your cupboards and under your beds. There are winds that talk to you and trees that whisper in your ear. We faeries are not something to laugh about. We are not pretend things. We are there with you. We do not like pink dresses and cute little cottages made out of mushrooms. We know you know these things. It is why I am talking to you now!

When Cyril's postcard arrived, I had a great vision of a terrible flood covering the earth. I saw yellow waves, floating rubble and the deaths of countless thousands. More than the starving children of Éire had in earlier times, this vision paralysed me. I did not know who I was or whether I was in faery or animal form. I saw a sea of blood that covered the earth down to the South Lands. I found myself accompanying Cyril back to the North on a ship full of young men going to war.

In the middle of summer, I saw a terrible cold come to earth and freeze everything. And in all this I saw a fruitless tree that the frost had turned into a healing force, its sweet grapes were medicine. I saw how this tree drew in the young and adventurous ones. All sought to eat its fruit. But the fruit left an after-taste of innocent blood spilled.[51]

How can I possibly put into words what all of this means? Yet I must. I have to tell you so you will recognise the pattern for yourself. But I cannot teach you. You must see in your own way.

Many people did not have Djuraindjura to protect them. The meaning of life, the true worth of land, sea and sky were lost. That is why you and I must change the world. We must stop the world from fighting. We must make good from bad.

Imagine wild dogs, sad and mixed up. These are times when things are going wrong, these are times when people make great mistakes. There have been many of these times of conflict and war. How can I explain? As I look into the future and the past there are many tales to tell. At the same time, there is nothing to say. When too much is made of the sacrifices of war and conflict you know that something is wrong. For no-one who has lived in "bully beef cottage" wants to dwell there long.

The free grandchildren full of their own strength and vitality had to decide for themselves. In the north so many were encouraged to fight by shaming and cajoling. Printed words on paper sheets with photographs and big letters appeared. They said to men if you do not fight you are a coward. The reverse was true. But this was the first time that a man or a woman could decide for themselves. In the past, whether you liked it or not, you did what you were told. You did not think much for yourself. That was the last thing you thought about. You thought of a monarch or an obligation or a debt to pay... so this new right to decide whether to take up arms was something powerful and fearful. Idiot barons now welded the minds of men together and made them stupid.

Only a few chose to go against the newspaper headlines and to challenge the thoughts of their friends and family. Grand and wise Vernon was one. He set a pattern for his son and the coming generations. Through these great wars and torments, Honor's strength and feeling of wildness would come to more people but did the world have to be covered with blood for this to happen? Some think so but I am so weary of war, it never achieves anything. There is so much more to tell. Yet how can I possibly tell? Hold this in your mind - life and youth are something sacred and pure to be nurtured and treasured. Let no harm come to young people. Let the old protect and discipline the young so that they can protect themselves. Always listen to your elders, you will know the ones to listen to most. It is difficult to explain why Cyril, Christopher and Mary's grandson, ended up at war. How was it that in just two generations so much had been forgotten? I think it was partly because the new land created a false belief in strength and youth. The new country had virgin soil never cultivated except by forests and nature. The first crops that were planted were abundant. The sunlight, the sea and the work in the fields made the children and adults very strong. Had they only been more attuned to the land! Had they felt what had happened to the first peoples all around them? And yet the relatives of the first peoples were also signing up to go to war! These peoples who had lost so much marched off to war because they were promised equality and on the battle field they died equally. So I say to you, child, beware of these times of madness, know your own heart and never be afraid to let it guide you. Call on your invisible guides, let them speak to you.

The Martins now spread across the country. They were a great gardening and farming family. Even Michael could not say why his nephew Cyril and his brother Serge enlisted to fight. It took him to the most famous battle of the young nation - a battle of defeat and idiocy - where the first young crop of beautiful boys was sacrificed. It was here that many family lines crossed. Cyril was wounded seven times and finally repatriated home. But the Tolls, who would cross the family lines far into the future, lost their great future leader and heir. Later Norman Baird the great man of the Daintree and the custodian of Yalanji languages would enlist to gain respect that could not be won at home. He would come home with new knowledge and understanding. Out of everything bad something good must come. But it is too high a price to pay.

I WAS LEARNING SO MANY THINGS AS A DOG. Sometimes as I ran across the stringy bark plains and savannah lands I thought I might explode with joy. We dogs had been on this continent for a very long time.

Much longer than anyone knows. We were giants who traversed the earth, what you now call dinosaurs, but we were much more than that. It was our job to safely take spirits to other worlds. Our calls would let everyone know that we were on guard patrolling the landscape, sniffing the ground and feeling for people of poor spirit or bad blood. One day I sensed the west wind bärra was blowing me new knowledge. I followed it. It was blowing across Arnhem Land to Caledon Bay. There I found a strange man. He was not an ancestral being but a hero of another kind. I spent many nights near his camp. He named me Tiger and I achieved renown as a hunter amongst the Dhayyi and Djäpu warriors. It was I that supplied the food for the camp. Gaminyarr became my master. I was his faithful companion and hunter. But we were drawn together for many reasons. This was a time between war when the world seemed to stop in its orbit. Thousands were out of work. The promise of a fairer land where an ordinary man and woman might be comfortable seemed to disappear like a puff of smoke. In Europe, great hope and great evil vied with one another. And in the north of the Great South Land, in Djuraindjura's county, there was outrage. A great leader and diplomat Wonggu, following the teachings of Djuraindjura, had repelled invaders to his land. New intruders, some Australian, some Japanese began to commit crimes against women, to steal and abuse their privileges on Yolŋu territory. Five Japanese men, two Australians and a policeman were killed. They had underestimated the strength of the dog and the shark. But now I began to sense that the outrages of Van Diemen's Land and New South Wales would be visited upon the Yolŋu. It was this that drew me to gaminyarr. In Bayini's spirit we had to create a new possibility and to work with Woŋgu to bring about peace and prosperity. It was not just the threat of intruders that disturbed Arnhem Land. War between clans, rivalry for women and territory was exacerbated by the new ways of the world. A new mission had been established at Millingimbi. It brought sit-down houses, machines, fans, cool rooms, tobacco, steel and new ways of the world with new ancestral beings. Rivalries were created.

New competition for goods and machines became evident. Gaminyarr and I broke through many worlds. We saw the bleak worlds of missions, museums and governments and blind police. We saw too that war was tearing the Yolŋu clans apart. With Wonggu's help we began to create a spirt of peace across Arnhem Land and to prepare the barricades to protect people. Gaminyarr developed a plan which had the full force of Bayini and Djuraindjura's spirit and he prepared to deliver it to the seat of government. Arnhem Land was to be created as a reserve with full segregation of outside intruders to preserve the Yolŋu social and family structures. There were to be no compounds nor stations but the preservation of the full nomadic cycle of life and homelands.

Patrols were needed to prevent unnecessary war and attacks between clans. Leprosy and yaws, two diseases that were too common amongst the people, were to be prevented by the creation of mobile medical services. No police constables as "protectors of Aborigines" were to be created. We wanted these principles to be expanded across all of Australia and gaminyarr called for the development of a national department of native affairs. It was to be forty years before our call was heeded! There is one thing we faeries understand. Even if the world must wait, the vibration has to start. We started the vibration and it challenged even the most progressive and benevolent minds. That did not matter. The direction was established. The new wind was blowing. That was all that mattered.

"WAKE UP, YOUNG FELLA, WAKE UP." There in the packing cases was a beautiful young boy sleeping so deeply. He was dreaming of Dungala, of the great bends and currents, of swimming and diving and of playing beneath the ancient river gums. A great flock of white cockatoos was wheeling across the sky. "What is your name?" came the words into his mind.

Sleeping so deeply at first the boy could not answer. As he opened his eyes he saw the face of a great and loved gentleman. Somehow, he knew that his dreams had taken him along the river to a new place in life. "My name is Douglas, sir, Douglas. I come from Cummeragunja and I want to return home." With those words, a great life adventure was beginning.

"Well you can't stay here. The police will have you in the lock-up in the wink of an eye. You better come home with me."

The generosity of spirit of Éire that I longed for and mourned returned in those words. No Australian of Irish origins could ever turn away a young man so lost and so far away from home. Young Doug had ridden a truck from the orchards of the Goulburn Valley seeking adventure in the city. I could hear a great melody. The faery hosts were singing. They could see in this young man and this great Irish man a love of sport, cricket and football, that would make their families' lives intertwine. New light was emerging. This young boy was one of the Cummeragunja greats. He would thrill the man, himself a champion, with fleetness of foot and intuition. But we faeries could also see in this young boy, wiping sleep from his eyes, a great advocacy and passion emerging. He would become one of the family in the house on the fledgling oval at Princes Park. It began to rain as they walked down Swanston Street, then through the cemetery. But the man was smiling to himself at the young fellow. "And what do we have here?" were the words that greeted them as they arrived home. "This is Douglas of Cummeragunja," Tommy Warne told his wife, "He will be staying with us for a while." Peeping around the corner was young Grace. "Oh, my goodness," she said. "I will run the bath. Mother you can find some clean clothes." The next day the boy and the man and his sons would continue their harrowing with dray and horse. Tommy's cow paddock would become a great sporting arena on which the young boy would excel and fly. He would test the knowledge and understanding of the Irish men. He would move from Carlton to Fitzroy later on a principle that in itself would create a lineage going back to Cummeragunja for his kin. But now he was one of the family. Family ties would form, balloons would rise slowly at funerals making young men of the future ponder their heritage and dynasties of warriors across races and in groups. There was magic there. It would play out in the generations to come. It would flow and merge and disappear and come back stronger. I can see them now walking against the rain with dray and cart on Princes Park creating a great destiny. There were so many other pathways intersecting here too.

THE LEADERS of the newly federated nation of Australia were, like all politicians, part tosspot, scallywag, part scoundrel, part under-dog, part genius used-car salesmen. They could not hear us or understand our messages to them. A conman took his fellows on a boat ride and convinced them he had written the draft constitution. All meaning and purpose flew out the window. Conservative fools who wanted their words to imprison every generation into the future held sway. A mediocre nation was formed. Revolutions rocked the world. The workers were seizing power. Workers' parliaments were created in the capital cities. It was the beginning of a century of blood. In 1917 twenty-six members of the extended family were machine-gunned. Their crime was to have been recruited to work for a king. It was too far away from me. I could not even hear their cries until decades later. A war of the world began and lungurmarr unwittingly blew it towards us. I often wondered about the family I had left behind in the South. Gaminyarr too wanted to go south to his home. I began to retrace my footsteps.

It was Ivy who I first found. She was Michael's daughter and had taken all of her grandmother Honor's cautions and instincts to heart. Her family had borne pain in their sinews. She wanted only to create a house and garden, a home, a refuge. Her children and grandchildren only knew that she had many cousins from Van Diemen's Land. She never ever talked of her great grandmother, grandmother or grandfather and the great journey they had made from Éire. She hid the pain as her grandmother had wanted. She even became a member of the Church of England. It would take generations for her family to know of her Irish Catholic past. She wanted only to have a home for her children. She gave no clue to the past.

Leopold Karel (the secret Russian Jew) saw Ivy playing cricket in Preston. A place where his own mother Helene had shaped and developed parks, streets and thoroughfares. The lines of family were again being re-shaped. The St Petersburg boatswains, the French mariners, the Cummergunga Invincibles and the Irish convicts were meeting across the fault lines of history. Are you surprised at this? From the holds of the convict ships came an incredible and ineluctable force. Powerful women with determination in their every fibre were shaping the land. Women playing cricket! For these daughters of women with the spirit of lions, physical sport seemed luxurious and fun. Ivy wanted only these simple pleasures. To feel the joy of throwing a ball, playing a game. Did Nathi see in her the life he wanted so desperately to build. Like his mother he was a man who had great plans and abilities. But in these tumultuous times one false move sent you back down the slippery dip.

Leopold Karel and Ivy planted apple, pear, peach, nectarine, plum trees in great lines down the hillside along Wetherby Road, Doncaster on the outskirts of Melbourne town. At any other time and place great rewards would have followed. But it was 1930. When the trees bore their first fruit a great and evil wind was blowing through the world. Fortunes were lost. Empires collapsed. Leopold Karel could not find anyone to buy his first crop. Boxes of apples were given to those who did not have enough to eat. Leopold Karel now found it hard to pay his bills. He had built a great house for his family. He had built it stick by stick. It had great white columns and high ceilings and stained-glass windows. But the money was just not there. In quick time there were five children and as they grew up it worried them to hear their father, who had worked so hard, so agitated about paying bills. After so long the anxiety had not subsided. The great lines of trees so healthy and strong and productive had to be sold. The young family managed to hang on to the house. Leopold Karel was declared bankrupt.

I was hovering over as this great gale was blowing. I said in his ear: "These things do not matter. Please know this and do not worry." But Leopold Karel thought only that he had failed where his own mother had succeeded. He felt as if he had let his family down.

Ivy always had a kitchen that was full of food. It had a whole wall of bottled fruit. She would spend summers canning fruit for the winters. Her kitchen walls were lined with jars of apples, peaches, nectarines, plums, marmalades, jellies and preserves. Her vegetable garden fed the family. It was a wonder to behold. A milking cow was in the stalls and it became the children's daily chore to fill the milk tin every morning and evening.

Ngumaydierdidini:"Church can do a lot of good... but then the Church must allow you to talk up if you're right... (That never happened at Cape Bedford?) No. If you start talking up for your right, you go. Go leave the place." [52]

WHEN YOU KNOW THE WINDS, YOU CAN CALL THEM. I watched the Yuin people whistle up the west wind so that they could see the waves and throw their nets far out to sea. On a very hot day the old people would call in a southerly buster to cool the land. A wind bringing thunder and lightning would come from the south west saturating the dry ground. But the wind now blowing through the world was something no man controlled. The rule of kings and queens was giving way to the rule of machines and great companies. This wind brought ruin and then war. Something was happening to me, something I had never felt before.

I was finding the air suffocating. Was I dying? I found myself unable to fly, unable to walk or run. I was desperately slithering... the sea was drawing me. With every ounce of strength, I pushed myself over grass and sand. Then, oh the joy of the sea... In I dived and suddenly I had all the power and grace of a bird. I could feel myself changing. My arms, my legs, my blood was transforming. All I could feel was joy at moving with the tides and currents. I looked around me and a paradise of blue water surrounded me. I was breathing water and it was propelling me forward. Suddenly I had another feeling I was being examined by a large fish. Instinctively I shot out a black spray and made my getaway.

I knew exactly where I had to go. I was speeding through the ocean depths consumed by the thought of reaching a special rock, a special place where wise men and women would come to talk.

But I found myself turning around. I wanted to go north but I found myself following the ocean currents south along the great barrier reef. I was on the Torres Strait Highway and I could see above me fishermen and canoes. I knew this place from the coral and the coconut fronds and cycad nuts in the water. I was coming to the place where the rainforest kissed the reef. I was coming to that river of tears where peace was replaced by war in an instant, where a great cyclone had wiped from the earth every building and shelter. I knew this and felt it and heard the old men and women calling the storm to the infidels who had turned back a thousand years of land management and careful guardianship. I saw the opium dens on the river banks. I saw the hotels overflowing with grog. I saw the rifles and horses again in my mind. Then with a flash it all disappeared. The mangroves still grew.

The dugong came again. The mullet still followed their ancient path ways. The infidels disappeared and the town of evil struggled to paint its walls. It had to begin again. Why was I here?

The moonlight came and phosphorescent particles glowed in the water. I found myself drifting past sleeping crocodiles down to Jepsons Crossing. It was early morning and I could see soldiers on the bridge. I could see a man with a great flowing beard and Willie and Ernie and Walter. A crowd had gathered now. The soldiers were herding the whole community on trucks they were heading for the wharves.

I heard someone say: "When this war is over and the danger is past, you can come home again." I heard a whistle and saw that down the river a steamer was coming. Where were they taking these families who had already endured so much? Did they know that the cold of the interior was a death sentence?

I saw the soldiers set fire to the houses. I saw the farms and the church destroyed. Why? Why? Why? Lutheran, lutheran, lutheran... war, war, war, Germans... could they really believe that there would be collaboration with Japanese invaders? I had seen the great planes coming and going all night. They were flying to Gove/Yirrkala... and then north. It was dog eat dog again. Out there in the jungles underneath the flight path was Leopold Karel stringing wires from tree to tree. Hunting dogs were howling on the wharf. Old people were crying.

147

Young men, like young men in times of war, were excited for all the wrong reasons. That night I followed the steamer down the coast to Cairns. Two hundred and eighty five rainforest people were herded off the steamer and onto a train. I could hear them talking. No food for three days. Such a short time to pack personal possessions: were we enemies again? It was madness. Worse still, it was murder. At Townsville, the group was separated. Fifty people were taken to Palm Island - the place that Aboriginal "troublemakers" were sent. In this case it was a blessing because the rest of the group were sent farther south to Woorabinda Aboriginal community, 170 kilometres south west of Rockhampton. As I lay among the sandbanks my mind travelled with them. I could feel the cold, pain, anxiety. Chill is a terrible thing for people who have only known warmth. Despite the discomfort there was trust and solidarity with each other. My mind snapped to other trains and to other men, women and children being taken away. This was a terrible time in the world. The people accepted that they were being taken for their own safety. But to be taken so far south and so far inland? To be so ruthlessly moved without any care and preparation? Ignorance piled upon ignorance.

I heard the crying at night. Bäru's little baby was the first to die. Sixty died within the first year of flu, German measles, cold and hearbreak. It was seven long years before the people came home. Seventy people died during the long exile. The men worked alongside suspected enemy collaborators and other Aboriginal men across Queensland on farms and roads. It was sobering and educative. The Lutheran mission of Hope Valley would be forever changed. After much advocacy, slowly the men returned then the families. One by one the houses and buildings of Hope Vale were built by men and women of courage and endurance. The steel of a young leader was being forged here. I saw him too enduring so much of this on his own, away from his own family. His slow and rising anger was carefully tempered by wiser minds. But his own grief could barely be contained. At Hope Valley and Hope Vale Garray was a curse and a blessing.

I too could hardly endure the pain. Each night my tentacles extended out over the land to give comfort to the grieving families and strength to the community. The people dreamed of my presence. I lived amongst the starfish, seahorses and coral. The tide was taking me somewhere else. I had grown to such a size that even the sharks did not challenge me. The fish made way for me, they knew that I was a magical being. After each of the rainforest people had started the long journey home, I too made my way up the coast. I was travelling, thinking and dreaming and wondering when some understanding might prevail between the people of the land and the newcomers who were so ignorant and destructive.

LEOPOLD KAREL HAD NO LOVE OF WAR and a working man's instinct for distrusting government and officialdom. But war would give him a chance to redeem his debts and to regain his honour. He could escape the bitter-sweet views of the great orchard he had so successfully planted. Now it belonged to someone else who would enjoy the fruits of his labour. The first owners of farms so often lose out, on their shoulders others are carried and succeed. War would give Leopold Karel income for his family. He was one of the first to enlist. Over the next five years he would travel the length of the Australian continent on the whims of generals. He would tread the jungle paths of New Guinea and feel the futility of war. He crossed the trails of Dhapa, Gumminyarr, Raywala but they could not recognise him nor he they. Like Cliff before him he came to be a fully paid up member of Bully Beef Cottage. Like Leopold Karel so many warriors of the first peoples sought succour, recognition and gratitude that they could not receive in the normal workings of life.

I flew into the great battles for Lae. I talked to Leopold Karel there and I planted knowledge and gratitude for this wild land. His sons and daughter would later come to live in this land ravaged by war and they would repay some part of the debt these soldiers owed. But the bigger debt and understanding would take so long to understand. It was beyond the politics of nations and the conventional diplomacy of civic men and women. It was a knowledge that came with the play of wind and sun on water - a looking beyond life where colours formed and spirits merged. Across an oval, fireballs chased children, thunder filled the skies and rain beat on the roof of an open-air cinema. Sacred Lyn carried to the Datsun, car accidents, hammers dropped from trees a childhood of teasing forging unbreakable bond between father and daughter -a greatness transmitted from one to the other. A little boy walked through the rainforest singing "ga gong mello ganda sei" at the top of his lungs to the delight of his companions... "Walkabouti go long Chinatowni... for suppose you like long me you can wait for ten years more man he karangi karangi het he lose em money." Frankie Lee and Stevie Low, Rawali Ali, Tiana Illa, Stephen Lamocki. I will come back and find you.

What good, at these times of war and misery, comes from the pain of a family. Nothing, nothing, nothing - I thought to myself. Ivy had named her oldest boy Michael after her beloved giant of a father. She loved this boy. He was a symbol, a sign that things could get better, that life would change. He was the eldest. A boy to take the place of Odysseus. A boy that Ivy looked to when things needed to be done, when work was to be done, errands to be run. His brothers and sisters would look to him too. One day with all the spirit of youth he dived and violently hit his head on the bottom of a swimming pool. "It's nothing," he said. But suddenly he could not stand. Over time headaches blinded him. Ivy's instincts told her it was something serious. But how could this error of a split second have such profound consequences? She looked up at the bottled fruit on the wall and prayed to God. These were times of profound reflection. In the hardest moments of grief, she found something in the simple giving-up to the man from Galilee. She struggled to get Michael to doctors and to hospital. She would move heaven and earth to support her son. The other children fended for themselves. At this time, each of them found worlds within worlds. Stan would build and finish the empire his father started. Daedelus would be the greatest of teachers. He read the covers off books, learning with a hunger and a passion that would open other worlds and possibilities beyond his great great grandmother's wildest dreams. He too would traverse the old country and learn of the Dublin maestro and the wandering knight. `Once upon a time there was a moo cow... Tra la la la, Tra la la la di, Tra la la la... the brush with the maroon and green velvet backs. One for Menzies brass balls, one for Evatt. 'I'll kiss you back to life my sweetness.' He would marry Grace's daughter, Helen of Troy, Queen of country towns and grass courts and beautiful backhands and forehands and lobs and smashes and volleys for whom young men would swoon and build empires, and they too would produce their free ones, tookoo, sacred Lyn, the laurel of New Haven linked to an ancient African dynasty of scholarship and dreams and, of course, Dame Tara who made mothers weep and even through all time, Honor, singing as she sewed and weaved the future all together in a quilt of many colours and hues. Sweet Sue would rebuild her mother's world, with new colours, new recipes, new gardens mother of the remarkables wife of the great Bill. All would catch a hold of something. Dante would run like the wind and emulate the feats of her mother. Children following Macassan traders to Beijing and whalers to North America reconquering the world. Joe Dylan would yet build plantations and create his own dynasty of law and life and politics. Another Christopher would come to the highest judicial spheres – a premonition of his great great grandfather. And these freedom children too would discover that the world which seemed so large was so small and so fragile. Their destiny was to see beyond the great generation that rebuilt the world after war had torn it apart. To see the spirit in the land and earth and sky and stars. But when Leopold Karel received news of Michael's illness and death and Ivy sat numb and unfeeling in the hospital... it was a pain too great to bear. Something in both of them died. Leopold Karel, like Honor turned to drink to numb his brain. But Michael came to his father and said, "You are a great man." He came to his mother sleeping and waiting so patiently in the hospital and said, "I love you so much Mum, thank you for all you have done." But they could not hear him properly at this time when so many were dying. It was up to me to preserve his love and to write it into the life journey of all of the children and their children and the children's children. The name Michael became an agony. Young Dante wanting to ease her mother's pain named her son after her beloved brother and her grandfather. He too did not grow into manhood. It was as if only the memory of a man with Size 13 shoes, the eldest boy who was a born leader and the child who was the very spice of life, could not exist on the normal plain of life. Like their namesake they became immortal in the lives of those who came after them. But please do not ask me if all this was for the greater good. I who watched over a flood of tears and pain will never see any reason in this pain. All I can say is that at these times of inconceivable death and darkness when people blamed each other and themselves, kindness and gentleness ultimately prevailed. Spirits rise.

All over the regions where gold had been found and the newcomers had built cities and towns, the wise ones of the Waltheruung, Yorta Yorta and Camileroi took shelter. Somehow they found ways to love and regroup again. If you stay in the household of an Aboriginal family you will find a great halo of consolation and love all around you. For King Billy and a thousand elders, Ivy and Eric's pain was endured without limit or abatement. It was an ongoing nightmare. Death was the great event of life... one returned to the ancestors and to family, to a place at one with the land. In the midst of this great mortal pain that had been inflicted on the first peoples a great force was emerging. In time people would see that these were the greatest of men and women. They had survived an era when great monsters roamed the earth, when oceans froze and continents divided and again they were emerging.

Their extraordinary wisdom and grace was becoming apparent to even the thickest heads and hardest hearts. The signs were everywhere. How I enjoyed the beauty and strength of the Cummeragunja Invincibles as they played the game of their ancestors with new rules and in an enclosed space, against their Irish and European counterparts. They embodied the wild winds, the heart of the sun and the mighty quality of the great Dungula. They were undefeated and undefeatable. They demonstrated to their families the spirits of the ages.

These were the great generation of re-builders and re-makers. They would build homes, lives and purpose. Memories of them would never fade, they would inspire their children and children's children.

When Leopold Karel returned, his reward for staying alive was malarial fevers and arthritis, an honorary discharge from bankruptcy, a job building sporting stadiums, bowling alleys and retention of the precious house and block at Doncaster. He and Ivy had triumphed over adversity but Michael's death hurt them deeply. His sons and daughters worked in the orchards that surrounded the house. They had a knowledge of every variety of apple, peach, plum and pear that was the envy of newer growers at the Victoria Markets. I took the love and pain and sewed the very best of thoughts in grandchildren and great grandchildren. I was with him as he chauffeured his tookoo in his green EK Holden motor car surveying childhood streets of Preston, Young and Jackson's bar, the Port Melbourne docks, the Upper Yarra picnic areas, and his Collingwood school. Expelled from that school nati! "What did you do?" "Lets not go there shall we. Cut the kindling tookoo for the evening fire! Diverting cars from the Nepean highway through the nasty school. Serves them right." I listened as he talked of bullock drays and running away as a child. I was with Ivy as she held tookoo's hand and led him up the hill to the church on Sundays in his detested school uniform, playing the protestant so well she was the protestant's protestant. Leopold Karel's church had become the pub. Children growing. The young prodigy Daedalus won scholarships that would take him to the highest heights. He learned to fly. In their own way and their own time so too did all the children and grandchildren. All were released. The pain and suffering dissolved slowly and surely. One day Daedelus stopped in at the Doncaster Inn and he heard, in another room, his father boasting of the young man's achievements. He had to stop and pinch himself. Leopold Karel had been the one to criticize the child who always had his head in a book. There was a scowl sometimes on his face and yet there was magic in this man. I knew it to be so. I placed the magic in his grandchildren and through them his sons and most importantly his daughters came to know how much he loved them.

Things were not always easy between Leopold Karel and Ivy. It was the tension of a woman for whom the garden was enough and a man who dreamed great dreams. Perhaps too it was the tragedies of the past from the West country and St. Petersburg vibrating across time. Ivy was content in the garden her ancestors had been denied. The garden would soothe Ivy's pain and comfort all those who came after her. Leopold Karel had seen much, he dreamed, in his own way, of a republic of good where the efforts and ingenuity of man were justly rewarded and where every person could develop their abilities and skills without end. This tension between Leopold Karel and Ivy may be seen by some as unhappiness in these times where people ask themselves about happiness - but it was the stuff of life. She never left his side and in the end he saw Ivy as when they first met. So much had passed between them and was symbolised by their union and children. Irish and Russian dynasties would merge in the great jigsaw puzzle of life and criss-cross again with Germany, County Mayo, County Clare and the wild Westmeath territory. Descendants of the white trash of Europe and England had learned to fly. The question was now could they see!

"We had come to believe that in the search for wholeness in the Aboriginal community, a place for Jesus of Nazareth as a person of social and political sorrows must be found."[53]

"DJAMBUWAL! DJAMBUWAL!" The children came running from the beach at Yirrkala. "Djambuwal! Djambuwal!" Men and women looked up from their work and came out of their houses. It was Djambuwal! An enormous willy-willy and water spout was coming from the ocean up the beach. It was heading straight for the tin huts that were newly erected in the community. By-passing all the houses it fell upon Buramara's house, picked it up, twisted it in the air and then dashed it to pieces against a tree. No sooner than it had arrived, the great willy-willy vanished without a trace. Everyone was stunned.

Buramara was in shock. Soon the new Fijian missionary Kolinio told Buramura that it was a sign from Garray that he needed to dedicate himself more to the church. But the white-haired wise men and women were quick to tell Buramura that his work with the church had angered Djambuwal and that he was neglecting ceremony and the stewardship of the lands. There are times when things seem to lock up and time stops still. The sea is smooth like silk and there is not a breath of air. On the far horizon clouds can be seen forming up. Be careful of these times. More often than not there is a willy-willy or something even bigger coming. Just like a bird hovering in the wind currents, a slight change, a tip of the wing and soon you find yourself hurtling into places you least expected. Things stand still and then the forces of life and time are too great to bear and change comes at a rapid pace. Wild winds snap the tops of a thousand thousand trees. Great rains come and flood the earth. The new land was seemingly in the grip of the old order of things. Gaolers, police and orders from across the seas determined how men and women lived and what seemed to matter. An evil bureaucracy enveloped the first peoples. Letters had to be sent to government officials to buy the most basic tools. Wages were withheld. Rights ignored, sytmied and trampled upon. It was denial of the primacy of being and it would curse the newcomers for generations to come. Great men. so-called, had imposed their names on the new landscape: Melbourne, Sydney, Brisbane, Perth, Darwin.... But beneath the surface great forces were at work. The spirit of the land, the people of the land were always there influencing, changing, working even from the most peripheral places. I could feel old empires twisting. A gale blew in the homelands of Europe, in the Americas and across the world,. It was 1947, the great Balanda war had ended. Like a willy-willy balanda planes and air crews and an enormous array of machinery had come and gone. They had left something that would last through the generations that would bring hope, but also enormous problems and grief. It was an all-weather landing strip upon which great planes could land. They were strange these balanda people, they would build in war what should be built in peace! New problems and dilemmas were emerging. The white-haired men and women contemplated the great dimensions of life and land and now this new spiritual figure called Garray? Was it a trick? Who could be trusted? The missionaries were impressive. They brought metal, steel, light, cold and great machines that could shape the earth. The missions were protected zones at a time when a great primordial war was also being fought between the Yolŋu themselves. Warriors asserted authority over lands and life. Some great men and women stood out. Bäpa Edgar and Bäpa Sheppie and their wives were among them. If your heart is true and your mind is open it does not matter if you make mistakes. Oh yes, they made mistakes and had false thoughts but in the end they too saw the majesty of the people. They too felt as much adopted as they were themselves. I was with them in so many thoughtful discussions. Both of them were workers in the same spirit of gaminyarr. They were balanda men of high degree. They seemed to understand the primacy of Yolŋu ceremony which held the world in all its dimensions together! I watched all this. It was the beginning of a great jigsaw puzzle coming together. I saw how on the balanda side too adjustments were being made. As great battles of metal and guns were fought all around and as planes took off from Gove runway - primordial attacks, death adder night raids with blood, bone and spear, were occurring. In 1948 calls for peace began to be heard. Baraltjana Barrarwanga visited Djäwa Dhäirrŋu and new plans were made. Baraltjana had witnessed the carnage waged on the Warramirri - men, women and children, and he had given up his dug-out canoes to save the few survivors. They in turn gave him custody and responsibility for looking after their lands.

Baraltjana made his way to the place where the fire burnt beneath the soil and established the first of the modern homelands. This was again never understood or acknowledged. For time it did not matter. A great alliance was forged with "Sheppie." But it was Baraltjana who cleared the mangroves, cut the airstrip and built the houses and the school. On this ground, this waŋa, a new future that linked the past and present would be founded. One day people from all over the world would come to learn and discover the ancient ways, the ancient magic of the land.

Change was occurring across the earth. I found myself entering another dream within a dream. I was in Switzerland in Easter 1948. I watched a young man free in thought in a great and beautiful building. He told a woman of three kinds of love: a love that ignores the reaction and violence of man and does not react; a love which is active without aggression;and a love that counters a murderous attacker with intense humanness. I saw the great woman's eyes watching the young man intently and then over-flowing with tears. To talk of this love at this time and this place sent a vibration all over the world. Tears flowed for opportunities lost and opportunities regained and reimagined. At this time men and women began to say, as they had said before, never again. Never again will the world be plunged into such carnage, blood and tears.

Hearts and minds were filled with the children of the future. As ever there were great blockages of ego and selfishness. But the purity of vision of this young man was also flowing to the South Land, something was changing. Honor and Lalla's combined ethics began to slowly transform the life of men and women. Money belongs where it is needed. It is never rightfully owned by a person. It was becoming common to ask for a "fair go" and to enquire of a "mate," a fellow, an equal, a person who understood what it was like to stand in your shoes. No person who was stranded was without help. No stranger who came asking for food could be turned away. When adversity struck, everyone pitched in. These were wonderful things that began to unfold but there was still this aliveness to the land. This willy-willy wind also picked me up and blew me through time and space. It was propelling me here and there. It propelled me to Lalla Bakitju Gunda and Ḏilkurrwurru Wataŋgurr to Djalu, to Bruny to Gikal and Mata Mata to Wallaga Lake to Kangushot and Paddy Roe and Joe and Ronnie standing on mother Theresa's country. I slept with stingrays and turtles. I rode with sharks and watched with crocodiles. I saw the canoe paddling from the east guided by the morning star. I was not in one place in time. I flew from Honor to Christopher and Mary, to Michael and Annie, to Ivy and Leopold Karel to great great grandchildren and to the junctures of great families.

Sometimes I just wanted to run for the joy of running. I would stretch out to full stride across boundless river plains. When I reached a certain speed, I would not know who I was and I lost all sense of my body and soul. I would then find myself drifting in space. I became ḏamala, djuṉmal - whistling for the tide - ŋakŋak, wälmut - great dhuwa birds of prey watching over land, sea, earth. At these times I would see the whole earth spinning. Years would flow by. Babies would be born. Lives would expire. I saw the greatest ceremonies on earth performed by the Yolŋu to help mothers, grandmothers, fathers, grandfathers move across djiwarr' to Baralku - the land of the morning star. I saw too the last breaths of Honor, Christopher, Mary and their children.

I saw their spirit move into the night sky to play freely amongst the stars. I loved to watch from my place high in the clouds. I saw earthly tears and celestial joy. I watched as new little babies were formed in the wombs of women and I saw the joy of fathers learning of new lives that they had created. I saw a man and woman hunting. I saw the man throw a boomerang at dharrgadharrgayun. I saw djanda shrug off the boomerang as it hit his shoulder. Then I saw the mark of the boomerang on their baby's shoulder and the knowing look of Rover and his wife. I saw a stingray come towards the spear of a great man. I saw that man sharing his meal with the great men of Walmadany. I saw the baby that would change the vision of the newcomers and help them to understand the nature of the land. I heard the whistle blow as the boat left the pier. I saw the great American calling again. Mahkarolla looked up, waved, then lowered his head again. He was crying . It was the last time the two men would see each other. I saw a man track down his children to Bomaderry. I saw him working as a market gardener. I saw that he was not allowed to speak to his sons. I saw the hand signals they devised and the two shillings he would leave on the rock for them.

I saw Leopold Karel years into the future waving his walking stick with a handkerchief tied to it on the wharf at Port Melbourne. I saw the Daedalus' tears flowing freely knowing that it would be the last time he would see his father. Years would fly by and I would return with the wind through the places and people of the South Land. I could hear the pulse of the land. I could feel the vibrations of the people. Would they learn and come to understand? Would they come to know the secret of this place that the future of the world depended on?

Gaminyarr and Woŋgu had sensed the dangers all around them. Their achievement in protecting their people against all odds was immeasurable. There was precious space and time to negotiate with the police, the conflicts, the trade and the war of the newcomers.

Woŋgu and the men of high degree had time to think. Now I saw Barratjuna and his family paddling their canoes from Milingimbi to Mata Mata. It was a new beginning. It was the end of war not only in the Balanda world, but in the Yolŋu world. The agreement with Djäwa Dhäwarrirrŋu and the men of high degree meant ceremonial duties and land stewardship would fall to new custodians and the offerings of the new world could be examined from a position of strength. After the long journey of many days and nights the real work began. By hand the family members started to clear a place to land boats and an airstrip. One by one they cut and pulled out the mangrove trees. Then the work began clearing the land for houses. Two miles square of bush and scrub was cleared. Slowly houses would be built, a school, a clinic, burial grounds, mango trees would be planted. This place would be a centre of culture and a point of intersection between the new world and the old. The djäma begun in 1948 still continues, every day, day by day. I am telling you this now so you can recognise this and honour the creativity and vision of the elders and their families. It was not only Mata Mata. Across Australia in cities, towns, remote areas, on the beaches and in the old missions, preparations were made to hold the knowledge of the land.

Through the homeland movements across the North, through the reincarnations of the missions of the south, ambassadors, emissaries, philosophy and most of all ceremony and performance began to be prepared so that the world could start to appreciate and know the beauty and grace of the first cultures of the land, the oldest of the world. Ḏilkurrwurru Wataŋgurr and Lalla Bakitju Gunda's vision and far-sightedness was there behind this so that the leaders and thinkers knew how well-prepared they had to be. In this land that came to be called Australia, first nations people found ways to negotiate and repel the relentless drive and ignorance of the newcomers.

Of all the things that the newcomers brought - engines, electricity, refrigeration, steel, medicine, processed food, sugar and a myriad of other technical and social innovations - it was Garray - the lovely one, lord and master who was most impressive. In the ceremonies and rituals of the church was something that could be respected and recognised as valuable. There was also here over the seasons of life a uniting of hearts. In the late summer of 1860 a clergyman read a story of a boy who had been found wandering in Melbourne. The boy was adopted by the Reverend Lloyd Chase. Willie had been left an orphan after his mother had been shot and killed in a settler raid. Children hearing the story jumped up. One of the boys was Willie's brother, the other his cousin. They had seen Willie's mother fall dead. In the midnight the boys took the unbelieving clergy man to Willie's mother's grave. Willie had died of tuberculosis alone in a strange land far away but his spirit came home with this story.[54] At moments like these in the Wimmera, in the Pilbara, in the Kimberley, in New South Wales, in Queensland and in Arnhem Land lines crossed, salt and freshwater came together.

This Garray was the newcomers' ancestral hero and guide. He was the foundation stone of laws and life! In the songs and hymns and in the little rituals of the cross, something could be recognised. Across Australia the work of philosophically and intellectually placing this ritual within the first peoples' worlds had to be done.

It was strange that the representatives of Garray did not have white hair. They were young and had to be taught language, culture and knowledge. Not all people could be trusted. After much thought it was agreed to adopt the newcomers into the family structures and system of knowledge.

Then like babies they would learn, first slowly then quickly. Like clearing the landing strip at Mata Mata it was a slow and painstaking job filled with frustrations and tough tap roots that had to be pulled out. For many decades, wise men and women adopted and educated so many newcomers. When they were adopted and became family members they would not be like seaweed drifting around with the tide, up and down the beach and out into the ocean with no direction. They would have a place, duties and obligations. Slowly they would have understanding.

In the thoughts, dreams and long discussions the balanda world came to be understood. Garray had come after the Djanggawul and Barama and Laindjung to help people learn to love each other and to re-order families and clans. "So, this was what the newcomers had at the centre of their seemingly mad activities and this song *Onward Christian Soldiers*. If the newcomers wanted to learn we could help them deepen their knowledge and philosophy and improve their ceremony and appreciation of this host of family members that made up the sea, sky and land. We could even help them improve their singing! And certainly their dance!" These thoughts emerged on more than one occasion.

In 1948 in the north things came to a head. Well, it had started much earlier. A man from Chicago was the first to come, even before gaminyar, and began recording stories. He was Mahkarolla's confidant. The knowledge that was given was written down in books. It was like the people were being studied as insects from a great microscope. The turning point came after the recordings and photography of the great ceremonies became known. Cowboy movies had been shown throughout the war years at open-air theatres. Now the cameras came into the sacred areas. A hush came over the crowd as images appeared of sacred objects that only men of high degree were allowed to see. It was death to see these objects in normal life, now everyone had seen them. Was

161

everyone to be killed? How was it that the uninitiated balanda strangers had gained such access? For many old men and women this was a sign of disaster. But in so many other ways the teachings of the new missionaries had challenged the old ways. Marriage, relationships, family groupings, names, reasons for war and hostility were also challenged by mission life. Houses in one place, food that could be stored, machines, lights, all these things brought new questions. There was good and there was bad. The slow revelation of knowledge over the course of a life was now to occur in an hour!

I was flying high following rivers. I came to see the clay - white and red. I came to see ochres - yellow, red. I came to see the dyes of the earth - purple, red, green and white. I saw the white clay of Gi'kal, Yari and Walmadany. Two ceremonies were calling me. I saw Christopher's great grandson talking to an old man at his graveside, asking for advice and guidance. I saw him at Gik'al with women whose hearts were troubled, painting the white clay all over. White clay can help ease trouble. It can help purify the mind and ease pain. It can change the patterns of destruction and war.

I was taken to Skull Creek through the bubbling waters of the Mill Stream. I saw the precious life-giving water in the dry country the Pilypara. I saw twenty men and women walking. I saw one hundred.

I saw hundreds walking across the hot desert sands. At this time in the West it was illegal for Aboriginal women and men to congregate. I saw them coming secretly Ngarla, Kariyarra, Ngarluma, Yindjibarndi, Nyamal, Nygangumarta, Warnman, Kartujarra, Manjilyjarra, Nyigyaparli and Palyku men and women weaving across the country to Skull Creek. I saw that old man Karriwarna. He was looking into the future. I heard his voice and mind asking: "How is that we can work all day and into the night for flour, tea and blankets?" I saw his dream of a day when the Pilypara lands would be returned and the best of both worlds would emerge. A great action was planned that would rock the European world.

White clay was leading me here. It was showing me the pin pricks in trees that were the guides to food and delicacies. Little did I know that these little insects were angels that guarded life itself. They were its essence and its vitality. As I searched my mind it suddenly came to me that here in the dry desert country Karriwarna and his countrymen and family were leading the way. The lawmakers took a different path here. Only under the most exceptional circumstances would newcomers be allowed anywhere near ceremony. Traditional law was enforced under pain of death. But I saw senior lawmakers talking to a balanda. He was a saint with all the failings of a man. The ceremonies went on for six weeks. It was 1942. I saw all of the law makers and communities agree that if Aboriginal station workers were not paid proper wages then at the same time Aboriginal workers would walk off the stations on 1 May 1946. Over four years the pastoral bosses of the dry country were asked to pay their Aboriginal workers proper pay and they refused. Seven or eight hundred stockmen and their families walked off the cattle stations after 1 May. Under the pretence of going to the Port Hedland races a great group of men and women formed and never went back to the stations. Hundreds of station workers, their families and elderly relatives moved to the famous 12-mile camp outside of Port Hedland. The people "yandied" for tin and gold to make cash and lived off the land for food. Over the next decade I saw the courageous men and women learn, against great adversity, to run their own stations and mining companies. I saw their fight carry on and on. I saw so many Aboriginal station workers unpaid, waiting and dying before justice was done. How could this be?

They could not beat Karriwarna. He won his people's land back at Yandeyarra, Yarrie and 12-Mile. But the battle for rights and justice in the pastoral industry goes on. The Christian soldiers did not march or see justice here. Governments were too narrow. In the distant future other people won their country back. But these great symbolic events sometimes disguised the plight of the ordinary people and still the ceremony and knowledge of the people was not known. The law continued at Karupar, Jinparinya and Yandeyarra but it was time the newcomers knew of these things, knew of the land and the knowledge of the sacred places. "We call the land 'mother' because everything come from that," Karriwarna whispered. The world depended on knowing the deep law and wisdom behind this thought and it was this thought that like lightning sent me with white mud on my forehead and hands hurtling back across to the North East.[55]

I found myself being drawn once again to the fish that swam around the rock and to the rock, to the manda islands. I was following whales back to these warmer waters. All of us travelled silently thinking and dreaming as we travelled. Then one day I reached my special rock. I could hear the discussions.

"These newcomers believe that land can be possessed by holding a piece of paper and a flag. We know that this is not the case."

"Time will tell."

"These strangers act as owners but walk as strangers on the land. The land does not recognise them."

"And yet this wangarr-being Garray offers us something new. But who is to know? Some of the balandra are kind and good and want to learn. Others are cruel."

"Let us help these good men of Garray bäpa Sheppie, bäpa Edgar. We will let them know how we hold the land and the sea through marr." "We must involve them in ceremony. We must adopt them into our gurrutu. These balanda strangers have already filmed our raŋa and sacred objects. We must now let all our people know of the confidence and certainty of our land and sea knowledge."

For many weeks and months, the conversations continued. A great and heated debate continued. The missions at Millingimbi, Galiwinku and Yirrkala had buildings, gardens, machinery, roads, refrigeration and a new peacefulness that allowed communities to grow. It was not a question of sitting back. The leaders had to take the initiative. They had to show their power and knowledge. At last I saw the men carving and painting. A great concrete slab had been poured outside Sheppie's church. One by one the raŋa appeared. Njambi created a yirritja pole with the wisdom and story of wimari. Djunmal created ŋadili presiding over Burabu spring.

Galŋawiri, Gaguba and my beloved Ḏilkurrwurru Wataŋgurr created three poles signifying djanda on the djuda at Jelaŋbara.

Surely the strangers would see this and know the power of the ancient wisdom! Then followed gandalma at Daliŋura created by Badaŋga. The great woŋgar beings Laindjuŋ-Bemidji were carved by Badaŋga as gyrinal at Cape Wilberforce. Njambi and Badaŋga showed Gundanamgaurumiriŋju at Ridarŋu and the flooding rain which split the rock sending out pieces to the different clans uniting them in ceremony and knowledge. Mejameja and Woibaŋa carved the Ṉnkaraŋura icon and story. Njambi and Badaŋga created Laindjuŋ's pointed wedge. Then Badaŋga, helped by Buramara, created a sculpture that combined the best of Christian and Yolŋu law. Gidbaboi and Badaŋga created the journey of walu across the sky. Baidju created burulu associated with Luŋgudji at Arnhem Bay. Marabai created djuda at Marabai in Buckingham Bay. Paintings of the stories of Yirrkala and Bremer Island, Rabaraba at Bibila and Waramiri, stingray at Bibila, Djaŋgawal brother and sister, Djaŋgawal sister as ŋgainmara conical mat, the Djaŋgawal at Jelaŋbara, a dream of minerals in the country around Arnhem Bay and the conception of a boy in a whale and burala. Finally, a pulpit, djalwagduarau, was created and the several posts around the assembled raŋga represented mangrove fish. With all this it had begun. The road, a million roads, had been opened to explore.

When the raŋga first appeared, many people could not go near them. It created controversy and even panic among the people. It was almost too big to comprehend. Some could not bear to stay in the community and left immediately. Normally women and those who were not imitated into adulthood could not enter the nharra ground. Now all that changed. The detail of the stories and sacred objects were not told. But everything was visible, open and not secret. The ideas of the leaders did not unfold in the way that was planned. There was one law in the Yolŋu world. But for the balanda there were many laws that constantly changed along with the people who enforced them. Even those who loved Garray did not follow one law! Did all

165

these different balanda bungawa have to be explained the law? It seemed so. But now at least Bäpa Sheppie and Garray had been adopted and incorporated and the power and knowledge which each family group and their elders commanded was revealed. There was no going back. Substance and meaning would be discussed and debated for many years to come. This would be a foundation and a start.

I lay now for many years sleeping happily in my watery domain. In the settlement of Galiwinku there was a period of calm. Bäpa Sheppie and the church understood through the sacred objects that families and homelands were primal and important. Sheppie heard of Barratjuna and his family cutting their new homeland by hand. He admired their courage. He heard of a woman home schooling at Gi'kal and began to help with whatever resources he could. Sheppie understood what people would later forget again and again. Wäna was the centre of everything. The sacred raŋga vibrating outside his church reminded him of this every day. I was happy with the thought that deep law and wisdom of the people of the south had begun to emerge at this one place at this one time. But mine was a troubled sleep.

Kananook
(Sweet Water)

AFTER THE ERA OF BLOOD AND DEATH, they paved the paradise. It was supposed to be the era of prosperity and good will. But it became an era of invading ants. The coat of arms is all wrong: emu and kangaroo. These are only yiritja symbols. Where are the dhuwa animals? No wonder things are out of whack and unbalanced. Emu and kangaroo people cannot marry. How can anything be productive? All these problems simply increased the need for waŋa.

> When sheets of ice line the paddocks
> Fog persistently hugs the earth and will not rise
> I realise how much I miss you
> Your body turned brown by the Greek sun
> My grumpy discomfort stems from the lack of you
> When my mind fills with thoughts of your nestly form
> A pleasure envelopes me
> Makes me whole
> Keeps me warm
> Is it the heat flowing from you
> All this way?
> Perhaps.
> But more it is this force unfathomable
> That overcomes all differences and obstacles
> You are my home. Please come soon.
> Free yourself of lesser things.

Let us make our new coat of arms with ŋerrk and ŋaṯili.[56] Then things will come good. Power clans are something that the balanda have created. They make kings and queens but there are no kings and queens in our world. There are no votes or shows of hands or white boards. Our decisions are made with our hearts as well as our heads. We feel things. Things are not right.

It is no good for anyone. How can people really know the country? Who will sing for the country buried under so much steel and concrete and glass? Someone will tell them a story just to get access to land.

The town lagoon is Galpu and all these things change between grandparents and grandchild anyway. There are more than one yirritja and dhuwa clan. Do you think because we were the last to come from the bush we are stupid? No, the opposite is true. It is the land that guides us. Who guides you?

Jimmy Gurruwiwi came out from the bathroom. Gunydjulu ran across the ceiling. Little stamps "Danger: asbestos do not remove" stared down from each of the corners of the living room at No 12. It was better than sandflies and tents at East Woody but these houses were a death trap and they too would be bulldozed. Jimmy's T-shirt and clothes reeked of smoke and spirits. He was very weary: burrumunuŋ!

"I am starving for ŋarali'."

None of the family members asleep on the floor stirred. Outside, the Birritjimi dogs were barking. It was 8am. Some of the children were making themselves breakfast in the kitchen and getting ready for school. Jimmy's long day/night of the soul was ending. He found a spot on the floor and pulled the fleece blanket marked 'Elvis lives' over himself and promptly fell into a deep, snoring slumber. From the kitchen gentle, melancholy words floated through the house.

Wuyupthurruna dhawal Galapuŋu
(The ancient place Galupa)
ṉirrpounydja ŋarraku ŋähinana
(has disappeared from my sight)
nhenydja ŋarraku djirrmi`yurruna
(my mind is crying)
manhanhayurra bäya Bekuḻŋura
(you flashed in my mind a spark)
ŋirrpuŋura dhuwalinydja, bäpawala Banunydjiwala
(back where the Macassan cymbals crashed that memory of my father Banunydji)[57]

Dhamalingu: Bama to Yolŋu, Yalanji mataka, no electrics, manual, 100 series, across the Gulf: land of dreams that last life

168

times.. Mossman 224,440, Innot Springs 224,634, Croydon 225026, Mt Garnet, Purple Pub 225,204, Burketown 225, 423. Hellsgate Roadhouse 225,607, Booroolola 225,938, Highway Inn 226,335, Lookout Central Arnhem Hwy, 226,668, Caltex Nhulunbuy 227,315, Mata Mata 227,440.

WRAPPED IN THE CLEAN LINEN SHROUD, frankincense and myrrh filling the great tomb, the sacred body hovered. Nothing is too much to hope for. A dead grain of wheat gives new life. Crying with Liyapidiny, merging the sacred, adopting balanda, showing them the way, sharing knowledge. Yapa and dhuway - mother and child - preparing the stingray - washing the toxins away, creating the partnership, unlocking the balanda mind.[58] Singing and crying unlocking the accumulation of grief for all who have gone before and arising in a new dimension. Gurtha burning all impurity and misunderstanding - burning beneath the runway and the sea - forming a place to meet and talk honestly and freely. The fire that burns, guarded and contemplated by the sacred dogs. Looking into the future dreaming of all that is good coming together and the eternal vigilance and djäma involved.[59] Head and tail of the bäru and the crying of the dhuwa women bringing about the perfect synthesis of yirritja and dhuwa.

M-m-m-
Y-ä-ä-ä-
Gulandgdja nhungu badiwathhura
(Your blood lit up the sunset sky) [60]

AFTER THE GREAT WARS OF THE WORLD when nations pitted their armies against each other, there was a time when peace prevailed and men stopped killing each other. But they did not learn to stop killing land, trees, soil, animals, fresh and salt water and air. It was a false peace. Men now worked at a fervour to wreak havoc on the earth. This was a time when mokuy once again roamed the earth moaning their dissent. It was not only the Yolŋu who noticed the walking dead that started to haunt the landscape. Earnest and honest men worked hard and beneath their toil great horrors occurred. The new Frankensteins were farmer politicians, engineers, hard workers for the free world.

New leaders emerged out of the fog of depression. They were angry and they saw their father and grandfather's despair. The ancestral fire was coming back from Mata Mata. Its temperature could never diminish. No water could put it out.

Leon: "It walks abroad; it continues in its ravages; whilst you are gibbeting the carcass, or demolishing the tomb, terrifying yourself with ghosts and apparitions; your house is the haunt of robbers."

Yuwrrala: "I saw bulldozers rip through our sacred heartland. I watched my father stand in front of them to stop them clearing the sacred trees. I saw him chase the drivers with an axe. I watched him cry when the sacred waterhole was bulldozed. I saw him suffer with the land. The land is life."

Larrpan: "Return to the homelands. I want these mining graders for roads. We will build houses and schools. We must strengthen the defence of our sacred areas so this can never happen again."

Wesley Wagner: "I will enter that most perilous congregation of devils. Give me strength to support our people!"

THIS WAS SOMETHING EVEN WORSE than the first coming of machines. Now great monsters devoured whole mountains and rivers and valleys. Human beings could hear each other's screams but they could not hear the screams of mother earth. They could not see the difference between a natural palace of beauty forged over the millennia and a flat piece of ground pushed together by plates of steel propelled by engines. After the century of blood, human beings were in love with their own power to shape the surface of things. They could not see the deep forces of life and love and the connectedness of the family they were destroying. I was hovering in the ocean but there was a great current growing in strength. I had seen and felt times like this before. The war was over but no-one saw the great continent of pain that was inflicted on the people of the land. The wicked, ignorant greed that had been imposed on the countryside was still on the move and the spirit of the land was fading. In the South Land there was a paradise of ancient wisdom that was precious beyond value but the newcomers could not comprehend it. People in their hundreds, then in their thousands, then in their millions congregated in this ancient land. They had no comprehension of the culture that was tuned to the land and went back to the beginning of time. It was right there in their grasp, the paradise garden. The recorded history of the world was nothing, a mere speck, in the South Land there were thousands of years of life and mind to understand. Slowly, slowly a kind of collective awareness was forming but many blocked their ears. The madness of the European world was once again coming fast and hard. Little boxes of concrete and brick were built on sacred lands.

Ribbons of bitumen cut through the heart. Explosives detonated the oldest sculptures on earth. Many simply did not want to acknowledge the brutality, absurdity and stupidity of the invasion of the ancient life. The winds of time were blowing me here and there across lives and loves and contests and pain. Garray's law and Yolŋu law were one thing but the actions of men, courts and police and the way in which money and power worked were another. I began once more to feel myself changing. I heard rumblings and again I found myself drifting. I was moving away from the manda islands. I was getting angry and unsettled. My skin was becoming rough. I felt power bristling through my body. I was a hunter, the greatest hunter, the most powerful being. I felt the scars on my back where fire had once burned me deeply. I was bäru and my country was calling me.

AS I LAY SILENTLY WAITING I was absorbing my names Djubuyma, Gadumitjpal, Guryinmurru, Bakandjarri, Dhupundji. I could hear the lapping of the sea... and I saw the old man sitting under the great dharpa. He was my bapurru. I was his protector and he was mine. He was mywäwa. I loved him dearly. He would stand by his land because the land and he were the same. It did not matter what enticements were offered. I watched him. He was in shock. His heart was filled with grief. He had saved a great tree, an acrial to the cosmos,

171

and these fools could not even see it. Its roots spread down far beneath the earth bringing the power of the land to the air. He sat there watching the carnage all around him. The monster was devouring everything. But he had saved the dharpa. Was it enough? The tracks of the ancestral dog were being wiped away. The fresh water springs beneath the sea were being dug up and pillaged killing all of the life forms that lived there.

A great pond of toxic sludge would accumulate. Year after year, decade after decade. All this was all around him in his mind and in his foresight. He could not leave the dharpa. He was paralysed with grief. Just as had happened in the cities and towns all over the Great South Land the spirit was there and the people stayed thinking, meditating, dreaming, singing, dancing, trying to restore the spirit again. It was a monster like no-one had seen before. Minnyere of another kind! Its blood was acid, its breath was poison and it went on devouring everything in its path. I had seen destruction before on the other side of the world. But not like this. Machines of human death now became machines of earthly destruction. How the monster had grown! How greedily it ate! How ruthlessly it swept away all in its path!

"Old man," I whispered. "I will cry with you here. I will cry for you and for me. I will cry for this world coming and the world past. But let us not cry too long. We have survived and we will live with our hearts broken. Eventually they will see. We must hunt and go to war in different ways."

I saw the old man walk away and I saw him consciously bring an energy that would flow into his sons and daughters and granddaughters and grandsons. In absorbing the pain, he had also created a great aspiration to teach these newcomers their errors and to let them understand their own stupidity.

Go ŋilimurru nhina yarrarrayun
(Come let us sit lined together)
Yolŋu Bandirriya dharwulŋuruna
(ancestors at Bandirrya under the dharwul tree)
wäŋa marrkapmirri wäŋa marrkamirri
(beloved country, beloved country)

ŋarrakaŋu boṉal nherranhara gapany gopulu
(on Gumatj ground a site cleared by me).[61]

I heard the explosions. It was disturbing me. Deep into the earth steel teeth drove. It was a spear driving into my body. I cried and writhed with the pain. It was unbearable. Could no-one hear me. I swam away from my bäru sacred dreaming place into deeper waters and waited crying silently.

If there's wind, the Toyota offers shelter...[62]
It is best to enter the magic kingdom slowly by road. Winṉikamu Mossman 334,145, Mareeba 334,224, Mt Garnet 334, 354, Georgetown 334,569, Mt Croydon 334,714, Normanton 334,869, Alexandra River 335020, Leichardt River 335,021, Burketown 335,092, Gregory River 335,126, Hells Gate 335, 267, Calvert River 335,427, Borooloola 335,607, Lorella Springs 335,772, Butterfly Springs 335,842, Western Lost City 335,849, Limen Bright 335,681, Cox River 335,381, King River 335,918, Port Rogan 335, 959, Didi Baba 335,972, Mountain Creek 335,975, Yalllimanji 335,979, Roper Bar 336,036, Nhumbulwar Barge 336,026, Central Arnhem Highway 336, 484, MM turn-off 336,613, BP 336,843

SOMETHING WAS PULLING JIMMY ALONG CAPE MELVILLE ROAD. In the midday sun he tramped as the steady stream of flags and neon lights passed on the road. None saw the solitary man walking. He passed the empty dongas in the mining compound. Someone in the YBE bus waved as it turned off the main road.

"Baman' walala ŋuli marrtinja wäŋakurru ḻukuy."

Along the path he continued. After fifteen minutes he reached his resting place.

"Marrkapi. Ḻarra dhuwala manymak Yolŋu."

And there he curled up near the memorial stone and under the shade of the dharpa he fell asleep. He felt comfort sleeping there with his waku. Wreaths and blankets lay all around. The `irriwi from fires and the rubbish of the daily pilgrimages and camps were strewn beneath trees. Later when the heat of the day diminished he would walk down the long track, past the blue stone quarry. He hoped his wawa might pass by and pick him up. But not today. On he walked, past John Flynn Drive, left into Beagle Circuit, right into Arnhem Road then down Mathew Flinders Way to the grounds of Gove District Hospital. Family members were there underneath the trees. His yapa was inside but following mirriwi he did not enquire as to her condition.

"Nhämirri walala? Wanha ṇatha? Ṇarra djäl ṇathawa."

Soon hospital sandwiches and sweet biscuits were shared.

"Wanha Winfield Blue?"

"Yaka Winfield Blue."

A worn tin of Log Cabin tobacco was passed around. Soon the tin was empty.

THE OLD MEN AT YIRRKALA WERE UNSETTLED BY THE EVENTS AT GALIWINKU. They meditated long and hard. Bäpa Edgar did not have to be convinced of the deep knowledge of the Yolŋu. He had accepted his responsibility as a family member. Now he too slept uneasily. He had heard the news of the monster. This was a time when the people of wisdom would be ignored and scorned. Once again there was talk of transporting the community away. But the network of understanding that crossed the Great South Land was growing. People could not be thrown from their homelands. This was deeply instilled now in the feeling of the people black and white. With this the old men began again to paint. Dhuwa ga yirritja in magnificent panels. The story of Djaŋgawal on one side and Laindjuŋ-Banaidja on the other side. This time these paintings would not just guide representatives of a church trying to understand the law of a people in a new region. This time the panels would guide a nation. They would come to shape the laws of the newcomers. They would grow in power year by year. They would unlock a wisdom and knowledge of the land that the world would come to respect and learn from.

It was the power of the monster and the ignorance of the balanda men that made the old men paint with their hearts and minds. I had heard of the man who painted a church ceiling with

174

a spirit of love and divine magic. Now the old men painted for the world to see the nature of things and the deep forces of the universe here in the lands between sunrise and sunset.

It was just as it had been all those years ago in Éire. The earth was being pillaged but this monster had become clever. It no longer ran over the people willy-nilly. This monster promised a golden future to all who would feed it. In the peace time, the machinery that had been deployed for armies would now bring housing, factories, workers, jobs, prosperity, science and progress. The size and scale of the monster would fill people with awe. The best Swiss engineers men of precision, would create a monster of beauty. The world's largest aluminium mine and processing plant - a dream of bosses and workers - would modernise this ancient backward land. The monster would inhabit 20,000 hectares of Yolŋu lands. A forty-two-year lease with the right to renew for a further forty two years. The monster would build a beautiful town, swimming pool, a power station, cargo jetties, schools and hospitals. All the monster required was the top three metres of red bauxite soil over 20,000 hectares. You will never even notice it has gone! For forty two years the blasting and ripping of the earth continued. The old people fought, lost the battle and won the war. Land rights were born.

But it was no consolation to those guardians of the sacred places that were now blown up, scraped up and disintegrated and spun out across the earth in pots and sidings and automobiles. The young people did not want to live. Many threw themselves into alcohol, gambling and the superficial allures of the new world. The old people watched television looking for signs that things might change. They too learned to turn off because what was happening all around them was too painful to contemplate. The sirens would sound and the rumbling of the explosives continued day in and day out. Mighty Djumbawal watched. The willy-willy that came to Yirrkala on that day was alerting the old men and women of these coming catastrophic events.

From my hiding places in the deep holes and wells of the beaches, in the muddy waters I watched as politicians came. I

175

saw them work with the old men. I saw the combined power of Garray and Yolŋu rom. Then of course there were us faeries and ancestral spirits working in concert together. We would lose and we would win.

ALL OVER THE SOUTHERN LAND the monsters came. But there were few old people with the forces and wisdom of the old men and women of Yirrkala and the miwatj lands. These men and their stories and their ancient rom became a beacon of hope for all in the world. Without knowing why, thousands came to look with the awe at their paintings and to contemplate their meanings within meanings within meanings. The greatest painters of the world looked with awe at the abstract well of meaning that had no end. Great scientists, anthropologists, wrote their treatises as if they were studying insects. Even the Swiss engineers and mining bosses were changed and touched by the tears of the old men and women. As Garray was adopted, old men and women were using these scientists to get their messages to the people of the world. How funny it was to see the earnestness of the scientists and to feel the humour of the people. At night, they would talk of these men and women with their recording machines and cameras. They stood outside the ring of knowledge and the participation of dance, song and life watching with eyes for the world but they could not see. Only when they slept, only in their dreams did they really understand. They were being used as the vehicles of communication as the preservers of knowledge and wisdom in this world of monsters. They too were being changed. They too were learning to cry.

At this ancient temple of life where there was so much destruction the old men and women meditated and dreamed too. They dreamed and they worked with the ancestral beings to change these forces of destruction into new forces of life and love. The vibrations they sent all over the country could be seen in the great parliament of the Federation. The sons of the old man sitting beneath the great dharpa would be heard all over the world. Their messages in great waves of music, dance and power words - mother and child - would sink into the consciousness of evil and transform it to good.

Can you see this old man and his dharpa transmitting to you what you need to know? In the end, he was more powerful than the most powerful of the machines. His wise messages were flowing in the midst of the foolish era of machines and monsters. All over the world in Papua New Guinea, in West Irian, in Alaska, in Africa, in the islands of the Pacific, in South and North America, in Europe, in Japan and China, in Tibet, a vibration had begun that would never be defeated.

It had come too through the lines of Honor's family. When märipulu Grace entered into my consciousness it was a happy day. Douglas had changed her in a quiet and gentle way. She came from a long line of magic families of an Irish dynasty. When she walked in the Fitzroy Gardens then we faeries would come out to play. We danced behind her and music filled the air. The birds and possums would come from everywhere. She naturally attracted the most gentle of spirits., With her husband the quiet teacher and thinker, she changed consciousness of the mainstream world. For them no war was worth fighting in. Each plant and animal was respected. They were learning to hear the spirit of earth. They were people of learning and light and they picked up the vibrations of the old men of Yirrkala even before they could put words to what they knew.

I heard a shimmering song through the ages, a war song, a lullaby, fathers and sons:

Underneath the lamp post by the big lagoon
Lived a little crocodile his name was Chenier
And he liked to play all day and night
He was a fright a great delight
He was the little crocodile
His name was Chenier.

Kananook (Sweet Water) was the name of the street where they purchased a small block of land. Grandmother Grace would not allow the spirits of this block of land to be disturbed. Only the space where a house was to be built could be altered. How Leopold Karel and his son laughed at Grandmother Grace when she insisted that the banksia trees and ti-tree were like precious women who could not be touched. Yet Leopold Karel and Grace admired each other. Leopold Karel was weary of war and banks and engineers. They sensed each other's deep intelligence and they knew somehow that they were creating something special in the lines of their blood. It was not just them. For these things were happening all over the South Land. There were many Grandmother Graces and Leopold Karels, all of them were sensing what was special about this great land. The natural world was a temple of nature carefully nurtured and managed by people of great wisdom for thousands of years beyond the reach of written words or manufactured things. Yes, it was overdue. Yes, it was so late and tragic. But it was a start.

I came to little baby tookoo on this land as a vibration. I saw his beautiful ŋänḏi playing a game on grass for the beauty of the strokes and movement. For over all of the generations I too had come to understand the nature of the land as a dog, as an eagle, as an octopus, as fire, as a willy-willy, as bäru. I allowed this little boy to play with the spirits. I helped him to feel with all his being the way the land all around him was being swallowed by monsters. I saw Daedelus learn too of the things that are beyond the senses of ordinary mortals. At night, he sang and recited poetry and contemplated the writings and words of the great thinkers that had evolved since the time of his great great grandmother Honor and his great grandfather Christopher. Together this father and this son wrote words that would one day come back to them. 'We walk as strangers on this land." In these words, a great yearning was felt. A great feeling of wanting to belong and to understand. In the midst of the dullest, most ignorant monsters this great force was being created.

Baby tookoo began to see without even knowing it. He was living in a dream-like state. He could see the ancient fish traps along the creek. He could see the ancient lands where hunters came for eggs. He saw the way the hunters looked after all things. He saw them burning. He saw and felt the beauty and the peace of the people who lived here for such a long time beyond books and history. Baby tookoo was like so many little boys whose parents had come from this land, who was now of this land too. The earth was talking to him too. One day in a dream he chased a dog across a road. He did not see the oncoming truck. It hit him and dragged him. Horror and bedlam prevailed. Little sister Lyn hid behind the fence not wanting to acknowledge what was happening. She saw his shoe fly up in the air and come falling with a thud on the ground. Ha! Ha! Not even a truck could hurt me for I was bäru and even a truck was just a dent on my skin. In the hospital as the nurses and doctors tended to the gravel rash and cuts, the little boy felt the pain of the ancestral fire on his body. It was a pain that swept through his brain like waves and in the fire he saw the primeval patterns and felt the spirit underneath the earth and understood the importance of the ancient homelands and of the return of the families to Mata Mata and Gi'kal. All these things were planted in him. He would never stop when others stopped. He was driven when others tired. He would work without knowing why.

This little boy was a new spirit. I tell you this so you know that you are not alone. I was not alone in my journey from Éire. Many spirits came with me, after me. We were all coming to this South Land to learn how to save the world. There is no place where the consciousness of men and the universe is so closely united. The absurdity of the monster being built on my sacred dreaming site can be seen now. It was like bombing a sacred cathedral. You can see this now - I know you can. You can see this now because the spirit beings that are with me are also with you. You have your own inner spirit. She is with you teaching you, talking to you, learning with you and helping you to respect everything around you.

JIMMY ARRIVED AT CENTRELINK just before closing. He waited patiently for the attention of one of the women staring into her computer kiosk. He shuffled in his pocket for his Westpac card.

"Yaka rupiah."

"What is your client number?"

"Yaka client number. Ŋarra dhuwala Jimmy Gurruwiwi, No. 12 Wallaby."

"I can't help you without your client number."

"Yaka client number. Ŋarra dhuwala wäwa Djalu."

"Let me see your bank card."

She took his bank card and typed his name into her computer system. It was 4.25. She looked up at him. He was very irritable.

"Okay. Have you been applying for jobs? It says that it's been over a month since you reported to Centrelink."

Njarra djal ŋathawa ga ŋarali!"

She waited for a moment. She looked at the clock and then she looked at Jimmy.

"Yes, you have? Okay, I have cleared your breach. There should be some money in your account by about 7pm. Okay, all good," she smiled at him reassuringly. "We have to close now. Off you go."

Jimmy closed the door behind him. He walked over to Endeavour Park and sat down under a tree. Family members were signalling to him from the Woolworths car park. Yaka rupiah he signalled back to them.

THE CHESTERFIELD CIRCUIT ENTRANCE to the walkabout hotel is divided into two paths. One is for visiting balanda, yolŋu buŋawa and their families, the other entrance is the doorway to death. At 7.01 pm Jimmy had withdrawn all of the funds he could from his bank account and, after a brief purchase of ŋarali', he had entered the doorway of death and begun drinking.

Sergeant Ray Ray was in town chasing kava dealers. At 12.30 he received a phone call from the Walkabout Hotel. There was a disturbance.

When he walked in the door, Jimmy was standing on the bar with a pool cue.

"Makarrata," he said pointing to a tall mining contractor still dressed in his florescent shirt and trousers. He was brandishing the pool cue like a spear and suddenly he threw it striking the mining contractor in the thigh.

Luckily it did not penetrate the flesh but in a flash Sergeant Ray Ray had grabbed Jimmy and manhandled him to the floor.

"Jimmy! You are out and, mate, no way you are coming back in here." With that he pushed him out the door and into the night town air.

"Do you want to spend the night in the watch house?"

"Yaka."

"Get on your way then and if I see you on the streets I'll charge you and it'll be the watchhouse."

Sergeant Ray Ray thought of the over-crowded cells and wondered how he could fit Jimmy in. Better he walk home. Enough trouble for one night and Sergeant Ray Ray had bigger fish to fry.

Jimmy didn't need to be told twice. He disappeared down Franklyn Street and on to Gandalathami beach. There he lay down, keeping a safe distance from the lapping water. Some hours later Jimmy began the long trek home. I am following the pathway of the wititj he thought to himself. No, this is the wuŋgan path, he corrected himself. As he walked he thought of the ancestors who had made this trek before. He cut in front of the town lagoon and thought briefly about spending the night at East Woody. Yaka Riratingu, Yaka Gumatj this is sacred Galpu land. This is my land. This is my wealth. Too many sandflies! As he walked down Jasper Road he looked at the land cruisers and boats parked in every house. He thought of wurrguluma. The family would have to hunt for food. Manymak, there will always be wurrguluma and there would always be enough to go round. Manymak ŋathawa ŋarrra djal, yaka junk food, he thought as he walked.

A GREAT FIRE WAS BURNING. It was burning under the land, under the sea. It was burning so hot that no-one could touch it. It burned underground. It burned so hot like lava from the volcano. I felt my scarred back and dived deeper, waiting there silently, patiently. Even the monster could not separate me from my country.

"The land for us is like our mother. We are born from our mother and we finish being buried in the land. See, it's just like

181

we went from mother to another mother, something like that."[63]

"....you can see the Old People, long dead, living in their descendants."[64]

Wukun: Asleep on the sandbank I could feel myself rising, lifting off the ground. I was floating. Out on the horizon I could see the shock on the faces of the fishermen. A plane was landing at Mata Mata and the pilot saw me sleeping there on the sand bank. Nothing special about that. But I was rising, lifting off the ground. I was changing again.

I was no longer the great predator. I was not a bird, not an animal, not a spirit. I had become one with the wind. I was gathering up the moisture from the sea. Now drifting over the land, the rain was falling. I was drifting, gathering up and then letting go. I was feeling the earth's breath in and out. I was over forests. I was over lakes and rivers. I was bringing life to deserts. I was moving over the lands and seas watching over the world. I was lost in a world of shapes and endless patterns of light and dark. I was going with winds and following the rhythm of the earth. It came to me as a lightning bolt, the absurdity ownership and possession of land that had taken hold in the minds of men and women. As I watched over oceans and earth renewing land with life-giving rain I saw the imbalanced emblem. Yirritja only! No Dhuwa! Selfishness and possession, one-sided stories. In the thunder, I flashed back into time. I saw Honor with no house or land stealing to feed her children. I saw Christopher protecting a family from being evicted from their cottage. I saw Michael and the police. I saw men fall under fire from soldiers. All this fighting and fussing over something that could not ever be owned. I saw this hunger for safety and a place to call one's own. And there below me was Dilkuwurrurru, Gurritjiri, Djalu, Jason ga Terence and the Galpu song men and dancers. I saw them singing and dancing my movements. I saw the absurdity of ownership of land. I saw the monsters all over the land taking the best of the earth and turning it into aluminium and steel.

I saw the Galpu song men singing into the metal to help the world understand what was in that metal, the red bauxite of Galupa and the red iron ore of the Nyamal lands.

KANANOOK ESTATE symbolised advancement but created so much destruction. California bungalows transcend Victorian terrace houses and inner-city slums. Little boxes built on half acre blocks. Concrete, bitumen and glass empires trying so hard to erase the spirit of the land. But even here the spirits were talking. The burned little boy was with four sisters: Sonia, Dawn, Evonne and Sandra. They were playing records that echoed in their souls across time. The little boy saw for the first time the reverie of women and he fell in love with all of the Coles sisters. But the girls were in love with the man from Memphis. "Like a river flows surely to the sea/Darling so it goes/Some things are meant to be/Take my hand, take my whole life too..." "Dreams come true/In blue Hawaii/And mine could all come true/This magic night of nights with you." From the needle of that little record player came a vibration that merged with the yidaki all the way up to Arnhem Land. Wäwa Bararrwanga met the great one. Where? In Darwin? In a dream? In Las Vegas? I don't know but they did meet. They taught each other something: moves, singing styles - and something crossed over. Like "Skeetah" Davis in Morobe or "Pee Wee" Whitewing in Cape York, souls fused, entities merged, wheels caught fire.

The mediocrity of surburbia, the plastic lives, the gully traps and sewerage spewing out, all this still could not kill the spirit of the land there. The burned little boy could see it clearly. Black and white televisions, the Ed Sullivan Show, I Love Lucy - cutting edge, nature strips and pavement. Endless steps avoiding cracks. There was a Vauxhall Velox in the driveway. A big pipe crushed father working on the roads. Freddy Griffin broke collar bones. Dingo the dog barking at Mrs Minogue.

The faithful Loys drink-truck dragging the boy along the bitumen. In the hospital, the fire of Mata Mata. Yang Yang in the ti-tree glowing and hiding and playing, showing the ancient fish traps and grass lands, the nests and hollows where a thousand thousand stories were told.

William Buckley, walking past endless nourishment, starving. Mischievous, adventurous, Kennie Stagyard, Gary Slack, Nicky Mortimer, Malcolm Beaman - the beautiful Coles sisters 'love me tender'.

A typewriter tapped in Pitt Street... a little boy was crawling in the bracken with his friends... they were weaving the stalks together to make fragile cubby houses up on the north coast of NSW... "Believing that many of the difficulties encountered today by Aborigines arise from discrimination against them"... clack, clack... the roneo machine went round and round...

They had built great sails of concrete on the point where the mullet ran. It was a grand palace from the deep imagination of the world and it was pleasing and it fitted. I could hear a great voice as deep as the great Mississippi River. I could see a great grandson singing Bayini. The songlines were slowly connecting again. This was always a place of great performance and song and dance and music and a hundred thousand campfires. The great warrior Pemulwuy and the great ambassador Bennelong were smiling with me in the stars. We faeries and spirits were coming together. We could weave magic even in tiny minds who thought only of money and cement. That was our job.

We Celtic faeries and dreaming spirits have a wicked sense of humour. It is good to laugh. A new culture was emerging from the most unlikely places. It was fun to make magic amongst those who painted concrete green so they wouldn't have to worry about plants and grasses. In these places of control, we created wildness and frivolity. The salt of the sea squall would take the edge off even the hardest concrete and even these great monuments of vain men would blend into the land.

Boiling clouds and pale light made the world softer and unreal. The calm that comes to fishermen and those who are slowly dying would also be here. Dolphins and whales would sing to them. As I moved through time I looked out and saw so many things... all of the cruelty and suffering... all of the dreams of freedom... We sprinkled our faery dust at many times and places.

So many things happened in this time when I was a cloud looking down on the world.

There was a man who carried over his dreaming in paintings to help the newcomers see some of the magic of the land, His paintings were ladders to see. Like Douglas he would sow the first seeds of understanding and like Douglas he would take on the hypocrisy of the world and defeat it. One day a young queen was touched by his presence and she too saw in the paintings the ancient lore of the people. She had grown up with the red cedar furniture all around her. "Sheeeeee" they would cry. You see even to this childhood monarch, so far away from the cold rainforests of NSW and Tasmania. the ancient trees could talk and tell. When she met Albert, a tingling went down her spine. Lalla talked through the timbers to another queen of an empire that had conquered worlds. But there was a greater force. Albert too was sending the first signals back over the seas to Éire and the islands of the great North seas.

This queen recognised us and the error of her ancestors. She knew in her heart that the people of the South Lands stretched thousands of years beyond her ancestral royalty lines. She had never expected to be a queen. She had seen her father rise as a stoic fighter against tyranny, she had seen parliaments echo with speeches about the rights of the common man and she had wondered about the role of kings and queens. Now in her old age she thought of Albert. A Yawuru man from Broome invited her to watch the sun come up. As the warm rays came up over the Kensington Gardens - my original faery playground - the white bearded man talked quietly of the women singing in the day on the ancient southern continent.

On through the winds of time I travelled. There were times of conflict and pain when men and women from the Great South Land were no better than the convict ship bullies. Little by little a culture of love and sharing overcame death and evil. The greatest torments brought new determination. The newcomers were also enduring pain. We faeries were there on the battlefields of Turkey and France. We were there in the muddy hills and rainforests and in places where men worked as slaves and were marched over terrible distances. In all of these times of death and cruelty a new spirit was emerging. It was there in every wise-crack and laugh in the face of pain. We faeries were there to perform little miracles of understanding. When sour-mouthed journalists and politicians talk only of facts and proof, beware. We send little birds and animals to open closed minds. Sometimes it is a shaft of light that shines through a window and touches a politician or magistrate's head at a crucial time. Sometimes it is a little boy or girl lost in nature, climbing trees or running along a sea shore.

I see a little girl in the branches of a great fig tree above the harbour. I see her watching the commuters going by under the branches. I see her falling in love with the gardeners and the birds and the animals. I see the brutal men and the cruelty. I cry for her and with her. Magic comes in waves. I return her now to grace. I free her from her pain. Do you know who she is? She is all of us.

And there too is the beautiful fortune teller teaching children to fly. Why would you want me to wash cups and saucers when I can teach you to fly? Follow my wet footsteps across the smooth rocks of the ancient river and up into the sky. Let us play there amongst the clouds and the stars and the moonbeams.

We can turn on good and evil within ourselves It is our choice. Choose to turn on your best feelings at the worst times. The land will heal you. Can you hear this message in your heart? These are the next steps in the future of our world. Our quest is only limited by our thoughts and what we can imagine. Dream it and it will come!

Remnants, fragments, endurance, courage, survival - I saw so much. I saw two little boys growing up. I saw Arrimi being cheeky. He would taunt his pursuers again and again. I saw him disappear and appear at will. He evaded the most skilful trackers and brought *mayi* and spirit to those who were confined in missions. I saw that a young boy would also learn this trick of being able to disappear and appear at will. He would help to win back lands and rights that had been taken away. Sophisticated lawyers and statesmen were learning from those who lived at one with fog, midst dust, insects, marsupials, crocodiles and wild country.

I saw the baby tookoo standing in a park one day. I saw him sense something. A man with no schooling other than the great melody of his ancestors came to the podium. He was quite an upstart this young well-dressed Irish-Australian. He had a bit of the malarkey. We faeries gave him the ears for great music, eyes for special beauty and a gift of eloquence from the Ages. The words flowed out of him. "It was our failure to imagine these things being done to us. We failed to ask – how would it feel if this were done to me?" I could hear Honor stirring in her grave. It was still an admission of failure from a point of superiority. It was enough for this time. Through these words understanding would come. I could feel the reverberations even in my world. The great orb was changing, slowly the philosophy of the ancient ones was re-emerging in the fabric of the country and its laws. There was so much now to do.

WHEN THE EARTH AND MOON come close it is a special time. In the north west of the Great South Land on certain nights the moon's beams form a ladder and we faeries can make the journey up and down into the galaxies. The faery folk and spirits all make the journey here.

If we tried to fly up on our own it would take us many years to reach the moon. But when the moonlight ladder forms, the magic beams take us into the heavens very quickly. Some wise people can also fly up into the heavens. These things are well known. The Yawuru sand dunes are a cross-roads for the magic of the world. Here on the coast of the first sunrise so many spirit beings congregate to make their journeys upwards and downwards. For us the silvery ladder to the moon is like a wonderful invisible current. The silvery moonbeams make you feel so light and alive. They are beams of prosperity and life. As I climbed the ladder ever upwards the moonbeams embraced me and I bathed in them. My thoughts became one with the silvery light. I looked down and saw that on earth secret ceremonies were being held all over the land. I could see a special lady painting the stars so that children would know of the places where the grandmothers camp in the sky. I saw a grandson writing a song for his grandmother. He wrote of how much he loved her and of how she looked after him as a boy.

I knew I had to go up into the heavens. I think you can guess why. I wanted to visit the grandmothers at their campfires. Ha! Of course, you know these fires. Can't you see them? There are a million, million campfires. I had to find Lalla Bakitju Gunda's fire. I was getting weary of the world. I wanted to rest at the campfire and talk with old man moon who gently guides plants, oceans and people. He brings babies into the world and germinates seeds from plants. I sought his counsel and I wanted him to bring something new into the world.

There is a special knowledge of women that is celebrated in the moonlight. It is not for me to tell you of these things. As time goes on mothers and aunties will talk to you of the wonder of the moonlight. They will talk to daughters of many beautiful things and they will talk to their sons about the sacredness of women and the role of men to love, honour and always protect their mothers, sisters and wives from any harm.

But my business was with old man moon himself. Men had grown very clever but they had also become thoughtless. As I sat at his campfire old man moon, Gidja, told me a story. It was how he came to be the protector of the rainforest world - where the coral reef kisses the great trees - in the north of Australia.

"I was once a warrior. My brother was Mali (the fruit bat). We lived for a long time as brothers. But we knew there was something wrong with the world. It was all the same, full of men. We fought each other and other men who came into the rainforest. We hunted roughly.

"Worbu (the hornet) and Mullima (the wasp) would enjoy stinging us because we were so disrespectful of the world around us. It was like a giant comedy and everything stayed the same.

"One day I talked with Mali. I said, 'we need to change in this world.' But Mali was not really interested. When he went hunting I began trying to cut out new beings from the flat rock at the falls of the Roaring Meg. But the rock would not respond.

It was too hard. One day Yalangur (the eagle hawk) went to sleep in the rock near the falls. 'Yalangur I want to make you a new force in the world.' I looked up into the night sky and I could see the distant glow of campfires. I asked for the guidance of the grandmothers and Yalangur began to change. All of the forms and shapes of a woman welled up inside his body.

"Babies emerged from Yalangur's new body. It was the beginning of a new world. At first I kept my secret. But I could not keep if for long. Oh how wonderful Yalangur and her babies were. They brought fire from the stars, they prepared fine white flour from the poisonous cycad nuts grinding and washing them to remove the poison. They caught mangrove worms, hunted for oysters, yams and other delicacies.

"I could not keep my secret for long. Others began to search for Yalangur and soon they found the glow of our campfires. The warriors were furious with me. They chased me down the river spearing me as they went. Each time they thought they had killed me I dived into the river again and again. At Kauwai where the river meets the sea the warriors finally pulled me from the waters and there my spirit turned into a giant rock that is still there. My spirit sought refuge so I took a bone from the blue-tongued goanna that was shaped like a boomerang. I threw it far out to sea. At first my light was quite small but then it grew larger. I became the moon and I appeared and disappeared like Gidja the warrior in the river. I formed light in the night.

"From my starry heights, I watch over Yalangur and all her offspring. The warriors took wives and formed camps and clans and divided up the rainforest world into two great divisions Dabu (the scrub bee) and Wallar (the forest bee). Marriages, land, relations were determined by these two grand orders.

"No-one owns the land. Responsibility for stewardship, physical and spiritual maintenance transfers over time back and forward across the kin groups of mothers and fathers and grandmothers and grandfathers."

I began to sleep in the stars dreaming of beautiful little girls growing into women. Gidja's voice was slipping away in my mind. I slept so beautifully and no dreams came to me that night. When I awoke I knew that I had to find Lalla and Honor. On earth, they had never really seen me before. I loved them both so much. I knew that all the hurt of their lives had disappeared here in the moonlight. My heart had been broken by Honor but also by the pain and suffering of Lalla and her people. When they saw me here in the moonlight they could see me in my purest form. As I flew, lifted by moonlight, into the galaxies and to the place where Lalla and Honor had their fire I knew that something wondrous would happen. I came around the celestial pathway and there we saw each other for the first time and at the moment we also saw the great mother earth in the far distance. We merged with each other, we flew with each other, we rejoiced, we sang and we became as one with each other. Our spirits became one with the earth. Now do you know why people fall in love in the moonlight? Why it is so magical?

It was not just me who had made the ascension that night. Thousands of faeries made the journey to find the children they had loved, to see them again and to allow them to see who they really were. This is the special quality of the Broome stairway, it is a ladder to the universe beyond. The spirits and forces of the great mother were evolving and changing. Just like moonlight and the great invisible pull of the moon across the earth so our spirits and thoughts were moving the world. There are so many forces at work. There are cyclists, whales, ships and great carnivals, beautiful dogs, and many animal spirits all revolving around the night sky bringing their special charms to earth. From high in the galaxies, great empires, kingdoms, battles and monuments slowly fade into space. The tides, the land, the seasons, the stars, these are the certainties of the world.

Over millennia, Lalla and her people had devised a way for the people to look after land over many generations continuously forever. As I merged and played with the spirits of Lalla and Honor I saw how the magic of the land was loved, respected and it was a part of the way people lived. I saw how young boys were initiated into this knowledge. I saw the women singing the new day and worshiping the changing constellations and campfires of the night sky.

As I sat at Lalla Bakitju Gunda's campfire in the stars, stories began to tell themselves. We could fly where we wanted in time and space. On the top of the mountain at Karupur was Kangkushot. He knew that the important caves and places were saved but looking down from the summit the old man was dizzy and sick in his stomach. He put his hand on his heart and prayed to himself that he had not dishonoured the land. He thinks of the great blind snake that left Marapikurrinya never to return again when it heard the propellers of the first giant ship come into the harbour. At Marble Bar, Henry Whalebone was talking of horses. Willie Jumbo looked over the horizon and saw a bush turkey. I could see him returning to his family with bush tucker. Cyclones would lift caravans into trees. The desert was home. Like Pundul trees they would build slowly and surely a different way. They would win back control of the land using the newcomers' own laws. They would challenge the strange ideas that one man or woman can own a piece of country, a slither or a whole territory, and pay for it with paper money. How stupid and bizarre? No wonder there was so much war and conflict. No wonder these people were so violent. The old man was reciting power words Jinpinya, Yurlukunya, Marntinya, Purraka, Watarra.

We must stand up to people who will call us fools when we see the beauty of a mountain is more valuable than a great polluting, violent world of glass and machines. We must stand up to people who want to cause harm to people, animals, land, plants or water. This is not something to take lightly or a quest without thought. Of course, we can shape the world but we must do so gently and with more than just money and selfish human interests in our minds and plans.

I remember Lalla sitting so quietly on the shore at Bruny. In her own time, knowledge of these things could not change the course of the newcomers. But now with the vision of the moon, things were changing. How could she tell of these things to people who were so sure, thoughtless and ignorant? She saw her own men die trying to stop the ignorant destruction of her country. There was just a glimmer of hope in the friendship and knowledge of Honor who had seen something similar and tragic in Éire. It was this little spark or glimmer that I held onto over the lives of the children and grandchildren and which I now transfer to you through this story.

We faeries are part of the magic of the land. We were the spirits of Éire and Europe. When machines and industry came, people stopped believing in us. Great populations were set loose to wander the earth without purpose or place. Men and women became laws unto themselves. Great wars and fights over territory and the produce of the land began. The world was spoiled and men and women's hearts became hard.

The spirits and first peoples of the Great South Land reminded us faeries of our ancient magic, they taught us about how men and women could look after the world and then the world would look after them. Men fought for a perfect form in Éire to capture the politics and welfare of all. It was like capturing sunshine. The more elaborate the catching device the more perfectly it failed. I saw the hypocrisy of 'recognising' the first peoples of the Great South Land - in their own country - now overrun by newcomers. The old ones laughed and said the land already recognises us, but it does not know who you are. This is the problem.

Lalla Bakitju Gunda was holding my hand. She beckoned me downwards once again smiling. She showed me a young man and his wife spearing a stingray. The stingray swam towards the man with a spirit in its heart. It begged the old man to spear him and to unleash the spirit within. The young man and his wife shared their meal with old man Walmadany and the last people of this land. A child of the stingray - a grandmother - would be born and she would hold the knowledge of this precious land of the first sunrise. Like Kangushot the family would carefully document the names of the places, creeks and camps. How Lalla beamed to see how the family would save this precious land against all those that sought to damage it. This time the story would come out and the land would survive.

We faeries wanted something more than politics and survival for our own original lands too. We learned this so perfectly from the people of the South Land. We wanted the spirit of the land to be restored and respected. After that things would take care of themselves and people would know how to live. Go back to the sacred times of each place and each region and restore the feeling and knowledge for the land.

In the cities, in the towns, in the regions and in the remote areas – a great new dreaming was emerging. In Van Diemen's Land, the original peoples had retreated to the islands. Now they returned with great force to preserve the natural estates of the land and the seas. On the south eastern coast, the people had scattered and survived where they could. Now they too returned with power and vision. We faeries worked with the friendly spirits to remain with the children and to restore their languages and knowledge. From far high in the stars I saw sacred places in the middle of the cities and towns where families knew they would be safe no matter what occurred nearby. Alongside the great hallmarks of European civilization, little camps often unacknowledged and unknown, carried on.

There was not one place where the Aboriginal spirit was vanquished. The land was never taken, never conquered, the first peoples were prevailing. There were times of great sadness, battles, defeats and tragedies, but as in the millennia before the coming of the white ghosts, the people survived. In the forests and the coasts sacred knowledge was stored in the stone and the trees and the sands. In the north and the centre, the old ones sang great ceremonies of survival. Slowly, slowly the European civilization would take on this spirit. How ironical that from the peoples who were thought to be lost, subtle ideas and concepts changed the world. The people of the South Land were changing the world. The world was beginning to see.

I give you these things that I see from the stars but I cannot tell you the full story. It is not possible. I can only put you on the right pathway to learn. When you have white hair and if you try hard... you will begin to see more and more... The stories I tell you have many layers.

You have to earn the knowledge in your life. Many people can never go beneath the surface. They have not been taught to dive or to think that there is something more to the words on the surface of a story. When you are old and have white hair, I know that you will have dived. At each part of your life you will see more. For every stream, forest, river, beach, valley of the Great South Land there are stories. Dive into these stories. As you dive you will learn to think, you will hear the world spin and the vibrations of the star. You will know how to live well and wisely.

HORROR OF THE STUTTERING TAVERN KEEPER and the bricklayer with a hump in his gut. Spare and meagre brains on toast. Flop on the seamy side. Phoenixed in the car park. Crass, commercial, economic imagination washing brains. Yeasty days. Fosters. XXXX, Victoria Bitter. Super phosphate. Glyphosate tea tipped into Tim Finnergan's coffin. Arise Vegemite man. Refrigeration. Power. Renovations. Caterpillar boys neatly carving up the land. Horror of the nation of the same people living in the same place. Plastic seas. Epoxy water table. Parasites eating living flesh, plundering the wealth, corrupting the good. Who will sweep away the suitors? Mediocrity is the logical curse of the terrible journey and confrontation. A strong white race with strong bones born of cattle and sheep bone gnawing. With embarrassing arrogance and ignorance, weakness is confused as strength. Win at all costs sledging, rude, superficial victories. A young person with instincts intact flees. Garbage dump. Industrial utilisation of urine. Coles. Woolworths. MacDonalds. Greedy politicians, huddled over their vats of fat, guard their disgusting spoils. They train their siblings and children to take their places in white fat jelly collection. Queues of waiting aldermen attend mindless meetings saving swimming pools. A nation of committee meetings in which the lowest common denominator prevails. A criminal with a smattering of classical knowledge never caught, presides over premiers, prime ministers and the corporate world. Killing horses with hammers, eugenic racist calculations and the destruction of children. Cleaning contracts for city buildings go to those who provide the political favours. Used car salesmen, property developers, fashion moguls, newspaper editors - potpourri of unimaginable blandness - spewing out of glowing boxes across the country. The mindless

194

woe and depression of a million small business managers complaining about the help, the country, the costs and the first peoples. The taste of oysters brings the forces of life. Wititj, burrmalala ba`aŋaw'yun gapu cleaning the land. Slaughter by ideas and knowledge the evil sloth.

GALPU WOMEN GATHERING OYSTERS AT GI'KAL: as it was in the dream so long ago, as it was since time immemorial. With them, Honor's great, great, great great grandson, baby tookoo, the spirits of his ancestors walking with him.

Oh yes, her aunt was very fond of oysters...[65] he thought happily. Beautiful, large, generous black-lip oysters were brought back to the clifftop. Eucalyptus leaves were quickly gathered for a short sharp fire. Some mangrove herbs went into the shells. Enormous: One oyster a meal. How delicious they were! And the looks of satisfaction, smiles and laughs were something to behold.

He had brought flowers and she had liked that. Then on to the famous Tathra oysters with fresh rolls behind the sand dunes.

–Don't tell my brother... O no thank you not in my house. It's just a shed.

–I would love nothing more.

–Tattoo?

–Where?

–Your dragon, it's beautiful.

–Oh that. Yes. I want a snake next.

He had only once seen the spirit being. She had come to him when he was at the rangers' accommodation on Wuyal Road. He was sleeping with the door open. It was a mistake to do that in the magic kingdom. But it was his way. Sleeping on the verandah of the clinic at Mata Mata in a swag, old man walking stick had played a trick on him.

–Dhuway, something jumped on me in the night. It felt like someone was lying on my swag.

–Ha! You should know who that was. He was annoyed at you. You didn't come for the funeral.

–But I wrote the testimonial.

–Yes, galay we read it out. But it's not the same. You have a duty to be there for the funeral. He was annoyed.

That night I slept, and on many nights since, I have slept beside the grave.

–Sorry for letting you down dhuway.

–That's all right, galay. I will keep you safe.

Talking things through. Never had that chance with father. But I told him I loved him in the emergency ward. Some mysterious cloud of healing and comfort. After all the rivalry and trouble between us. It would have nice to give him the full ceremony and to sing and dance his life. I saw his spirit in the stars. Know he is safe. But it's taken so long to recover. Don't think anything has gone back to normal even after all this time. I miss him.

–I now sleep beside your grave, father.

–I will keep you safe, son.

She came again at Bawaka.

–Come with me.

Lost, meandering across the sacred sand dunes and into the Arafura swamp. Single men are an easy target for the luscious lips and bling, buŋ'puŋdhun

Muah! Smack! xxx! Chup! Schmatz! Mats-muts! Umma! Chu!

–Wake up everyone!

The crusty prison guard angrily came out of his tent.

–On parade everyone! Get up!

–What's wrong Ray? Its 3am.

–You know it's a privilege for you to be here at Gulkula. So, whoever has brought their wife into the camp has jeopardised the situation for everyone! So, whoever has done it, own up now!!

Midiku and the elders staying in the camp gradually emerge to hear all the commotion.

–What's the problem? There are no wives in this camp we are sure of that. What exactly have you heard or seen?

–I heard kissing outside my tent and I saw a woman's figure in the moonlight.

At this the old ladies begin to laugh. Slowly the laughing infects all of the prisoners and even the other guards start to chuckle.

–Don't you laugh at me! This is a very serious matter and tomorrow all of us will be on the way home to Berrima. Mark my words.

–Ray, you have seen Bayini, midiku finally exclaims. You have seen a ghost!

At this Ray's eyes widened. He knew that midiku and the elders could be trusted. They were acknowledged to be one of the best things that had ever occurred within the Territory prison system.

One of the guards whispered to the other:

–Wait until this gets out. Ray's ghost!

–That's enough for one night. You men (pointing to the guards), I don't want to hear a word of this ever again. Everyone get back to bed, we have a long hard day tomorrow!

But word soon spread round the camp - tough old Ray, salt of the earth, who called a spade a bloody shovel, had seen a ghost. It was on. The stirring continued for days, weeks, months years. Indignant, bad-tempered, stony-faced Ray - somewhere beneath that tough exterior, he quite liked the idea of Bayini.

"I'm writing this because I cannot speak
I'm writing this as an endless word
Fails to be heard."[66]

BIRDS WINGS FLUSHED HIS FACE. The vibrations sent a shiver as he lay on his bed. In and out. She was looking for a safe place to nest for the winter. It had rained overnight and everywhere there were calls. She had a white breast and a black head with grey wings, a stout dart of a beak. Who was she?

Birds bring messages. Dhuwa birds: N̠atili Nowra, Garrukal', Galuwukbuk, Mundjirr, Yirrita birds Malawid̠wid̠i, Ganyiri, Bilitjpilitj, Murriyil' in the morning, all through the day.

Auspicious to be fanned by the wings of a wild bird in bed. Gindi Gindi... the meaning will slowly emerge...

Bird feathers, string and wax... a way out of the nightmare of history. What is the prize? New eyes to see! New brain to think! New ears to hear! New fingers to touch! Flying high, higher than high again.

Two sisters, four sisters, seven sisters... Two sisters unjustly blamed poor James for the death of Rev. Flynn. It hurt him badly, under the blankets pretending it was Christmas, back then on 1 July 1895. Selfish, guarded, ungenerous - the four sisters never really let anyone into their confidence, unable ever to really trust a man, hang on for the ride and jump off when the time is right. Sirens drawing unwary sailors onto the rocks. Sins of the fathers. Pleiades. The seven sisters are always hunting in Djulpan. See them with turtles, fish, freshwater snakes, yams and berries. See them when the food and berries come out, travelling through the sky until the season. Then come the wishing brothers travelling west keeping the seas abundant. The sisters' fires can be seen in the northern horizon. This is the signal for the mosaic of ashes to appear once again.

Wish upon a shooting star. Walking down the road, when all else fails, there are the stars. They led us to this homeland, 'camp', 'hearth', 'country', 'everlasting home', 'totem place', 'life-source', 'spirit-centre'. Don't forget that! The hundred-million-star bed so precious and perfect. Who knows what happens next? Trust the stars. Who could ask for anything more? But always ask.

I LOOKED FORWARD AND BACKWARDS IN TIME and heard a thousand children's verses. In times of war, hunger and pain we had been there.

Faeries drink from buttercups.
Flitting about the little lights.
Little wattle faeries.

Dainty things.
Silver wing.

Loving summer weaves.
Little children dream.

Out of the creeks.

Touch me on the head.
Naughty sprite.

Sparkling. Waterspout. Scented bowers.
Flit away.
A daisy chain fastened to buttercup stalks. A little shoe.
Honey ices, fruit and dew. Friends to tea.
Mushroom houses. Red queen in the dell. Queer little figure.
Dancing on the lawn.
Our music is a cricket's sound. Where the still, dark waters lie.
Cosy bed.
Acorn chariots, summer bees. Prattling tongues.
Hearts all from heaven. An ambition to squint
At my verses in print.[67]

Luŋgurma too was here: whisky and water on the brain and iron in her heart. Wild and untempered, I saw her being patiently loved still. She was a one. I saw Honor and Lalla. I remembered the necklace of shells, running as a dog. meditating in the dharpa, feeling the Bayini spirit, learning, learning, learning over five generations. A great melody of everyman had been sung in the north of the world. Did it really mean anything with millions slaughtered? Slowly the wisdom and peace of the Great South Land is being understood? I saw the missionaries late at night trying to reconcile Garray and waŋa. We adopted you! Waŋjuk was proclaiming proudly. Were they the first to truly ponder the lost paradise with all its meanings? Probably not, but theirs was the important crack in time. I saw the old men wrestling with their consciences. The idea of one man or woman made no sense if they were not intimately connected to their family of clouds, dharpa, insects, animals and the deep heartbeats of the earth and the sea. Now another melody was being sung from the ancient southern continent. It was a melody for the world and for you. It was a melody of the ancient peoples of the land. Little children began to hear it. In the trees overlooking the harbour a lovely little girl heard the melody. And in the foreshore of Port Phillip Bay a little boy was picking up the vibrations from the trees. I too am singing through them to you. I saw the summer storm come to the beach where the children were playing. Everyone was sent scurrying. The beach emptied. It was a lovely chaos. On the harbour, the south westerly buster blew small white caps. In the north, this wind was called manuŋgarri or rawarraŋ. A lone seagull balanced in the air juggling the wind. It was just as it had always been. The old people knew that when the gusts of wind and rain made the water dance there was magic and energy all around. Change was coming from North to South and West to East. I saw how newcomers were accepting and understanding the natural order of the land. I saw a time when people from all over the world came to tune in to the spirit of the many sacred places. I saw how more and more human beings would appreciate this sacred natural world that had been preserved and nurtured for tens of thousands of years. A new spirit was also welling up in my faery soul. I spent more and more time in the dharpa. I merged into their cosmos. I was changing and so were all of the faeries that had come from other lands. The pinks and greens and bright tartans started to become blues and ochres and yellows. Just as Mary's children began to merge the lands of their ancestors with this new place, faeries began to merge more and more with the spirits of the Great South Land.

I occasionally made faery rings but I liked more and more to sleep within the dharpa with other spirits of the land. You can sometimes see faery lights bobbing about the horizon or through the forests as faeries and spirits play chasey through the night sky. I could no longer be a guardian that played at the bottom of the garden or perched invisibly on children's shoulders. putting thoughts or dreams into their minds. Mine was a new kind of dreaming. To find me, to find magic, humans would have to tune into the land. It was here that the wisdom for a better future would emerge. One day I became one with the trees. I am still here waiting for a child's voice to invite me to play. I am here with the wise grandmothers waiting for you to ask about the deep stories, to learn about the winds. I am waiting for you to ask me about the changes in the seasons. I am waiting for you to ask about the flowers and the sounds of the birds. King Billy Wasaga is with me here. His prophecy is unfolding. Watch over the lands and seas and feel them watching over you. I can feel Lalla Bakitju Gunda's smile warming my heart. So many departures and arrivals over all these years. 'The whistle blew. We started to leave the pier. I called. He looked up, waved, then lowered his head again. He was crying. That was the last time I saw him'.[68] A new magic is evolving. There will be many twists and turns. Many adventures and ups and downs. There are still so many things to learn. But we will have to leave those stories for another day. Just remember that when you feel lungurrma on your face or feel the rough bark of a banksia tree or the narrow slithers of ti-tree or the majesty of the paperbark, or when you hear the twitter of little birds singing to each other, remember, I am waiting for you to ask questions. When I hear you ask I will send dreams and feelings into your heart. Ask away and I will always be here in the dharpa waiting for you. We are only just beginning here as we end.

"What are these birds, brother? {the sisters} asked. And the man told them that the birds are the whistling ducks. The ducks lifted their dark wings and rose from the water, flying low over the spreading lagoon with heavy wing-beats at first, then rising higher and higher, flying round in growing circles, piping a strange sweet song as they flew. Then they returned to the water, planing down one after the other in close formation."

Description of part of Larrtjana's, Ngailmil, Damalmirri, Dhuwa panels of the famous Yirrkala Church Panels. Every tiny design has a meaning and a story. They are Australia's greatest monument, our Sistine Chapel, our past and our future. Ironically left out in the weather for a year by a misguided churchman, the two twelve foot by four foot panels are now a world heritage treasure and can be viewed at Buku-Larrŋgay Mulka gallery at Yirrkala. Every Australian should see them.

Ann Wells, *This Their Dreaming Legends of the Panels of Aboriginal Art in the Yirrkala Church*, University of Queensland Press, 1971, p. 26

End Notes

1 Gangoilma, "Dreaming Man and Manya", 1946, ETP.2052, Macleay Museum, University of Sydney, Berndt collection

2 James Joyce, Poem XXXV

3 Homer, *Circe and the Cyclops*

4 Ann Wells, *This Their Dreaming Legends of the Church Panels of Aboriginal Art in the Yirrkala Church*, UQP, p. 16

5 James Joyce, *Ulysses*, Section 17, Ithaca, The Modern Library, p.52

6 Ann Wells, *ibid.*

7 Dorothy Porter, Akhenaten, *By Royal Decree*, Picador, p. 29

8 James Joyce, *Finnegan's Wake*, p.7

9 Ann Wells, op. cit., p.56

10 Munggurrawuy Yunupiŋu "Lany'tjung - Barama & Gulparmun" circa 1960, IA26.1960, Estate of Munggurrawuy Yunupiŋu. This painting may be viewed at the Art Gallery of NSW

11 James Joyce, *The Dover Reader*, p.520

12 Rumi, *Birdsong*

13 The words Bakitju Gunda come from Batumbil and Doris Burarrwaŋa. They mean literally "very wise rock" and come from the Gumatj dialect. These words are used with permission and are not used in every day language. This phrase has symbolic meaning for learned Yolŋu men and women. Lalla (literally, "lady") is a (Moroccan) Amazigh title of respect. Special thanks to Djillawurr for this. Lalla is also one of the names that was used by the great Tasmanian ambassador, Truganini.

14 *The West's Asleep* - an anthem of Irish nationalists and the Young Ireland movement nvoking the indomitable spirit of an even older period in Irish history.

15 The words Ḏilkurrwurru Wataŋgurr come from Batumbil and Doris Burarrwaŋa. They mean literally "leader of the people" and come from the Gumatj dialect. These words are used with permission and are not used in everyday language. This phrase has symbolic meaning for learned Yolŋu men and women.

16 Rudolf Steiner, *Bees*, Anthroposophic Press, 1998

17 Birrikitji Gumana, This is a description of a painting that may be viewed at the Macleay Museum, University of Sydney, P2118, Yiritja

18 Baṉumbmirr, morning star pole, Jack Mirratja, Ramingining, Australian Museum, E77868

19 James Cook, *Account of the New Wales Coast*

20 David Collins, *An Account of the English Colony in New South Wales,* Vol. 1, 147, 1798

21 Birrkitji Gumana, "River at Gäŋgaṉ", 1947, *Yirrkala Drawings*, p.49, R.M Berndt Collection, Yirritja, also see Birrikidji's yirritja Church panels, Buku-Larŋgay Mulka, Yirrkala and the series at the National Museum of Australia,

"Tortioses and Fresh Water Crocodiles", "Narra Ceremony", "Stingray Dance" and "The Sacred Law-Givers for the Yirritja People of North East Arnhem Land".

22 Milirrpum Marika. "Djanggawul at Mauwulanggal" 1967. Natural pigments on bark 163 x 63 cm, Museum and Art Gallery of the Northern Territory

23 James Joyce, *Finnegan's Wake*, Faber & Faber, London, 1939

24 William Butler Yeats, "The Countess Cathleen in Paradise", poem

25 Woŋgu Munuŋgurr, *Thunder men at Durarydbi (1946)*, Djapu mala. Macleay Museum, University of Sydney. Dhuwa

26 Peatsai O'Callanain, Craughwell, East Galway in Thomas Kenneally, *The Great Shame, p.105*

27 Munggurrawuy Yunupiŋu, 1947, "Arnhem Bay at Gudaidj-bingaru". This painting may be viewed at the Macleay Museum, University of Sydney. Yiritja

28 Stanislaus Joyce, *My Brother's Keeper*, pp.103-4

29 Mithanari Gurruwiwi, "The Great Snake Story", 1962. This painting may be seen at the National Gallery of Australia, Dhuwa

30 S. Pigram, Saltwater Cowboy, 1997, Pigram Music

31 Bol'ŋgu', Djambuwal (the Yolŋu Thunderman) ... there is one song cycle for Bol'ŋgu' for the Dhuḍi-Djapu clan. There are different Bol'ŋgu' designs painted for each (of the) clan-based sites for the Dhuwa clans: the Ḍätiwuy, the Ngaymil, even the Riratingu and the Djapu". Gunybi Ganambarr, *Yirrkala Drawings*, edited by Cara Pinchbeck, Art Gallery UNSW, Buku-Larrŋgay-Mulka, 2012, p.47

32 Inspiration from Yothu Yindi, "Milika", *Freedom,* Yidaki by: Milkayngu Mununnggurr, Makuma Yunupingu and Bunimbirr Marika. Song is Rirratjingu clan song about the moon fish and a rock called Mandula sacred to Rirratjingu people. During Buŋgul (ceremony) we always imitate the fish. By imitating the fish it gives the warrior the power of the ocean and the timeless rock. Song is dedicated to the father of land rights and Rirratjingu clan leader Malpinytjingu Marikag who passed away in 1993, the International Year for the World's Indigenous Peoples.

33 See Mithili Wanambi, *Guwarrtji ga warrawada (Hawksbill Turtle and Milkfish)*, 1970, National Gallery of Victoria, 0.146-1989

34 Gulumbu Yunupingu, "Garak The Universe", 2009. This painting may be viewed in the Art Gallery of NSW, 208.2010

35 David Pigram, *Free, Under the Mango Tree,* Pigram music

36 Wanyubi Marika's painting of Djambawal may be seen at the National Maritime Museum of Australia, Sydney, 00033785, Dhuwa

37 Mathew Flinders commenting on Abel Tasman's charts of the Australian coast line in Eric Rolls, *Visions of Australia Impressions on the Landscape*, Lothian Books, 2002, p.4

38 *op cit.* p.101

[39] Banapana Maymuru, Yiṉapuṉapu, National Museum of Australia, H. Morphy, pp.252-61

[40] Louis Nowra, The Golden Age, 1985, p. 36

[41] Rudolf Steiner, Lectures, *Bees with an afterword on the art of Joseph Beuys,* Trans. Thomas Braatz, Anthroposic Press, 1998, Great Barrington, Mass, p.139

[42] This painting may be viewed at the National Gallery of Victoria, Tongue of the Fire, 1998, CMB, Ascession Number 1999.19. See also the amazing Ganiny, Ascession 0.75-1994, with Sylvia Mulwanany, Gumatji, Ascession No 1999.18 and with Elizabeth Djakminy Djang'kawu Story, Accession No 1998.146

[43] Mawalan Marika, 1946, Macleay Museum, ETP.2055 Dhuwa

[44] Narritjin Maymuru, "The Marawili Tree", 1977, Aboriginal Arts Board Collection No.2, Yirrkala, National Museum of Australia

[45] Geoffrey Blainey, *A Game of our Own The Origins of Australian Football,* Black Inc, 2003, p.1

[46] Henry Lawson, "As Ireland Wore the Green," *The Worker,* June 1891

[47] Henry Lawson , *Up the Country*

[48] R.M. Berndt, C. H. Berndt, *The Speaking Land,* "Dog and the Macassans", pp. 418-20

[49] Fiona Magowan, *Melodies of Mourning* Music & Emotion in Northern Australia, p. 130

[50] Bunbatjiwuy Dhammarindji, "Bul'mandji at Gurala", 00033806, Australian National Maritime Museum, Mäw Munnungurr, Mana, National Museum of Australia, 2007.0053.0959

[51] Carl Jung, *The Red Book,* W.W. Norton & Company, New York London, 2009

[52] Noel Pearson, "Ngamu-Ngaadyarr, Muuri-Bunggaga and Midha Mini in Guugu Yimidhirr HIstory, Hope Vale Mission (1900-1950)", 1986 in (J. Kociumbas ed), *Maps, Dreams, History,* University of Sydney, 1998, p. 225

[53] Edgar Wells, *Reward and Punishment in Arnhem Land 1962-63,* Australian Institute of Aboriginal Studies, Canberra, 1982

[54] Robert Kenny, *The Lamb Enters the Dreaming Nathaniel Pepper & The Ruptured World,* Scribe, 2007

[55] Jolly Read and Peter Coppin, *Kangushot The Life of Nyamal Lawman Peter Coppin,* Aboriginal Studies Press, Canberra, 1999

[56] Sulphur Crested Cockatoo and Red-tailed Black Cockatoo.

[57] G.G. Yunupingu, *Galupa*

[58] Gurrtjpi formed a creation path at Bäniyala creating springs. Wise one beneath the sands, waiting, deadly barb for enemies and those who do not respect the land. Yalmakany Marawilli, Maḍarrpa, Yirritja, Buku Larrṉay Mulka, Cat. 52557 Yiritja

[59] P. Batumbil Burarrwanga, *Gurtha,* Mata Mata, 2016

[60] "Burrminy's Easter Song" in Fiona Magowan, *Melodies of Mourning Music and Emotion in Northern Australia,* James Currey, Oxford, School for

Advanced Press, Santa Fe, University of Western Australia Press, 2007, p. 167

[61] G.G Yunupingu. *Gopulu*

[62] Martin Harrison, "The Coolamon" in *Wild Bees*, University of Western Australia, 2008, p.89 per kind favour BR.

[63] Kangkushot in Jolly Read and Peter Coppin *Kangkushot The Life of Nyamal Lawman Peter Coppin*, Aboriginal Studies Press, Canberra, 1999, p.187

[64] Noel Pearson, *Up from the Mission Selected Writings*, Black Inc, Melbourne, 2009, p.16

[65] "O no thank you not in my house..." *James Joyce, Ulysses, The Corrected Text, Random House, New York, 1961, p. 739*

[66] D.C.B. Moore, 2017

[67] Wendy Meaney, 9, 5 Audley Ave, Prospect, SA, *The Mail*, Adelaide, Saturday 23 April, 1939; Dorothy Keen, Brighton East,*The Argus*, Melbourne, Saturday 29 June 1939; Jenny Holmes, *The Argus*, Melbourne, October, 14, 1933 p. 10; Barbara Broadbent, 11, Macclesfield. *The Mail*, Adelaide, Saturday 12 January 1952, p. 10, Ethel Fitzgerald, PO Whittakers Mill, *Sunday Times*, Perth, 24 January, 1932, Mrs. Osgood, Burnie Tasmania, *Advocate*, Wednesday 21 October 1942 p. 2, "Seasprite," 18. Brisbane, 1929, *The Brisbane Courier Mail*, Thursday 11 July 1929, p. 21, Valerie Erleman, 8 1/2, Sydney, *Sydney Morning Herald*, Saturday 20 February, 1937, p. 13. Anon, Perth, 1935, *The Daily News*, Saturday 19 October 1935, p 3, Silver Mist, 7 September 1929, *The Blue Mountain Star*, Katoomba, Connie Wright, Perth, *Western Mail*, Thursday 29 March, 1930, Anon, Brisbane, *The Queenslander*, Saturday 8 November, 1924, p 45, Pat Catterall, 13. 1 Ruskin St., El wood, *The Argus*, Melbourne, Vic., Friday 16 March 1956 p 18 Peggy Drage, Perth, 1928, Clara Grant Duff, *Oakleigh Leader*, (North Brighton), Saturday 28 July 1894, p. 7, Robyn Allen, 60 Clive St, West Footscray, *The Argus*, Friday 18 June 1954, p 19 Challis Chave, *The Central Queensland Herald*, Thursday 25 January 1934, p. 52 Eileen Stapleton, Sydney, *Sunday Times*, 13 June 1926, p. 4, Ema Nitschke, Wood's Flat, *Murray Pioneer*, Thursday 9 December 1943. p. 7, Dorothy Kumnick, 13, Sullivan St, Inglewood, Vic, *The Australasian*, Saturday, 12 July, 1930, p. 46, Anon, Perth, 1935, *The Daily News*, Saturday 19 October 1935, p 3, *The Riverine Gazette*, Hay, NSW, Wednesday, 23 May, 1877, Poldy Bloom, Dublin, *The Shamrock*, 1877.

[68] W. Lloyd Warner, *A Black Civilization A Study of an Australian Tribe*, Harper, p.490

Paintings

Yolŋu paintings are the backbone of this book. They are inspirations for much of the writing, which is why many of the endnotes refer to paintings rather than written sources. For me the journey began with the Yirrkala Church panels but after that a myriad of stories and designs were explained to me or came from visiting places like the University of Sydney's Macleay Museum with Dr J Gumbula (now deceased) and other national galleries with Ms S D Gurruwiwi and the great grand daughters and sons of some of the original painters of Yolŋu designs and drawings. The great Buku-Larrŋgay Mulka, which is the home of the world heritage Yirrkala church panels, was and remains a great place of learning for me. It should be the first point of call for any research on Yolŋu art and culture. In all of this it is important to acknowledge that the use of the knowledge behind the paintings and designs is a very delicate matter. Even though many Yolŋu designs and stories have been published and commented on in a long line of anthropological text books and books about Aboriginal myths and legends and appear in national and international galleries and in paintings for sale and display in private and public spaces, the provenance of the designs belong to the clans and leaders of the Yolŋu people. It is notable that writers like Thomson, Elkin, Berndt and Berndt and Morphy have all written about the protocols pertaining to the use of paintings without permission and the divulging of information about the clan's mardayin (sacred law and ceremony). A decision was taken not to publish any Yolŋu images in this book apart from those of Mrs B Burarrwanga and her late husband because it is important to respect the original rights and knowledge that only comes from a long apprenticeship of learning within Yolŋu law and ceremony. It is also important to acknowledge that interpretations of designs in this book have no basis in Yolŋu mardayin unless noted. A distinction between garma or general discussion and accepted public use of designs and stories has tried to be respected on all occasions. (For a larger discussion of Intellectual Copyright and the complex intersections between Yolŋu and Balanda law please go to this discussion by Yiŋiya Guyala and Ms S D Gurruwiwi: http://www.cdu.edu.au/centres/yaci/pdf/Yingiya_Dhanggal_IP.pdf.) Some particularly inspirational public yirritja and dhuwa paintings for the author are listed below. It is important to see the paintings in person and to reflect on the meanings and stories and to dig deeper by talking respectfully and carefully to the senior leaders of all of the Yolŋu and other Aboriginal clans and nations. Each painting and design belongs to a clan and comes under the authority of a Yolŋu leader. My hope is that this book as an inter-cultural text will lead to Yolŋu authorities being recruited as guardians, leaders and interpretors to universities, the media and as a bridge to general Australian consciousness. Great thanks to the respective art galleries, museums and private owners for their help and support with this project. Very special thanks to Buku-Larrngay Mulka, the Macleay Museum, the Art Gallery of NSW, the National Gallery of Victoria, the National Museum of Australia, the National Maritime Museum of Australia and the National Gallery of Australia, and in particular to Djalu Gurruwiwi, Ms. S D Gurruwiwi, Mrs P Batumbil Burarrwanga, Will Stubbs, Andrew Blake, Djambawa Marawilli, Djawa Yunupingu and Banduk Marika.

Lak Lak 2 Burarrwaŋa, "Djunda," Gumatj mala, Buku-Larrŋgay Mulka 1326S, Yirritja.
Woŋgu Mununggritj, (sic. Mununggurr), "Thunder men at Durarydbi", (1946), Djapu mala, Macleay Museum, ETP.2051, Dhuwa.
C.M. Burarrwaŋa, "Ancestral Fire," Burarrwaŋa family Gumatj mala, Yirritja.
Mawalan #2 Marika, "Yalanbarra", Riratiŋu Mala, Macleay Museum, Dhuwa.
Barrupu Yunupiŋu, "Gurtha," 2.2010, 3.2010, 4.2010, 110.2013, Gumatj mala, Art Gallery of NSW. Yirritja,

Mawunbuy, "Burralku Spirit Country", (1946), Macleay Museum, ETP.2111 Dhuwa.

Bunuŋu Yunupiŋu, "Old Mangrove Stingray", (1946), Gumatj mala, Macleay Museum, ETP.2058, Yirritja.

Djalu Gurruwiwi, "Wititj", permanent collection, Buku-Larrngay Mulka, 1712P, Dhuwa.

Mithanari Gurruwiwi," Frogs at Mirrarmina", Yirrkala, 1966, Galpu Mala, National Museum of Australia,1985, .0259.0032, J. Davidson Collection No. 3, Dhuwa.

Joe Diembangu, "Wagilag Sisters Story", Macleay Museum, Millingimbi, 1980, UA1992.48, Dhuwa.

Mithanari Gurruwiwi, "The Great Snake Story", 1962, National Gallery of Australia, Dhuwa.

Munggurrawuy Yunupiŋu, "Arnhem Bay at Gudaidj-Binagaru", 1947, Macleay Museum, Yirritja.

Bangaliwuy Marrawuŋu, "Shooting Star at Dhuwalkitj", in *Yirrkala Drawings*, p. 72, R.M. Berndt Collection, 1947, Dhuwa.

Mawalan Marika, "Three Suns Story", 1946, Macleay Museum, ETP.2055, Dhuwa.

Birrikitji Gumana, "Macassan Praus", Yirrkala, 1966, J. Davidson Collection no. 3, National Museum of Australia, Yirritja .

John Bulunbulun, "Trepang-Bunapi", 2009, Maningrida Arts & Culture, in Trepang, China & The Story of Macassan Aboriginal Trade, Centre for Cultural Materials Conservation, 2011, p. 94, Yirritja.

Mungurrawuy Yunupiŋu, "Ancestral fire at Biranybirany", (1947), *Yirrkala Drawings* p. 142, R.M. Berndt Collection, Yirritja.

Bunuŋgu Yunupiŋu, 1947, "Influence from a Distant Land". *Yirrkala Drawings*, p. 133, R.M Berndt Collection, Yirritja.

Roy Marika, "Two Goanas", Yirrkala, 1982, Macleay Museum, University of Sydney, UA1992.46, Dhuwa.

Wanduk Marika, "Childrens Story", 1946, Macleay Museum, University of Sydney, ETP.2056, Dhuwa.

People, Places, Words and Meanings

Baḏaltja - fresh water tortoise – (Yirritja)

balanda - European, fair skinned people

Banaitja - creator ancestor - (Yirritja)

Baḻumbirr - morning star – (Dhuwa)

Baniyala- sacred homeland of the Madarrpa mala – (Yirritja)

Batumbil Burarrwaŋa - one of the master weavers and artists of NE Arnhem Land, Gumatj leader, custodian of Mata Mata and surrounding lands – (Yirritja)

bawuthu – generic Yolŋu term for wind.

Bayini - Queen of the fair skinned Bayini people, wandering spirit that leads men astray

bi`bi`thun - howl

Birimbira – thunder spirits - Yirritja snakes that stand on their tails and spit lightning into the sky – famously painted by Munggurrawuy Yunupiŋu – Art Gallery of NSW – IA19.1961

Birrikidji - one of the master painters of the Yirrkala church panels, Dhuluwaŋgu mala, father of Gawirrin, master painter, one of the visionary patrons of Yolŋu arts

bir'yun - shimmering light, illumination, knowledge

gatjirri/borrutj - sand fly – (Yirritja)

Bolŋu - thunder man (Dhuwa)

Buṉapi(') – sea slug, trepang

buŋgawa - boss, derived from Macassan word for admiral, leader

Bukaltjpi - Warramirri ancestor, warrior, dancer, philosopher (Yirritja)

burrkun – rope, possum-fur string

burralku – land of the spirit world, home of the morning star (Dhuwa)

daoine sidhe - little people of the hills

dhambaku/ŋarali' - tobacco

dhoku' - swamp paper bark tree – (Yirritja)

Dhuwa – one of the two Yolŋu moieties

Djambawa Marawili - master painter, leader of the Madarrpa
mala of NE Arnhem Land – (Yirritja)

djaykuŋ - file snake (Dhuwa)

didjpaŋgarr - spotted stingray – (Yirritja)

Djalu Gurruwiwi - elder of the Galpu clan, custodian of the
Dhuwa yidaki

djäma - work

Djambuwal - thunder man (Dhuwa)

Djankawu - ancestral creation beings of the dhuwa moiety of
the miwatj region – (Dhuwa)

djarrak - large white sea gull - (Dhuwa)

Djauwaldalwu - home of the lindaridj - (Dhuwa)

Djaykuŋ - file snake - (Dhuwa)

Djumayŋa - Macassar

Gi'kal - sacred homeland of the Galpu people (Dhuwa)

gaminyarr - grandchild

gamunuŋgu - 1) white clay, paint (Dhuwa) 2) yellow clay, paint
(Yirritja)

gapu-dha-yińdi - open ocean

gulka - ghost

Ganybu - fish trap – (Dhuwa)

Guṉburrku – midnight, middle of the night

gundawirwiryun - changing wind direction

Gunydju`u - gecko – (Dhuwa)

Guthaka - sooty oyster catcher (Dhuwa)

guwak - koel cuckoo – (Yirritja)

kananook - sweet water – (Boonwurrung)

ḻarrpan – spear – (Dhuwa)

Laintjung - sacred creator being – (Yirritja)

lindaridj - parakeets (Dhuwa)

`uŋgurrma – north east wind, season when seas are calm and
new growth starts, kingfish time, October- December,
(Yirritja)

mala - clan or family group of the Yolŋu people of North East
Arnhem Land

marrawili tree - a tree from the wangarr time, a cashew tree, a
casuarina – (Yirritja)

mayi - food (Gugu Yimidhirr, Gugu Yalanji)

Murnimiya - one of the hunters, lost at sea, now resident in the Milky Way, connected to guwak, (Yirritja)

marlwija - emu (Yirritja)

matjala – driftwood, also tripod masted sea craft of the Bayini era, great treasure

djaypila - moon fish – (Dhuwa)

Milliirrpum Marika - master painter and elder of the Riratingu clan, litigant in the famous Millirrpum vs Nabalco case that established the original foundation for Aboriginal land rights in the Northern Territory and Australia - (Dhuwa)

Ŋhaṯili - red-tailed cockatoo - (Dhuwa)

Njerrk - sulphur crested cockatoo – (Yirritja)

Nyapililŋu - ancestral mother figure of the yirritja, guardian spirit of paperbark and of women and children hunting in the bush, originator of possum-fur string – (Yirritja)

Raagapyarranne - Derwent River

Unghbanyahletta.- Mount Wellington

wakuwal - dream

waḻirr - sun

Wanyubi Marika - son of Millirrpum, master painter and chairman of Buku-Larrŋay Mulka – (Dhuwa)

wäŋa - spiritual home, place of peace, understanding and belonging

waŋarr- ancestral beings and their time

warawaḏa - milk fish – (Dhuwa)

warrŋgul - spear made with stingray's barb

wititj - olive python, rainbow serpent – (Dhuwa)

wuḻurrk - meteor, shooting star – (Dhuwa)

wuŋgan - dog – "Playboy" – sniffing around

wurrtjwurrtjmirri - emu

Yalaŋbara - spiritual and sacred home and centre of the Riratingu mala, Port Bradshaw region – (Dhuwa)

Yikuyanga - hunter, lost at sea, who resides in the Milky Way, connected to guwak – (Yirritja)

Yirritja – one of the two Yolŋu moieties

Written Sources

Debra Adelaide, *Serpent Dust,* Vintage, 1998

Catherine H. Berndt, "Prolegomena to a Study of Genealogies in North-Eastern Arnhem Land," Australian Aboriginal Anthropology, 1970

Ronald M. Berndt, *An Adjustment Movement in Arnhem Land,* Mouton & Co, Paris, 1962

Geoffrey Blainey, *A game of our own. The origins of Australian Football,* Black Inc, 2003

Geoffrey Blainey, *The Rush that never ended.A History of Australian Mining*, Melbourne University Press, 1981

G.C. Bolton, *A Thousand Miles Away,* The Jacaranda Press, 1963

Timothy Bottoms, *Conspiracy of Silence. Queenslands Frontier Killing Times*, Allen and Unwin, 2013

Buku Larrngay Mulka, *Saltwater Yirrkala Bark Paintings of Sea Country Recognising Sea Rights,* 1999

Wilbur Chaseling, *Yulengor Nomads of Arnhem Land*, The Epworth Press, London, 1957

Marshall Clark & Sally May, *Macassan History and Heritage: Journey, Encounters and Influences,* ANU, E-Press, 2013

Keith Cole, *Arnhem Land Places and People*, Rigby, 1980

Peter Coppin & Jolly Read, *Kangushot The Life of Nyamal Lawman Peter Coppin,* Aboriginal Studies Press, Canberra, 1999

Connor Cruise O'Brien, *The Great Melody A Thematic Biography of Edmund Burke*, Sinclair Stevenson, 1993

Day, Robert Adams. 1980. "How Stephen Wrote His Vampire Poem."*James Joyce Quarterly* 17 (2). University of Tulsa: 183–97. http://www. jstor.org/stable/25476277.

Kathleen Denigan, *Norman Baird - A Spark Within*, Balkanu, 2006

Ted Evans, "Arnhem Land: A Personal History," Talk delivered to the State Reference Library of the Northern Territory, 29 April 1987

Helen M. Gruger-Wurm. *Australian Aboriginal Bark Paintings and their Mythological Interpretation*, Volume 1 Eastern Arnhem

Land, Australian Institute of Aboriginal Studies, No. 30, Canberra, 1973

Louise Hanby, *Containers of Power, Women with Clever Hands*, Utber & Patullo Publishing, 2010

John B. Haviland, "That was the last time I saw them, and no more": Voices through Time in Australian Aboriginal Autobiography," *American Ethnologist*, Vol. !8, No. 2 (May 1991), pp. 331-361

John. B. Haviland with Roger Hart, *Old Man Fog and the Last Aborigines of Barrow Point*, Smithsonian Institution Press, Washington and London, 1998

James Joyce, *Ulysses*, Random House, New York, 1986 James Joyce, "All day I hear the waters," poem

James Joyce, "From Dewy Dreams," poem James Joyce, *Finnegans Wake*, online edition

C.G. Jung, *The Red Book Liber Novus A Readers Edition*, Norton and Company, New York, 2009

Grace Karstens, *The Colony A History of Early Sydney*, Allen & Unwin, 2010

Robert Kee, *Ireland a History*, Abacus, 1982

Robert Kenny, *The Lamb Enters the Dreaming Nathanael Pepper & the Ruptured World*, Scribe, Melbourne, 2007

Ian S. McIntosh, *Aboriginal Reconciliation and the Dreaming Warramirri Yolngu and the Quest for Equality*, Allyn and Bacon, 2000

Ian S. McIntosh, *Yolngu sea rights in Manbuynga ga Rulyapa (Arafura Sea) and the Indonesian connection.*

Fiona Magowan, *Melodies of Mourning Music and Emotion in Northern Australia*, James Curry, School for Advanced Reseamparch Press, University of Western Australia Press, 2007

Fiona Magowan & Karl Neuenfeldt, *Landscapes of Indigenous Performance Music, Song and Dance of the Torres Strait and Arnhem Land*, Aboriginal Studies Press, 2005

William Morris, *News from Nowhere and Other Writings*, Penguin Classics, 1993

Howard Morphy, "Mutual Conversion? The Methodist Church and the Yolngu with Particular Reference to Yirrkala," Humanities Research, Vol XII, No. 1, 2005

Howard Morphy, *Ancestral Connections Art and an Aboriginal System of Knowledge,* University of Chicago, 1991

Howard Morphy, *'Joyous Maggots': The Symbolism of Yolngu Mortuary Rituals*

Howard Morphy, Yirrkala Art An Exhibition of Aboriginal Bark Paintings and Carvings, Catalogue, 1976

Rob Mundle, Captain James Cook, ABC Books, 2013

Noel Pearson, *Ngamu-Ngaadyarr, Murri-Bunggaga and Midha Gigi in Guugu Yimmidhirr Hope Vale Lutheran Mission (1900-1950),* 1986 in J. Kociumbas, *Maps, Dreams, History*, Sydney Studies in History, No. 8, University of Sydney, 1998

Cara Pinchbeck, (Editor), *Yirrkala Drawings,* Art Gallery of NSW/ University of Western Australia, 2013

Howard J. Pohlner, *Gangurru,* Hope Vale Mission Board, 1986

Philip Ranlet, "The British, The Indians and Smallpox: What Happened at Fort Pitt in 1763?" Pennsylvania History: A Journal of Mid Atlantic Studies, 2000, Vol 67 No 3, pp. 427-441

Kevin Reed, *The Widows of Tullow and Outrages in Westmeath*, K & R. Reed, RMB 4580, Hamilton, Victoria, 3300 , 1998.

Roberta Sykes, *Snake Dreaming Autobiography of a Black Woman*, Allen and Unwin, 1998.

Rudolf Steiner, *Bees*, Anthroposophic Press, 2009

Donald Thomson, *Donald Thomson in Arnhem Land*, The Miegunyah Press, 2003

The Imperial-Royal Dream Book: Containing Intrerpretations of Most of the Dreams that visit the human family during the time of sleep, courtesy Ms. B Ross, R. Jones Printer, London, c. 1870

P.G. Toner (ed) *Strings of Connectedness Essays in Honour of Ian Keen*, Australian National University Press, 2015

W. Lloyd Warner, A *Black Civilisation A Study of an Australian Tribe,* Harper, 1937, 1958 reprint

Ann E. Wells, *Milingimbi Ten Years in the Crocodile Islands*, Angus & Robertson, 1963

Ann E. Wells, *This Their Dreaming Legends of the Panels of Aboriginal Art in the Yirrkala Church*, University of Queensland Press, St Lucia, 1971

Edgar Wells, *Reward and Punishment in Arnhem Land 1962-63*, Australian Institute of Aboriginal Studies, Canberra, 1982

Nancy M. Williams, *The Yolŋu and their Land: A System of Land Tenure and the Fight for its Recognition*, Stanford University Press, California, 1986

Gallarrwuy Yunupingu (editor), *Our Land is Our Life Land Rights - Past, Present and Future*, University of Queensland Press, 1997

Afterwords

Beginnings

This project had many beginnings.

First there was yapa- the stateswoman, linguist, ambassador and negotiator - Ms S D Gurruwiwi. *Quis est homo qui non floret.* She found her solace in Garray. And yet, yapa was a woman of humour not weeping... she would smile and laugh every time my jaw dropped at her stories. Many would congregate around her wherever she was, underneath the carport at No. 8 at Birritjimi, at East Woody, at Munch and Crunch or the 3cs, around the fire at Gulkula or at her beloved Gi'kal. Yapa's strength was legendary but her good humour was even more famous.

It was yapa who took me to meet the voice of fire, Mrs P. Batumbil Burarrwanga. Our first meeting was unforgettable. We shared a meal of stingray and I listened to the good humour and laughs of two of the great people of North East Arnhem Land. How lucky I was. The stingray bound us together in ways that I am still learning.

We have lost yapa now, but as the Yolŋu say, she is still with us every day. Her capacity to know her family on multi-dimensional regional and familial planes and to name her father's fathers back generations before Europeans settled in Sydney Harbour in 1788 was nothing special amongst her peers. But for me it was a wondrous and miraculous thing. Absorbing the different malas and moities and the way responsibilities for lands and estates switched and changed in an orderly fashion from grandparent to grandchild is a major intellectual exercise for an adopted balanda (non-Aboriginal person). Just comprehending the scope of living family members is a challenge. At one point, we set up a database to name yapa's contemporary family members and my energy waned after two hundred. This was just one panel of a grid that had multiple layers. Yapa would close her eyes, and without a pen or pad, or Google, recite the family members, leaving me struggling to spell and record names in Yolŋu mata. It made me ashamed to think of the deep family of Yolŋuversus the small concept of family within the European world. At this basic point of difference there was so much to grasp. The wonderful thing about yapa was she rejoiced in the differences and was so proud of her culture. Her generosity and laugh were wonderful things to know. They are the epitome of Yolŋudiplomacy, good manners and generosity.

Anyone who comes to know the majesty of Australian Aboriginal society and culture in a deep way is left with a feeling of inadequacy about contemporary Western, modern life. There are many, many questions that emerge about the place called Australia and the non-Aboriginal people who have settled there. How have we lost our magic? How have we lost our wäŋa-ŋaraka (home-country, sense of place, spirit of place connection to the land)? Why were we so märr-bambuma (spiritually weak/ignorant)? How did we lose our waŋarr (ancestral and cultural heroes)? How did we lose our bapurru (extended family)? How did we lose our buŋgul (ceremony)? Did we ever have these dimensions of life? How did we ride so roughly and brutally over this majestic culture that offers so many lessons about living and being on this earth?

This story had a second beginning on a bright Kangaroo Valley day while walking with a beautiful woman and her niece. In my garden, we came across a faery ring of mushrooms. My companion had a tough childhood but she knew the magic of the natural world was a healing force. Pointing to her niece my companion asked: "You're a writer, could you write a story about faeries?" In my mind, I was thinking, well, I am not that kind of a writer. But yes, I could write something that might include a mokuy (malevolent spirit), galka (sorcerer) or two! I began thinking of what I had learned about the spirits of this land. I wanted to write something that would be a great gift to this Aunty and her niece. Something that would bring them some of the understanding I had been given by my Aboriginal family and, in the process, some peace and happiness. I would

220

not write a pink faery story. Nor could I write one of those stories which have dumbed down Aboriginal culture for children or deadened them in an anthropological specimen jar.

How could a living ethos of this land emerge for children as well as adults? This became my quest.

I also wanted to write something that might bring Aboriginal and non-Aboriginal people closer together.

Magic was something that I think of whenever I think of Arnhem Land. The magic of the place is still there, maintained by the people in buŋgul (ceremony)and in every day life. The gift from my Aboriginal family members was to put magic back into my life, land and spirit. I realised we had lost that magic somewhere along the way and faeries were really the only ones who could explain how we came to lose it and how we could get it back again. It is hard to emphasise the extraordinary quality of the Yolŋu peoples. Ted Evans caught my imagination with these words he delivered in a talk to the State Reference Library of the Northern Territory in 1987 (*Arnhem Land: A Personal History*): "Rarely in the history of mankind has a people within the span of one generation, been required to make adjustments to their lifestyle which has impacted upon almost every vital element of their traditional world. The task has invariably taken its toll and there have been some victims, but overall the people of Arnhem Land have risen to the challenge with a vitality of endeavour that will surely see them maintain their pride and dignity that has been their inheritance from their ancestral heroes."

My Aboriginal family inspired me to work on my own relation with the land and to create a way for us all to work better together in the future. All this conspired in my mind around an *imaginary* story of my family, the five generations of Martins/Botsmans and Hogg/Warnes through the eyes of an ancestral being. The backbones of my father, grandfathers, grandmothers and their forebears are now part of the Australian land. Through events and deeds, big and small, evil and good, the substance as well as *the imaginary* of our collective life was formed. I wanted to find a link that would tie my Aboriginal family and my European family together.

This story is about the best of spirit overcoming the worst. My optimism in this is questionable. It comes perhaps from being born lucky, but also from an understanding of the power of Aboriginal Australia that seems to transcend life, death and the achievements of modern life. Surface events, great machines, technology, grand economies are impressive and seemingly all powerful. Yet the elusive, enduring Aboriginal spirit and mind - a gateway to land and space - is of more consequence to me. It seems to be more dependable, trustworthy and true against all the superficial mainstream stereotypes about Aboriginal society that have emerged since colonisation. The great freeways being etched through our regions and cities seem temporary. Something deeper lies beneath our surface world and I believe Aboriginal life is a key to it.

There was another beginning that I must also tell you about. My wäwa (brother) Djalu Gurruwiwi woke up something in my subconsciousness when he first played the yidaki into my heart at East Woody around the year 2000. Djalu consciously adopted me into his Galpu family as he has done with many others. In doing so he transmits something strong and wise to us. Many people have been *healed* by Djalu. He is the famous Dhuwa yidaki custodian of North East Arnhem Land. He heals with vibrations of sound. A feeling of great clarity pours through body and mind from his yidaki.

Djalu gave me the understanding that my first relationship with Yoŋu (Aboriginal people) was at Kananook in Victoria. How he did this only he can tell. But it came to me as a lightning revelation because I suddenly remembered I did have friends in my garden at Kananook. They were very real and very true and wonderful playmates. Grandmother Grace Warne and grandfather Vernon Hogg had bought the beautiful sanctuary of 32 Kananook Avenue where my sister and I spent our early lives. My father and his father built the house there. It was, on the face of things, just another suburban block and brick veneer house.

Thankfully Grace protected every *old man* banksia and clump of ti-tree on the block. Her will prevailed even in the most vicious and senseless period of suburban development madness. There at 32, and along the banks of the Kananook Creek, spirits played and sought refuge in Grace's sanctuary. I could also feel a deep foreboding along the creek which once was a paradise and had become a suburban sewer. Grace was an inspiring visionary. It was in Grace's sanctuary with my mother, father and sister that I spent my infant years. It was here, as Djalu explained, the trees talked to me. It was here that I first had contact with spirits and faeries. I still wonder whether Grace's time with the Yorta Yorta giant Doug Nicholls had something to do with all this or whether the trees talked to her too.

Grace's sanctuary could only last a certain time. 32 Kananook Ave like her haven at 8 Lindsay St Glenroy have now been turned into concrete and glass. But in my mind the possums, tiny wrens and wild spirits still prevail. They are waiting for all of us to understand that this sanctuary we destroyed was unique in the whole of the world. For Grace's sanctuary was a remnant of the oldest garden in the history of the world.

The carnage we caused is yet to be understood. People came from all over the world seeking comfort, safety and modernity. In doing so they destroyed sacred places of more enduring value than the pyramids or the monuments and cathedrals of Europe. It is perhaps the greatest vandalism committed by a small population in a very short period of time. It seemed of no consequence after the death and destruction of wars and the never ending 'progress' of cities around the world... but I felt it acutely then and now.

The things I felt as a child were ignited by Djalu, Dopiya, midiku and the Galpu people. In adopting me and my family they slowly opened my eyes to the magic of land, spirits and

223

ceremony. They helped me to remember and to understand the many dimensions of family.

Another beginning came through my dhuways Batumbil Burrarwaŋa and her brothers at Mata Mata, they taught me about how everything in the land, sky and ocean is family, not metaphorically, but really, actually and actively. They taught me the meaning of waŋa (spirit of place and home). The wonder of Mata Mata and Gikal, like the magic of Kananook came to me and this place we now call Australia opened over all of the generations. I could see plainly what was lost and what needed to be recovered.

Djalu says one mind, one blood, one journey. We all have a role to play in maintaining the continuity of the traditional laws of the land, in respecting the deep knowledge that is the provenance of Aboriginal men and women 'of high degree'. We newcomers and learners have an important job now to ensure that the buŋgul (ceremonies) that keep life, death and the universe in balance are continued. We must also ensure that the ceremonial leaders and workers who undertake the *djama*/work involved are as well-compensated as any civil, religious or educational order. It is not just about recognition, it is about supporting and being in partnership with Aboriginal people to ensure they are strong, secure and playing a leading role in the future of the lands we call Australia.

In all this, what began as a simple children's story became something for adults. It was also as if things that I learned as a small child could only reveal themselves now I am an old man. It was as if the true meaning of what I had experienced as a child could now be understood. Lots of things have happened as the story unfolded. Tears were shed. Hearts were broken. Great losses were felt. Battles were lost. Great friends have died. Great loves have come and gone. In all, the story kept on unfolding. It was at times unbearably painful and sad to write. But like a Kangaroo Valley fog that eventually rises in mid-afternoon, in the Christmas of 2015 I began to enjoy this tale and to think it might just be okay. I hope you think so too.

Acknowledgements

In the writing of this book there are a great many people who have helped me. Thank you to Karanda, Louise, Chase and the extended Walker clan for their great wisdom and generosity. Kevin Fong and the great Fong dynasty of Broome, Baamba, Stephen Pigram and the great old families of Broome were responsible for one part of the saga. Lew Griffiths and his family started another. It has been a privilege to walk a short way with Noel and Gerhardt Pearson. The things I have learned from them are profound and go beyond "politics" to life. Will, Merikiyawuy, Sienna, Rosalee and Arian were inspiring guides and forgiving and generous hosts. Will Stubbs has been in particular a gracious teacher. Thank you to Max Pearson for a thousand things. Paul, Kay, Adam, Belin and Daniel Briggs gave me sanctuary when times were tough. The Pearsons, the Roes, the great Lew Nannup and his family, Barry Taylor and Charmaine Tullock and their family, Willie Jumbo, the great Micko O'Byrne, Professor Langton, Gerry, Peter, Thomas, Bill & Nicole Moore have all helped me to see and write little bits and pieces. Sammy and Talarra and the gang from Habitat were friends at important times. Bill and Judy Moyle were truly inspirational and wonderful friends. The mighty McLeods and Browns of Wreck Bay, the Snowy Mountains and beyond – Bobby, Paul, Daren, and the wonderful Vida Brown and her family, most particularly Joe, are ever present in all of the writing.

Sonny Sims, Allen Madden and many other Yuin, Gadigal and Wadi Wadi elders inspired me, helped me and generously shared so much. The depth of their knowledge remains a treasure for the future to be appreciated and fully understood. Robert Chewying and his family have been wonderful friends through thick and thin as have the best farmers in the Shoalhaven region John Fisher and Dace Frejis.

There are so many family members and friends in North East Arhem land to acknowledge: Lisa Dhurrkay, her mother's pride and joy, Terence, Peter, David, Tony, Jason Gurruwiwi and their families, Damien Djerrkurra, Banduk Marika, Wesley Dhurrkay, Holly and their wonderful Marley. Rob Morgan and Elizabeth Aitken have been extraordinarily supportive of all of the Aboriginal community work that is behind much of what has made this book possible as has the inimitable, courageous and indefatigable Danny Gilbert. Djapiri Munnungritj was yapa's great friend and business partner they would meet in their business office on the beach at Biritjimi or Yirrkala. She and her husband Howard are inspirational friends and ambassadors. Djapiri continues the work of yapa in all its facets. Djambawa Marawili and his family showed me that in lines of sands are those elusive signs and symbols which the mainstream tramples over. A thousand helpers will come to Arnhem Land but Michael Macnamara at Baniyala has proved to be above and beyond them all. He is the living embodiment of the principle that small practical things and commitment make a difference.

Where would anything be without Lyn Gain and the wild Sydney Push? At a critical point in the road, Lyn and Valentine Press was there offering support and advice when no-one else would have bothered. Alex Podolinsky, the master of the soil, a wonderful teacher and mentor brought great blessings to Australia when he arrived. He too intuitively felt the spirits and call of places.

Budatŋga, Shakiera and Mahalia Munnuŋgurr and Whitney Yunupingu lived between our worlds and are inspirational young women finding a way for all of us.

Dogs have come to mean so much. Spinner and Keela are the guardians of Eramboo and Kangaroo Valley and my sanity. Then came the crazy Charlie and Waniulnga. Thanks to Batumbil, Gerry and Terry the ancestral dogs of Mata Mata appeared. Anchor, Ray Ray, Marlo and the Mata Mata pack were always there. The unforgettable Wally and Daisy are also forever in my mind. Dogs are angels - we just do not understand their role. Of course they have the capacity for ferocity for they alone must protect us when we make the final journey on our

226

own. Woo can you hear them coming... in the morning on the last day of the funeral. Many words came to me in the shed at Kangaroo Valley. Frogs, owls, crickets, snores of dogs and bat squeals were my music. At night I would dream and in the morning the words would come. Wadi Wadi spirits came to me from the place where flour was made, where babies were born and children played. They revealed to me from the past what eramboo (tomorrow) might look like.

I thank the Yolŋu clan leaders for their forgiveness, never-ending generosity and great knowledge. And to all Yolŋu, all Aboriginal people, I ask forgiveness for my mistakes and misinterpretations. I hope in stumbling along, others can learn a better way. I am eternally sorry and pray forgiveness for those of us who invaded and trampled so roughly over all of the sacred lands of Australia with such violent ignorance and arrogance. It still goes on. It is so long overdue to restore the ancestral connections and ancient ways as the foundation stone of the future. It is time for this rather strange and fragile constellation of political entities called Australia to forever recognise the primacy of the first nations of this land.

Finally as I think about the endurance and sustainability of families and the pain of writing I realise that it was my father Peter B Botsman - a man of firsts - the first of the Martin/Botsman dynasty to get through high school with such accomplishment, the first to university, a man who dared to take his family to Papua New Guinea, then to New York who gave me something important. My mother - who always followed her instincts, against the grain if necessary - also drove me on. My uncles and aunties on both sides of the family were vivid and colourful characters in my life. My cousins were also memorably etched into my life. In the last stages of writing, Jo and Melanie Ruchel thoughtfully reminded me of many things.

My beautiful and generous friend Gail Barker was the first reader of the manuscript who gave me great confidence. She called me during one of Brisbane's legendary storms and it felt like a conversation in one of the chapters.

Thanks also to my accomplished wäwa Dani and my yapa Lyn for her forbearance especially during moments of early childhood terror and Tarita for whom the world really is an oyster.

There are times when spirits flag and then along comes a wondrous, inspiring spirit and the essence of the story comes alive in real life - for this I am so thankful to Djillawur for so many things, so much inspiration, heart and so much love and soul.

Most of all I am grateful to my heroes Chenier, Dashiell and Declan who hold me together through thick and thin and whose strides in life always leave me feeling proud and admiring.

Peter Botsman
Easter 2017

www.ingramcontent.com/pod-product-compliance
Lightning Source LLC
Chambersburg PA
CBHW021010120726
47905CB00009B/2945